WRITTEN ON ICE

A DARK ACADEMIA HOCKEY ROMANCE

ICE AND SHADOWS
BOOK ONE

SMARDLINE S.

Copyright © 2025 Smardline S. All rights reserved.

The characters and events portrayed in this book are fictitious. Any similarity to real persons, living or dead, is coincidental and not intended by the author.

No part of this book may be reproduced, or stored in a retrieval system, or transmitted in any form or by any means, electronic, mechanical, photocopying, recording, or otherwise, without express written permission of the publisher.

Cover design by: @readingromancewithlauren

Editing by: @editingbyandrea

❦ Formatted with Vellum

PLAYLIST

Control - Halsey
Free - KPop Demon Hunters
Forbidden Fruit - Tommee Profit, Sam Tinnesz & Brooke
Daylight - Taylor Swift
Earned it - The weekend
Forever - Loreen
Wyd now? - Sadie Jean
Tattoo - loreen
Hard Place - H.E.R

For the girlies who want a black, broody hockey player with locs and tattoos.

DISCLAIMER

Welcome to Valcèrre

You've been accepted into one of the most prestigious winter universities in the world—a place where talent meets tradition, and secrets are buried deeper than the ice.

As a new student, you are expected to uphold Valcérre's standards of excellence: dedication, discretion, and discipline.

Restricted Content

The following material has been classified as mature and intended for audiences 18+. It contains contents that may be sensitive or emotionally intense, including:

- Explicit romantic and sexual scenes
- Strong language
- Grief, loss, and trauma
- Emotional manipulation and family pressure

Read responsibly. Valcérre University assumes no liability for heartbreak, obsession, or sleepless nights that may occur as a result of your enrollment.

Subjects of Study (Tropes)

- **Enemies to Lovers**
- **Black Hockey Player × Afro-Latina Figure Skater**
- **Forbidden Romance**
- **Found Family**
- **Forced Proximity**

- Dark Academia Aesthetic
- Mystery Beneath the Ice
- Twin Flame / Soulmate Connection
- He Falls First (and she doesn't know it yet)

PROLOGUE

SHADOW RINK

The Midnight Challenge.

THE MIDNIGHT CHALLENGE wasn't listed on any schedule. It wasn't acknowledged by any coach. It was never spoken of in daylight.
And yet, it existed.
A secret tournament passed down through whispers and bloodlines. Reserved for first-year students and invitation only.
The Challenge took place once every five years. Long enough for students to graduate, and for people to forget.
But it was never really about the skating.
It was a performance for the powerful. A way for the elite to watch from the shadows and decide who was worthy of legacy—and who wasn't.
No coaches, no fans. Only those powerful and rich enough to place their bets.
Win, and you would be rewarded.
Lose, and you might disappear.
Because the people betting didn't care who skated best.
They cared who survived.
And who followed the rules.
The rules were simple. And cruel.
Fall three times, you were out.
Get injured, the match ended—and sometimes your future with it.
Each challenge consisted of three nights.
Two qualifying matches.

One final round.
Then, one night, everything went terribly wrong.
They tried to bury the truth.
Called it an accident.
But secrets don't die.
Not here.
Not with me.
There are truths frozen within my walls.
Skeletons buried beneath my ice.
But some secrets don't stay buried forever.

CHAPTER 1

Luna

Welcome to Valcèrre

Have you ever wanted something so badly it hurts? And no, I don't mean ice cream, or Taylor Swift concert tickets, although I've never been to a concert. I mean the kind of want that turns into need and consumes your entire existence. You feel it in your chest, your throat, your bones, terrified that it'll slip through your fingers. That's what Valcérre is for me.

All I want is to show them I belong here.

"You okay?" Sophie asks from beside me.

I nod automatically, but I'm not. My chest is too tight, like someone is sitting on it, pressing all the air out of me. I haven't been able to breathe properly since we landed at that private airport thirty minutes ago. Because this is it. Valcérre has the best figure skating program in the world. I'm talking Olympic-level good. It's everything I've dreamed of since I was eight years old. Now that I'm here, I think I'm gonna throw up, because I can't fuck this up.

I stare out the window, hoping the view will help ease some of the pressure, but it doesn't. The trees are covered with snow. The sky's that pale, silver-gray that makes everything feel melancholy, as if the whole world is holding its breath. It's August. So, technically, it's the beginning of fall, but Valcérre doesn't care about the season. This Island is located in the

North Atlantic between Iceland, Norway, and the UK. It has one season. Winter.

Most people would hate that. My sister Rylee does. We grew up in the northern U.S., and she lives in Paris now. She's always hated the cold. The only reason she ever survived winter was because she was looking forward to spring and summer. Take that away? It'd kill her.

She said I'm crazy for choosing to go to school in a place where it's below fifty degrees all year long. I don't blame her. According to Sophie, the sun never shows its face around here. But unlike my sister, I don't mind the cold. At least I know what to expect.

Rylee still wanted to come, but I convinced her not to. She'd just complain about how cold it is the whole time. Besides, I needed to do this without her. She's been taking care of me since she was barely old enough to take care of herself.

I lean my forehead against the cold window, watching the glass mist beneath my breath. I press my fingers against it and trace the letters L U N A. Luna. I love my name. It's the one thing my mother got right. We might love a sunny day, but we all need the moon to light up our darkest nights.

"If anyone asks, you're my sister, okay?" Sophie's voice cuts through my thoughts again. "Because you are."

I glance over to catch her smile.

Sophie is my sister's husband Luc's little sister. He's the reason I'm here. She's also the first real friend I made after moving to Paris. She might look like she stepped out of a luxury fashion ad, but she's never made me feel like I didn't belong. We stayed close even after she left for school at Valcérre. She's a sophomore now.

I rest my head on her shoulder just for a second. Then the car jerks, and we slide sideways toward the edge of the road.

"Merde!" the driver curses under his breath, pulling the wheel right in time as we come to a stop.

A deer freezes in the middle of the road, wide-eyed in the headlights. I swear it's staring straight at me, as if we understand each other. Two creatures out of place and trying to survive. Then it runs away, disappearing into the trees.

"Apologies, mademoiselles," the driver says, glancing at us in the rearview mirror. "Are you both all right?"

"We're good," Sophie says, completely unfazed. Then she turns to me. "You okay?"

I nod, even though my heart's still in my throat. "Yeah, just wasn't expecting that."

She chuckles as the car resumes down the snowy road. That's when I see it. A black iron gate, barely visible through the mist. The closer we get, the clearer it becomes. On top, it says *Salvete ad Universitatem Valcérre* (Welcome to Valcérre University) in curly metal letters.

This is it.

"Welcome to your new home," Sophie says.

Home?

Home has never been a place for me. It's a feeling. The sound of my sister's voice on the phone. The sharp bite of cold air before a performance. The silence before my skate blades touch the ice.

The gate opens, and the fog thickens as the car drives deeper into campus. Dark stone walls cut through the haze, their spires vanishing into the clouds. I press my palms against my thighs, but my knees won't stop bouncing.

"Nervous?" Sophie watches me with a little scrunch between her brows.

"No," I say a little too quickly. Why would I be? It's not like this is one of the most elite schools in the world. The place looks like a fucking palace, and I'm just the girl who grew up in a two-bedroom apartment with a leaky ceiling. So I'm totally not nervous. I don't even know what nervous is. Never met her.

"Excited then?" She nudges me with her knee. Excited to

make a fool of myself? Sure. Pretty sure I'm wearing a sign on my forehead that says *she totally doesn't belong here.*

"I don't know yet."

"It's okay to feel both." She reaches for my hand and gives it a little squeeze.

We pass through the main courtyard toward the dormitories. In the distance, the main building rises from the mist. I've never seen anything like this in real life. It's massive, like an old palace, but also modern. Arched windows reflect the dim light, and dark stone walls stand against the rain-slicked courtyard.

"That's Ravensbourne Hall." Sophie nods toward the first dormitory ahead. If you can call it a dorm. It's more like a gothic castle.

It sits at the highest point of the campus, overlooking everything else. Its black stone exterior is carved in intricate designs, with massive, arched glass windows.

"The legacies live there. Kids of the founders, hockey stars, Olympians." She leans back on her seat casually. "They don't just belong here. They own this place."

"Figures." I swallow, and my finger tightens around the sleeve of my coat.

The car moves forward, curving around the lake. The water is calm and dark, swallowing the faint campus light. I wish I felt that calm, but inside me is like a storm.

Then a new building appears from the fog.

"And that's Wolfswood Hall." Sophie tips her chin toward the building with the polished stone pillars lining the entrance, where a valet in a black uniform holds the door open for a student dragging her luggage behind her.

"The elites stay here. Rich international kids, trust fund babies, children of politicians, movie stars." She smirks and nudges my knee again. "And us."

I'm staying here.

Except I don't fit in any of those categories.

The car stops, and the valet opens the door for Sophie, who steps out like she owns the place.

"Thank you," she says, fixing her coat.

I take a deep breath and force my legs to move. The moment I step out, the cold air slams into me, and my lungs welcome it.

My eyes drift toward another building, half hidden in the fog, at the farthest edge of campus.

"And that's Halloway Hall," Sophie says, following my gaze. "That's where the scholarship kids stay."

It doesn't look as luxurious as the other dorms.

I should be staying there. I applied for the scholarship, but I didn't get it. I'm here not because I earned it, but because Luc could afford it.

"Come on." Sophie slips her arm through mine, linking them together. "You belong here, with me."

I let her lead me inside, because if I don't, I might turn around, get back in the car, and fly back to Paris. Then what? It's not like I belong there either. That's Rylee's world, not mine.

Welcome to Wolfswood Hall.

We walk through the arched double door, and the smell hits me first. Vanilla, amber, fresh rain, and perfection.

Inside the lobby, students are talking in different languages, French, Russian, Spanish, Korean, and some I don't even recognize. Everything about them screams wealth.

A dark-brown desk stands in the center under the golden chandelier that probably costs a fortune, enough to buy a house with a backyard. Behind it, a woman sits with her black hair tied in a sleek, low ponytail.

She doesn't ask for a name; if you belong here, they already know who you are.

A towering arched window in the back reveals the courtyard and the nearby lake, and the snowy mountains in the distance. A grand fireplace carved from dark stone sits on the far side of the wall. Across from it is the lounge area, with dark leather couches, wooden coffee tables, and deep-burgundy rugs.

"Hey, Sophie, welcome back." A student smirks at her.

Sophie flips her hair with a lazy smile. "Miss me?"

"Not in the slightest." She laughs, shaking her head.

We step toward the desk, and I fight the urge to fidget. Instead, I shove my hands into the pockets of my coat, nails digging into my palms.

The lady hands Sophie her key card. "Welcome back, Miss Kingley."

Next, she hands me my key card as she studies me for a second. "Welcome to Valcérre, Miss Del Sol."

"Thanks." I smile at her, but her expression remains neutral.

I follow Sophie to the two staircases. She takes the one on the right, which I'm guessing leads to the girls' side of the dorms.

The stairs are crowded with students heading to their rooms.

"Her sponsorship deal is insane..." one student is telling a group of friends.

We stop in front of a door, and Sophie scans her key card before pushing it open. Inside, there's a girl sitting on a long brown couch with two burgundy leather chairs on each side. Behind the couch, there's a long bookshelf filled with leather-bound books. Across from them is an electric fireplace.

She looks up as the door closes behind us.

"Annika, this is my sister Luna."

"Hi." I smile at her.

She offers me a polite smile before returning to her phone. It's nice seeing another black girl. She looks mixed. Warm brown skin, almond-shaped eyes, and short, wavy black hair. I think she's Blasian.

Sophie loops her arms around me again, leading me toward the hallway on the right with three identical doors.

"This is yours." She points at the door with my name on it. "This one is mine." She nods toward the other door. "I'll let you settle in, and then I'll see you later."

"Thank you." My lips press into a small smile before I push open the door.

Inside, a bed sits against the wall, covered with deep-green wallpaper with gold filigree and ivy patterns. My eyes drift toward the gothic window with a view of the lake outside. I stand there, watching how the fog from the lake swallows the bridge that connects Wolfswood to Ravensbourne, before turning back to the bed.

My back hits the mattress, and I exhale through my nose, staring at the high ceilings with vaulted beams carved with intricate, twisting patterns.

I don't belong here. The only reason I'm here is because of Luc, but that doesn't mean I can't carve my own place.

I push myself off the bed and walk across the room to where my suitcases are set neatly beside the door. They must have brought them up while Sophie and I were checking in. I kneel on the floor, unzip my skating bag, and pull out my favorite pair of skates. The metal is cold and familiar against my skin as I drag my finger along the curve of the blades.

Whether I belong at this school or not, the ice will always be mine.

CHAPTER 2

Luna

I set two alarms and somehow slept through both of them. Thankfully, my ancestors decided to drag me out of bed. Don't ask me how.

After running across campus for ten minutes, I stand in front of the Aureum. The training rink, a place where only the strongest survive. The building is made out of dark stones, and on top, there's a glass dome curved like a grand palace, reflecting the stormy sky. Tall, arched windows line the walls.

Across from it, connected by a long glass bridge, is the Solenne Complex. That's where they hold the hockey games and figure skating showcases. There, reputations are made or destroyed. You have to prove you've got what it takes before you cross that bridge.

My chest feels tight, but not from the run. My body is used to that, from conditioning drills, morning jogs, and chasing down the bus back at home. This is nerves. I hate that jittery feeling clenching in my gut because I'm late on my first freaking day of official training. Just great.

Breathe, Luna, I repeat in my head, forcing air through the knot in my throat.

I run up the staircase, stopping at the last one to read the quote above the iron door: Vinvit qui se vincet (He conquers who conquers himself). I push the door open and step inside.

My skates are hooked over my shoulders as I sprint across the main balcony of the Aureum.

At the center of the building is the athlete lounge, a massive open circle beneath the glass-domed ceiling with a view of the sky.

A balcony overlooks the ice rinks, where coaches and high-profile guests usually stand. Below the balcony, we have the hockey rink to the left and figure skaters' rink to the right.

I should be heading toward the right stairwell. But the sharp sound of a puck slamming against the boards stops me in my tracks. My head turns instinctively toward the rink. Jerseys flash against the ice, bodies cutting through the drills. I should already be halfway down the stairs. But then I see him.

Number 7. He moves faster than the others, with an effortless kind of control, as if the ice bends to him. Then he turns, like he senses me watching him, and our eyes meet. They're unreadable at first, dark, and too intense for this early in the morning. But they drag me, and suddenly I'm not on the balcony anymore. It feels like I'm on the ice in front of him, like he pulled me into his orbit without moving a damn inch.

My pulse stutters, and everything fades. The sounds of blades scraping ice, the calls of his teammates, and the fact I should be on the other side of the rink.

His eyes narrow slightly like he's trying to place me. We stare at each other, seconds maybe, but it's long enough for my breath to catch. I tear my gaze away, breaking whatever that was, and rush down the right stairwell. What the fuck was that?

As soon as I reach the benches outside the skaters' rink, I drop my bag on the floor and kneel to tie my skates before stepping into the rink.

The moment my blades hit the ice, everything else disappears, leaving just us. I close my eyes, letting the feeling sink in. No matter where I am, this part never changes.

I fell in love with figure skating when I was eight years old. Sitting alone in the living room, watching a movie. My mom wasn't home, like the many nights before. I don't even remember the name of the movie. Just the girl on the ice. She moved like she belonged there, like she was free and in control at the same time. I wanted that.

I asked my mom if I could try skating. She barely looked at me before yelling at me to go back in my room. I didn't ask her again. Instead, I asked Rylee. And she didn't hesitate. She found me a class and bought me my first pair of skates.

"Luna." A female voice breaks through my memory.

I open my eyes and lock gazes with my new coach.

"You're late." She stares at me with an unimpressed look.

"Sorry, Coach, won't happen again." I bow my head slightly to show my remorse.

She gives me a look that says it better not.

I glide toward the center of the room where the other two pairs of skaters plus my new partner are waiting.

"All right, listen up. You've trained for this moment, but raw skill is not enough in pairs." The coach drifts around the ice, making eye contact with a few of us. "If you do not trust your partners, you will fail. If you don't match their rhythm, you will fail. And if you don't have chemistry, you will not last."

The rink is silent except for the sound of her skates moving against the ice.

"Today is a trial. We are assessing your ability to connect with your partner. Some of you will stay together, and others will not. There is no guarantee you will find a replacement partner." She glances at the clipboard in her hands. "You have thirty minutes. Run through basic footwork, spins, and lifts. We'll be watching."

No good luck wishes.

"Ready to impress, freshman?" He skates toward me.

Freshman? I fight the urge to roll my eyes.

Nicholas Laurent. He's a sophomore and my assigned partner. They put us together because our heights match. At five feet seven inches, I'm taller than the average skater, including the guys.

I reach for the small cross pendant necklace around my neck and press it to my lips. My sister gave it to me when I was six. She said it would protect me, and I always kiss it before every skating session. Call it superstition, but in my eleven years of skating, I've only had one accident that resulted in a minor head injury. And that just so happened to be the one time I forgot to wear my necklace.

"Always." I nod, forcing myself to breathe.

Ready or not, training starts now.

"Show me what you've got." He smirks.

We begin with basic steps, warming up to a simple crossover. One foot crosses over the other as we skate in a curve to build speed, our steps synchronized.

I take the lead and transition into a twizzle sequence—three fast, one-foot spins while gliding across the diagonal. My body moves on instinct as I bend my knee and extend my arms to stay balanced. Then I spin through each turn. One, two, and three. I stretch my leg back, shift my weight, and land on the outside edge of my skate.

Nico keeps up, his edges strong, but he started his twizzle half a second after I did and threw off our timing. It's small, and wouldn't be noticeable to anyone outside the rink, unless you're the coach or a judge. But on the ice, small mistakes matter, especially in pairs. Judges catch everything, and don't mention the fact that one slip can lead to accidents and injuries. I've seen it happen.

We come to a stop in the center of the rink. Nico places his hands on my waist, preparing for a simple press lift.

"Okay," he says. "On three."

I inhale sharply. This is where trust matters and instinct takes over.

"One."

I set my foot, ready to jump.

"Two."

His grip is firm, but something feels off.

"Three."

I jump, but his hands hesitate for a brief moment, and I feel it instantly, the split second of doubt before my body shifts too far forward.

I'm off-balance because he hesitated. And this is not new to me. I've felt that pause before. Most of my partners do it eventually. He probably thought I was too heavy for him to lift. But no matter how much I work out or how healthy my diet is, I can't change my body type. I'm not skinny, but I'm not fat either, not that there's anything wrong with that. Every body type is beautiful. I'm just that in between. I won't starve myself just to fit their mold.

I try to adjust midair, pushing my weight back, preparing for a rough landing. Nico tightens his grip to compensate, but it's too late for a clean save. My skates hit the ice too soon, too hard, and I stumble forward.

"You okay?" Nico mutters, running his hand through his short brown hair.

"I'm fine." I straighten quickly, shaking it off. I've taken worse falls. I can handle this.

We try again, and he gets me up this time, but the movement is shaky and unsteady. The trust isn't there.

I don't trust him to hold it. He doesn't trust me to land it.

We lower back down, and I let out a slow breath, trying to stay calm.

"Let's go again," I say.

Nico exhales, shaking his arms out. "Yeah, sure."

There's hesitation in his voice.

I swallow back my frustration, but my shoulders are tight, my fists clenched. We should be better than this. I should be better than this.

Don't fuck this up, Luna.

CHAPTER 3

Zayden

The first day of practice at Valcérre isn't about skill, it's about survival. This isn't just any hockey program. It's one of the best in the world. And the first practice? It's meant to break you. It's the same drill every year. Conditioning first. Nonstop suicides.

"Stretch it out, boys. Sixty seconds," Coach yells from where he's standing.

Everyone drops onto the ice. Some are on their back with legs up, and others are on their knees.

I place one knee on the ice with my stick in front of me before leaning forward to stretch my hips, rotating between the left and the right knee.

Then I switch positions, with both knees on the ice. I hinge my back, and my groin tightens before I feel the stretch. Next I add some hips rolls to help loosen the muscles.

"That's enough," Coach announces. "Now it's time to work."

A few freshmen groan under their breath, but no one dares say anything.

"Goal line. Let's go."

Every blade hits the ice all at once as we skate toward the goal line. We line up and wait for the signal. Then he blows the whistle, and everyone skates off.

Skate to the blue line, touch it, and back.
Red line, back.
Another blue line, back.
Full length, back.

Timed. No excuses.

"Again!" Coach yells.

We go again.

One of the first-year students trips and slams into the boards. Coach doesn't yell. He doesn't have to, because his disappointment is worse than his anger.

I make it back to the goal line ahead of everyone else. Some guys are hunched over, sweat dripping onto the ice. I'm not one of them, but I feel it, the burn in my legs and the tightness in my lungs. But I don't slow down.

Show no weakness.

"Aldenhurst gets a free pass because his dad's the coach."

The whispers start early. They always do.

"Bet if his last name wasn't Aldenhurst, he wouldn't even be here."

I don't react. I never do. Because I know what they don't. I've spent the last two years proving I belong here.

As the coach's son, team captain, and the only Black player on this team, in a sport where I've never been given the benefit of the doubt, I don't get to be just good. I have to be ten times better.

I don't have the luxury of making mistakes. For me, there are no second chances. Every shift, every game, every drill, I play like I have something to prove.

Because I do.

"You all need to shut the hell up," Jasper says next to me.

Silence.

He straightens, rolling his shoulders then nodding toward me. "Zayden's the captain and center for a reason. Because he's the best player on this team, and you know it. That's why you're running your mouths. Because you're pissed he's better than you."

The tension shifts instantly.

Jasper's not wrong, and they know it.

No one says anything after that.

And I don't acknowledge it, but the pressure in my chest eases a little. That's why he's my best friend; he always has my back. Not that I can't fight my own battles, but I don't usually waste my energy on people who have no idea what they're talking about.

"Number 76, get off my rink," Coach yells at one of the first-year students.

The kid doesn't even argue, just slowly skates off the ice.

We continue to 1v1 board battles.

Scrimmages.

Checking drills.

The entire practice is a war zone.

And I hold my own. I win my battles until Coach finally blows the last whistle. "Off my ice."

I skate toward the bench with the rest of team, looking for my blade guards. Some of the guys collapse onto the benches, chugging water like they've been parched. I take my helmet off, letting the cool air hit my face, sweat rolling down my back.

He's standing there writing notes on his clipboard, not even a glance in my direction.

Coach Aldenhurst.

My father doesn't say a word to me. Not even a nod. Like I didn't outskate every guy on this ice.

I walk past him without giving him the satisfaction of looking back as we head toward the lockers to shower before going to the lounge to refuel.

Twenty minutes later, we're at the lounge. There's a high-end café bar in one corner, stocked with high-protein shakes, high-carb breakfasts, fresh fruit, and recovery meals designed for peak athletic performance.

The air smells like rich espresso, warm oats, and toasted almonds from the high-protein bowls most players order. A few round mahogany tables are scattered around with plush seating.

Massive arched windows reveal the vista of the mountains in the distance.

Some of the players sit at the round tables, going over plays from practice and talking about drills. Others sprawl in the deep leather armchairs by the fireplace, stretching sore muscles. The rest of them sit at the café bar. Most are focused on their food, already mentally preparing for the next session.

Instead of joining them, I grab a protein shake from the counter and drop into a high-top table near the glass balcony, levitating above the ice below.

I don't mean to watch, just cooling down and letting my body recover, but my eyes catch on her.

The new girl. The one I caught watching me earlier. There's something familiar about her, like I've seen her before.

She's with her partner, running through lifts. She's different from the other skaters, and not because she's taller and thicker. It's something in the way she moves. She looks like she belongs there, like the ice is an extension of her.

I sip my shake, watching as they go for another lift. I know it's going to fail before it even happens. Her partner's grip on her hips is wrong. His stance is awkward with unease, and it's clear his balance is off.

And sure enough, he fumbles.

She barely makes it above his shoulders before he wobbles, forcing her back down.

She steps back into her position and tries again.

And again.

And again.

Her brows are pinched together, determination etched on her face. I recognize that look. The fire. The need to be better and the refusal to quit.

"Didn't take you for a figure skating fan." Jasper's voice breaks through my thoughts. I turn just as he drops into the seat next to me, one eyebrow raised.

I scoff, leaning back in my chair and gripping my protein shake tighter than necessary. "I'm not."

Jasper smirks. "Right."

I roll my eyes, tearing my gaze away from the rink. It doesn't matter. She doesn't matter. It's just practice. Just another skater on the ice. And yet, as Jasper starts talking about one of the drills we did earlier, my eyes drift back to her.

She's still trying. Still pushing through it like she refuses to lose. For some reason, I can't stop watching.

CHAPTER 4

Luna

Today has been a fucking disaster.

The rink is emptying, most of the other skaters chatting easily as they head up to the lounge.

I exhale sharply, rubbing my hands over my face.

It's fine. It's the first day. It's just practice.

But no matter how many times I tell myself that, it still feels like failure. The next group of skaters walks in as I switch out my skates on the bench—solo skaters this time. My eyes land on Anastasia, one of the top ice skaters at Valcérre. Everything about her is perfect. Perfect posture, perfect physique.

She takes a few minutes to stretch and warm up before starting working on her spins and crossovers. And I hate how she makes it look so easy and effortless. I look away, ignoring the sting of jealousy tightening in my chest.

I grab my bag, slinging it over my shoulder, and carry my skates by their laces as I walk out of the rink. I climb the last set of stairs, heading toward the athlete's lounge. I need food. Water. Something, God anything, to get my mind off how badly today went.

The hockey players are gathered at the bar near the balcony, owning the place like it was built for them. Some lounge at the high-top tables with their legs stretched out, others lean back against the countertop.

I recognize some of them from when I stopped by the

hockey arena earlier. However, only one of them catches my attention—again.

Even seated, he carries himself differently. Lean, powerful, and contained. The kind of posture that says he doesn't give a fuck.

He isn't loud like the others. He's not grinning, talking, or socializing like he belongs in the conversation.

Instead, he's quiet.

He's wearing a hoodie, the sleeves pushed up just enough that I catch a glimpse of a tattoo peeking out from beneath the fabric.

I look away and keep walking, focusing on the café counter. Food first. Then I can drown in my self-pity.

But then I hear them talking.

"Who's the new girl?"

"Nico's new partner."

Why are they talking about me?

"The tall one with the braids?"

"Yeah." A low whistle. "She's hot."

I stop mid-step.

Of course.

Not, *"She's a good skater."* Not, *"She might be a threat this season."* Just hot.

A laugh follows, and someone mutters something I don't catch before another voice cuts in. "Z, here got a good look at her earlier."

I blink.

Wait. What?

"Yeah, I caught him staring from the balcony."

"Maybe he's got a thing for figure skaters."

My fingers curl tighter around my bag strap, and my face feels hot all of a sudden.

"Relax. She's just another ice princess." His voice is completely uninterested.

I freeze.

Of all the things he could have said, that's what he landed on.

Just another ice princess, like I'm no different from the others. I'm just a cliché, another pretty girl on the ice with nothing to prove. As if I haven't fought for every damn opportunity I've had.

Screw this.

I step forward, gripping my bag tighter over my shoulder. "Excuse me?"

The conversation dies instantly. All the casual laughter and teasing disappear as every pair of eyes focuses on me. Zayden Aldenhurst—and yes, I know his name; everyone does—is still leaning back in his chair with his protein shake in hand, completely unbothered.

His eyes flick to mine as he studies me slowly, like he's taking his time deciding if I'm worth acknowledging. Something about him makes my skin burn with frustration.

"Didn't quite catch what you said."

His expression doesn't change. If anything, he looks more bored, like I'm inconveniencing him by standing here. And then he speaks. "Something bothering you, Ice Princess?"

A slow shiver runs down my spine. I hate how his voice makes my stomach tighten in a way that catches me off guard. How his words burrow under my skin, settling there like they belong.

I fold my arms and stare at him, trying not get distracted by the way his piercing brown eyes hold mine. "Just wanted to make sure I heard you right. Something about me being just another ice princess?"

A few of the hockey players exchange glances, one of them shifting uncomfortably. But not him. Zayden doesn't blink, or hesitate. "If the title fits."

I see red.

The audacity, the smug confidence. Like he knows exactly

how to get under my skin and enjoys every second of it. "Right. Because hockey players are so much better?"

"Did I say that?" His voice drifts through the air, smooth as the ice downstairs, but there's something beneath it, like he's waiting for me to react.

I should walk away, let it go. Instead, I plant my hands on the table, leaning in just slightly. My fingers brush his, barely touching, but a sharp, electric jolt crawls up my arm.

Zayden stills.

His eyes drop briefly to where my fingertips accidentally graze his.

My breath catches, and I push away, forcing space between us, breaking whatever that was. "Maybe not, but you sure as hell implied it."

"Look, Ice Princess—"

"Don't call me that."

His head tilts, just slightly. "Sensitive?"

My fingers curl into fists. I could throw my skate at his head right now. Instead, I exhale sharply, forcing my voice steady. "Enjoy your protein shake, Hockey Boy. Just don't choke on it." And with that, I turn and walk away with my heart pounding in my chest. I don't have to look back to know he's still watching me. "Hijo de puta (son of a bitch)," I mutter under my breath.

The cold air stings against my skin, but I hardly notice. My body still aches from training, and my mind is replaying a loop of every mistake, every missed lift, every whispered doubt.

And then there's him.

Zayden Aldenhurst.

Just another ice princess.

The words shouldn't mean anything. But they do.

I just thought that he, of all people, would understand. Even though his last name rules the school and his dad is white. He's still the only Black player on that damn team. He still has to be twice as good just to be seen as enough.

I've heard the rumors. That he's only on the team because of his dad, and no matter how good he is, they don't believe he's earned his spot.

I step into my dorm, drop my bag by the door, and let out a sharp breath. I should shower. I should eat. Instead, I grab my phone and press Rylee's name. It rings once before she picks up.

"Hey, sissy." Her voice is warm, soft, and familiar.

And suddenly, the lump in my throat is impossible to ignore. I flop onto my bed, pressing my forehead against my arm. "Why am I calling you instead of getting ready for class?"

Rylee laughs. "Because you're upset."

I groan. "I hate that you know me."

She shifts in the background, probably walking around her villa in Paris. "Rough first day?"

I exhale slowly. "You could say that."

"Let me guess. You're already doubting yourself."

I close my eyes. "Maybe."

"Luna!"

It's not a scolding, just my name, but it's enough. Enough to make my chest tighten.

"You earned your place there. You belong there. Got it?"

I nod, even though she can't see me. "Got it."

"So, what happened?"

I hesitate. I could tell her about practice, about the lifts, about how every muscle in my body still aches from trying too hard. But instead, I say the part that got under my skin. "Some hockey player called me an ice princess."

Rylee snorts. "And?"

"And it pissed me off."

"Did you throw your skate at him?"

I thought about it.

A laugh escapes before I can stop it. "No. Pero lo quería matar (No. But I wanted to kill him)."

"Then I'm proud of you."

I shake my head, staring up at the ceiling. "It just…got to me."

"Why? Because some guy who doesn't even know you said something dumb?"

"I just… I don't want to let you or Luc down." The words slip out before I can stop them, and as soon as they do, the weight in my chest feels heavier.

"Luna." Rylee's voice softens. "You could never let us down."

I press my lips together. "But—"

"No. Listen to me." She's serious now. That big-sister voice, the one she used when I was a kid and needed someone to keep me from spiraling. "Luc and I don't care if you win every competition or fall on your face a hundred times. You love skating, and that's enough. You are enough."

Of course, she said exactly what I needed to hear. I close my eyes and let her words sink in a little deeper.

"So get out of your head, baby girl. You've got this."

I breathe in then out. The pressure and the weight are not gone, but they feel a little lighter. "Thanks, sissy."

"Anytime."

Rylee is quiet for a second before she speaks again. "Have you talked to Mom?"

I hesitate just a second too long before answering.

"No. I've been busy." It's not a lie, not completely, but it's also not the truth. Because even if I had the time, I wouldn't call.

Rylee exhales. "Luna."

I know that tone.

"I'll call her soon, but right now, I need to get ready for class."

She sighs through the speaker but doesn't push. "So this hockey boy. Is he hot or not?"

I groan. "I'm hanging up now."

She laughs like she already knows the answer. "That's not a no."

"Bye. Te quiero mucho. (I love you so much.)"

"Yo también te quiero. (I love you, too.)"

I hang up before the lump in my throat gets any worse.

As always, the memories come knocking whether I want to let them in or not.

Six-year-old me was sitting on the couch, wondering if my mom was coming home. Rylee had just left for college, and I didn't know what time it was, except that it was dark outside.

I pulled the oversize blanket over my head. It still smelled like Rylee, sweet vanilla, but she wasn't here anymore. I didn't want to cry, but my chest ached in a way I didn't understand.

The little flip phone Rylee had given me was clutched in my hands. I opened it and dialed the first number. Mom.

The phone rang, but no answer.

I tried again, and still no answer.

I stared at Rylee's number, trying to decide if I should call her. Not because she wouldn't answer, I knew she would, but I didn't want to wake her up. She had school and work, but I called her anyway.

She answered on the first ring.

"Hey, Hermanita, you okay?" Her voice was soft, a little raspy from sleep. No frustration. No annoyance. Just warmth.

"Can't sleep. Can you sing me a lullaby?"

There was a silence on the other line, and then she softly began. "You are my sunshine, my only sunshine..."

I closed my eyes, my body curling deeper into the blanket, her voice pulling me away from the ache in my chest.

By the time she reached the second verse, my breathing had evened out.

I didn't tell her Mom wasn't home. Or that I was hungry.

I just let her sing.

The next morning, I woke up to the buzz of my phone against my pillow.

"Hello?"

"*Morning, sleepy head. Go open the door.*" *Rylee's voice cut through my sleepy brain.*

I slid off the couch, my small feet padding across the cold wooden floor. I paused for a second before reaching for the knob and opening the door. A little part of me was hoping to see Rylee standing there.

Sitting on the welcome mat was a brown paper bag. I picked it up and peeked inside. Eggs, pancakes, and a little container of syrup.

I closed the door and carried it with me back to the couch.

"*She's not back yet, is she?*"

I shook my head, even though she couldn't see me. "*No.*"

She inhaled softly on the other side. "*I want you to eat your breakfast and get ready for school, okay? The bus will be there soon to pick you up.*"

I could hear the jingle of keys. She was probably heading to class.

"*I have to go, but don't tell anyone, okay? I'll call you later.*"

"*Okay. Love you, sissy.*"

"*Love you, too.*"

I blink, shaking off the memory as I grip my phone tighter. My heart is beating too fast.

Why does this still affect me?

Why does a memory from over a decade ago still feel fresh?

I exhale, shaking my head.

She's trying now, and she's been trying for three years. But three years don't erase the fifteen that came before.

No amount of time ever will.

My phone vibrates, and when I check it, it's a message from Rylee.

> Rylee: He's totally hot.

I roll my eyes but smile anyway.

CHAPTER 5

Zayden

I watch as she storms off, her shoulders tense, and her fists clenched at her sides.

She's pissed.

For a second, I thought she was gonna throw her skates at me.

Jasper lets out a low whistle beside me. "Ooooh, the new girl has a spine."

I don't react.

"Is it just me, or is she hotter when she's upset?" Cameron adds.

That does get a reaction out of me, even though I try not to show it.

It shouldn't bother me.

But it does.

Because he's right, and I hate that I saw it, too.

Those brown eyes stared me down, full of fire and agitation that made my chest clench in a way I didn't like.

But I hate it more that he noticed, too.

He shouldn't be looking at her like that.

Shouldn't talk about her like that.

I push up from my seat and grab my bag with more force than necessary. I leave before I say or do something stupid. Cameron's still laughing. He has no idea how close I was to breaking his jaw over a girl I don't even know.

But for some reason, I feel like I do.

Jasper follows me, because we're going to the same dorm suite. I don't go outside. Instead, I take the underground route to Ravensbourne.

I scan my card as I reach the arched door. The light blinks green, and the heavy lock clicks open. Only legacy students have access. Fucked up? Yeah. But that's Valcérre.

The tunnel is quiet. That's why I take it. Most people use it only when it's too cold outside or during heavy snow storms. But for me? It's about the silence and the space to think.

Jasper walks beside me as we pass the arched stones. We couldn't be more different, even if we tried.

We are both mixed. His mum is Asian, and his dad is Valcerran. He has sharp features, high cheekbones, almond eyes, and golden skin. His tousled black hair looks like he rolled out of bed and still looks perfect.

People underestimate him. Too pretty, too casual, and too relaxed. But they forget Jasper Moon sees everything. He's two steps ahead while they're still stretching. One click on his computer and he will have everything he needs to destroy you.

Me, on the other hand, my mum is black British, and my dad is also Valcerran. I have my mom's brown skin that always makes me stand out on the ice and my dad's jawline and broad shoulders.

Jasper and I have been friends since grade school. Born and raised in Valcérre. He's the only one I let close. And even that, some days, is pushing it.

He hasn't said anything since we left the lounge, but I can feel him watching me. He knows better than to say something when I don't want to talk.

"So...are we gonna pretend that didn't just happen?"

I guess not today.

I don't slow my pace. "Nothing happened."

"Right." He snorts. "Nothing happened. Except you

responded instead of shutting her down. Which, let's be honest, is weird as hell."

I don't answer.

He drops it, like he always does.

That's the thing about Jasper, he pushes just enough, then backs off. Knows when I need silence, when I'm not ready to admit what's crawling under my skin.

Because the truth is? I should be over it. People don't get under my skin. But I can still hear her voice, still remember how she looked at me with those fiery brown eyes.

And that pisses me off.

I don't get distracted, or waste my energy on things that don't matter. My focus is simple: hockey and classes. That's it.

Valcérre demands academic excellence from all its students, whether you're the best player on the team or not. You keep up, or you fall behind—and I don't fall behind.

Once I get to my dorm, I should be getting ready for class. So why the hell am I sitting here, staring at my computer and looking her up?

Luna Del Sol.

Her name is a fucking contradiction.

Moon of the sun.

Two things that don't exist together but somehow fit her perfectly.

My fingers hover over the search bar for a second before I hit enter. A few competition results. Nothing too deep. That's when I see it, an article about Lucien Kingley standing next to his wife, and her sister Luna.

That's how I know her.

I scroll back to the image, staring at the girl I shouldn't recognize, but somehow do. She probably doesn't remember.

So, she's not a legacy. Not a scholarship kid. She's here because her brother-in-law is one of the wealthiest men in Paris.

I don't even realize how long I've been staring until the door swings open behind me.

"Mate, seriously?" Jasper walks in, eyebrows raised as he tosses his bag on the couch. "I thought you didn't do distractions."

I drag a hand down my face. "I don't."

He crosses the room, glancing at my screen before I snap the lid of the laptop shut. "Luna Del Sol," he says, with a low whistle. "You're still thinking about her?"

I don't answer.

Mostly because I don't have a good excuse.

Jasper drops onto the arm of the chair beside me, studying me with the kind of look only your oldest friend can pull off. I rub the back of my neck. The silence stretches.

"Just wanted to know who I was dealing with."

He raises an eyebrow. "And?"

"Nothing." I stand and head to the closet to change out of my sweats and into my uniform. By the time I'm done, Jasper's already waiting by the door, scrolling through something on his phone like he's not paying attention.

But I know better.

"You good?" he asks without looking up.

"Let's go."

He follows me out without pressing, and we cut through the underground tunnel toward the main campus. Stone archways and vaulted ceilings line the walls, the kind that hold secrets.

I keep telling myself I'm over it. It's been three years since the last time I saw her, and she doesn't matter. But when we round the last corner and head up the stairs that lead to the academic building, something shifts.

Like gravity just tilted and the air's thicker somehow. And then it hits me, mint with something soft and sweet underneath.

The same smell I caught earlier when she leaned too close to the table. Even after hours of training, she still smelled like that.

Like winter and summer. The same scent that'd been haunting me for years.

And there she is.

Standing just outside a classroom, her back turned, one hand adjusting the strap of her black tote bag, the other tucking a loose braid behind her ear as she laughs at something someone says.

I slow without meaning to.

Her presence hits me before my brain catches up, like I've stepped into her orbit again and forgot how to breathe.

Jasper notices. "Damn, what is happening?"

I don't respond.

He grins like he already knows something I don't. "I've never seen you like this. Ever." Jasper nudges me with his elbow. "You barely look at people, Z. Let alone burn holes in the back of their heads."

"I'm not—"

"Staring? Sure you're not." He glances back toward Luna. "I mean, I get it. She's hot."

The same heat from earlier that almost made me break Cameron's nose comes roaring back into my chest. It burns hotter this time, because this is Jasper, and I don't want him to look at her like that.

"Drop it," I say with the kind of tone that should make it crystal fucking clear that she's off-limits.

"Oh shit, I knew it. You like her, like her." Jasper grins like he just cracked one of his codes. "You think I didn't see the look you gave Cam earlier, like you were ready to beat the shit out of him."

"I don't like anyone."

"Except me, right?"

"I tolerate you, that's different."

He laughs, shoving his hand into his pocket, because he already knows the truth. I love him more than my own blood, and I would take a bullet for him without a second thought. Not that I'd ever say that out loud.

We're almost walking past her when Luna turns around, and our eyes lock.

Just like before, the world goes quiet.

Her cold stare pins me in place. Then she storms off like I never existed, leaving a chill behind.

Jasper jogs a step ahead, half-turned toward me. "She hates you. Like, full-throttle hate. That's kind of impressive."

I ignore him.

Let her hate me. It's better than whatever the fuck this is. The pull, the ache, and the way she's already under my skin. Better than the heat that flares in my chest when someone else looks at her.

Because I can't afford it.

CHAPTER 6

Luna

By the time the lecture ends, I'm starving.

My first Intro Psychology was supposed to be interesting. I like the topic when I'm not thinking about food. I forgot to eat breakfast thanks to my lovely little confrontation with Zayden. My stomach started growling so loudly halfway through the lecture that I'm pretty sure the girl next to me heard it.

Thank you, Zayden.

I grab my bag and follow the other students out of the lecture hall, into the hallway, and toward the bridge that connects the science building to the main campus.

My only goal right now is food, and my stomach growls in agreement.

"Okay, I get it." I pat it like that will calm it down.

I step off the bridge and into the main campus, past the library, heading straight to the dining hall, and then I freeze the moment I step inside.

Students gather around square wooden tables beneath grand chandeliers and high vaulted ceilings. The large windows offer a picturesque view of the snowy mountains in the distance.

Everyone looks like they belong here, and it's…intimidating as hell. I probably look lost as I stand frozen near the entrance until I spot a familiar face.

"Luna!" Annika waves at me with a big grin, and a sigh of relief escapes me.

We'd gotten close during orientation week when she and

Sophie showed me around campus. I learned her mom's Black and her dad's Korean and an automotive billionaire. But Annika? She's chill, real, and funny.

I make my way towards her, taking the seat across from her.

A few seconds later, Sophie slides into the spot next to her, rocking her uniform—cool-gray blazer over a white button-down shirt, blue, gray, and gold plaid pleated skirt, and black knee-high boots.

First and second years wear slate-blue blazers, while third and fourth years wear cool-gray ones.

I know what you're thinking. Why are we wearing uniforms like we're still in secondary school? Apparently, it's a way to show tradition, unity, and excellence. That's what the handbook says, anyway. As if dressing the same can erase the power games and politics happening underneath. We all know this is just another mask we're all expected to wear while pretending not to drown.

"Well, look who survived her first morning," she says, settling into her seat.

"Barely." I sigh dramatically.

She leans in, resting her chin on her hand. "So? How was practice and your first class?"

I groan, louder this time, letting my forehead hit the table. "A freaking disaster."

Annika snorts. "That bad, huh?"

"I got called an ice princess by some cocky hockey player like all I do is twirl around in circles or something."

Both girls blink.

Sophie sits up straighter. "Wait. Who?"

I lift my head just enough to glare at the table. "Zayden. Freaking. Aldenhurst."

That name gets a reaction.

Sophie's brows shoot up. "Wait, he talked to you?"

"More like insulted me in front of his team."

She and Annika exchange a look. Sophie leans in, dropping her voice. "You don't get it. Zayden doesn't talk to people like that. He barely talks at all."

I flop back in my seat, rolling my eyes to the ceiling. "Lucky me."

"I'm serious, Luna, if Zayden talks to you, it's because he likes you."

I think she missed the part where he insulted me, but okay.

Ignoring her, I pull out my phone to order lunch. This is my top priority right now. Yes, this is Valcérre. No standing in line. You order your food on your phone, and they bring it to your table.

Sophie continues. "Like, damn, you got the attention of Valcérre's hot, broody hockey star on your first day. Do you know how many girls around here have tried and failed to get him to even look their way?"

I groan. "They can have him. I'm not interested. I freaking hate the guy."

Sophie smirks.

Annika snorts, clearly not buying it. "Hmmm."

Before I can even tap confirm on my order, the air shifts, not colder or warmer but heavier somehow.

My thumb stills on my phone screen. My breath hitches, and a strange warmth flutters low in my stomach, as if my body knows something I don't.

I look up instinctively, and there he is.

Zayden freaking Aldenhurst.

He walks in, commanding the room without trying. His locs are tied back with a few strands falling loosely around his face. Somehow without scanning the room, his eyes land on me, as if he knew exactly where to look.

We hold each other's gaze for a few seconds.

A pulse beats hard in my throat. Heat crawls across my

cheeks, and I'm hyperaware of how fast my heart is racing, how breathless I feel for absolutely no reason.

I frown, forcing my eyes back to my phone and confirming my order.

Annika leans forward, raising an eyebrow. "Okay! What was that?"

"What?"

"Don't play dumb, Luna. We saw how you two stared at each other. That didn't look like two people who hate each other," Sophie says, grinning.

Annika shrugs. "You felt that, though, right? That weird tension or whatever that was?"

"No," I lie. I did, everywhere, on my skin, my chest, my pulse. "The only thing I felt was hate. I hate him so much that my skin boils whenever I see his stupid face."

Annika snorts into her water. "That's what we're calling it now? Hate?"

Sophie reaches for my hand. "Babe, this is a lot of hate, considering you guys just met. Sure, he was a jerk, but there's something more going on here."

I pull my hands away from her, mad for no reason. "There's nothing else going on."

Sophie leans back. "If you say so."

I sink lower in my seat, crossing my arms over my chest. I want to argue, but the truth is I have no fucking idea what's going on. But I don't have time for whatever this is. I'm here to focus on my skating and make it to the Olympics. Not get distracted by a hot, brooding, hockey boy—who I hate, by the way.

The presence of someone beside me breaks me out of my spiraling thoughts. An older woman in a black uniform places a tray in front of me with a grilled chicken and quinoa salad bowl and a bottle of sparkling water.

Everything here is so fancy, even the way they serve food like we're in a five-star restaurant, not a university dining hall.

I take a forkful of my quinoa and bring it to my mouth, chewing it slowly. It tastes good, even when my appetite is gone. I've already skipped breakfast, and I can't afford to skip lunch. After this morning's training, my body needs the fuel.

Then everyone goes quiet.

What now?

I look up as she walks in like she owns the damn school.

Anastasia Angelov.

Valcérre's very own ice queen. Three-time national champion. Her gray blazer fits her like a designer piece, and her long platinum-blonde braid swings down her back. Her black knee-high boots click against the dark wood floor.

Anastasia's mother was an Olympic champion, and her grandfather's name is on the training complex.

She ignores everyone's attention and boldly makes her way to Zayden's table. Her eyes move between me and Zayden, who's been staring at me.

Anastasia perches against his table, leaning close to his ear with a playful smile. Probably saying something flirty. Zayden nods but says nothing. He barely even looks at her.

"Oof. That's cold," Annika says.

I look over at her as she pretends to sip her drink instead of watching the interaction between Zayden and Anastasia.

Sophie chuckles. "She's been trying to get his attention forever."

I shove another bite of quinoa into my mouth like I'm definitely not watching or counting the seconds she lingers at his table.

She says something else, but Zayden doesn't respond as he pushes his chair back and walks away without glancing at her, or anyone.

Anastasia watches him, confused, before turning and heading toward our table.

"Uh...What's she doing?" Annika's eyes go wide.

"I think she's coming over." Sophie straightens her blazer.

"She's not—" I start, but then she's right here.

She doesn't look at Sophie or Annika. Only me. "Luna, right?"

I blink. "Yeah, hi."

"I'm Anastasia, welcome to Valcérre." Her lips curve into a too sweet smile. "I heard what happened at the athlete's lounge."

I guess word travel fast around here. "It wasn't a big deal."

"Hmmm, Zayden doesn't usually talk to people, let alone first years." She tilts her head as if she's thinking it over. "I get it, you're still new and don't know how things work around here yet."

Translation: You don't belong here.

I bite back the words that want to slip out, giving her a polite smile back. I hope my face doesn't betray me and she doesn't see the eye rolls I'm giving her in my head.

She lets the silence stretch before adding, "Anyway, I just thought I'd say hello. It's always nice to meet someone new on the ice."

With that, she turns and walks away.

Sophie grins. "Well, look at you."

I pick up my sparkling water and take a long sip.

"You've been here for two minutes, and you've already caught the attention of the ice queen, and the hot, brooding hockey star."

Annika laughs. "Honestly? That's kind of impressive."

"I'm not hungry anymore." I gather my things and push off the chair. "I'm going to the library before my next class."

They exchange a quick glance before standing and grabbing their things.

"Let's go." Sophie loops her arms through mine.

Annika slings her bag over shoulders as she walks beside me. She's the shortest of the three of us, barely five feet three inches.

We pass through the arched doors, down the hallway, and leave the dining hall behind us.

Sophie is right. It's day one, and I'm already caught in the middle of whatever this is.

I'm here to skate, everything else is a distraction.

Focus, Luna.

CHAPTER 7

Zayden

Practice ended thirty minutes ago. Most of the guys are already gone.

But not me.

This is when the real practice begins.

You don't get to be the star of the team by leaving early. Not when your dad's the head coach. Not when your last name is Aldenhurst.

People think I have it easy, that everything has been handed to me. They don't see this part. The extra hours I have to put in, or the way he talks to me when no one else is around. The constant corrections. The clipped disappointment, like I'm one mistake away from proving everyone right, that I'm only here because of him.

Because in this school, the Aldenhurst name isn't just legacy, it's dynasty. My dad went pro before a terrible accident ended his career. His father before him was a legend and the school director. His great-grandfather was one of the founders of the school.

The legacy runs so deep it's practically stitched into the damn ice. Except my skin doesn't look like theirs. And every time I hit the ice, it feels like I'm still trying to earn something that was written into my blood but never shaped for someone who looks like me.

So I push harder, skate faster, and hit harder, like I have to compensate for the fact my skin is not as fair as his. Like I need to earn what's already mine, even when I'm bleeding for it.

My legs are on fire, but I drop back into the drill anyway.

Sprint.

Pivot.

Tight crossover.

Sharp pass.

Shoot.

Top right.

It's still not good enough.

"That hesitation at the line was lazy," he calls.

"I recovered," I snap.

"You don't go pro by hesitating."

The words land harder than they should.

Go pro. Right. That's the goal, isn't it? Or is that just his goal?

He skates toward me, eyes stern on mine, and his voice is even colder now. "You're a third year, Zayden. This is the year that matters. You either want this, or you don't."

He studies me for half a second longer before returning to his clipboard like he's already written me off.

The whistle blows.

"Again."

My lungs are burning, my body's screaming, but I move anyway. Because if I stop, I'll have to ask the question that's been in the back of my mind for years now.

Do I even want this? Or am I just chasing approval from a man who's never once looked at me like a son?

What I need is a father, not a coach.

I finish the last drill in silence and wait for him to say something.

"That's all for today." Then he's gone like he didn't just tear me down for an hour straight.

No, *"Good job today, Zayden."*

I stand there for a second, stick hanging from my hand, chest still heaving. Then I skate off, slowly, pulling off my gloves as I go.

The locker room is empty, and my gear bag is still half-zipped where I left it earlier. I strip out of my pads in silence, peeling off sweat-soaked layers until I'm just in my base gear. My body aches, and my head's killing me, but it's nothing compared to the hollow space in my chest. I don't even bother taking a shower; I'll have one back at my dorm.

The metal locker door creaks as I swing it open. My jacket hangs inside, along with my backup hoodie and a folded beanie I've had since my first year here.

My eyes linger on the jacket for a second as my father's words replay in my head. *"You either want this, or you don't."*

Does he even care about me and what I want? Or am I just a legacy to maintain? I just want him to look at me, once, like a father, not a coach.

I grab the jacket and shut the locker harder than I need to. I take one more deep breath before pulling on the hoodie, shoving my hands in my pockets, and heading for the exit.

I don't take the tunnels, not tonight. It's quiet, just the way I like it. Snow flurries swirl in the dark like ash. A few students are walking between buildings. I cut across the glass bridge that leads to the dormitories, the frozen lake black beneath it.

Ahead is Ravensbourne Hall, bold and large with gray stones that look dark in the night. Tall, bare trees stretch upward like skeletal hands. From afar, they look like shadows. Behind them, the arched window expands high across each floor, glowing light coming from within.

I push through the heavy oak doors and step into the main lobby. The scent hits me first, cedarwood from the fireplace across from the velvet armchairs and bergamot.

The dining hall sits behind the lounge for students who would rather eat here instead of the dining hall back on the main academic campus. It's filled with broad walnut tables and chandeliers hanging from above.

I pass through without stopping, taking the stone staircase up to the third floor. It opens to the floor lounge—a shared space where students go to unwind and have fun. Each floor has one. This is where legacy kids like me do whatever they want.

The smell of cigars hits me instantly.

A few students sit around a grand chessboard near the fireplace, completely focused. Two guys are deep into their poker games. A tray of drinks sits next to them while cigars burn in a crystal tray, along with empty tumbler glasses on top of coasters branded with our school's crest.

To my right, a couple is making out in the corner, half hidden behind a towering bookshelf. Her legs hook around his hips, and his hands are everywhere.

Nothing I haven't seen before.

At Valcérre, as long as you keep your grades up, show up to practices, and do what you are supposed to do during the day, they don't care what you do at night.

You can drink, gamble, screw around. Just don't kill each other.

I make a left down the hallway toward my suite, swipe my key card, and step inside.

Three of us live here.

Jasper is in his spot on the armchair, feet resting on the coffee table and his laptop open in front of him as he types away. Cameron is shirtless on the couch with a girl on his lap.

I nod once and keep walking. My room is at the end, with a private bathroom and small sitting area. The door closes behind me as I lean against it and let my bag fall on the floor. I stand there for a few seconds, trying not to think about it, but my mind goes there anyway.

I used to count the seconds until I get home, especially after a rough practice. My mom would be waiting. One hug from her and everything would be okay.

Later, they would argue about how he was pushing me too hard, and he'd yell at her to stop babying me.

I pull away from the door and move toward my bed. My back hits the mattress, and I stare at the ceiling.

No headphones, no music, just silence, thick enough to choke me, but I need it, crave it even.

Silence means no yelling.

No father telling me I'm too weak or too soft.

No expectations.

I curl my arms around my myself like I can hold all my broken pieces together.

A soft knock breaks through my thoughts before the door pushes open and Jasper steps in, dropping into the lounge chair across from my bed.

"You good, mate?"

I let out a groan instead of answering.

"That bad, huh?" He leans forward with elbows on his knees.

I exhale through my nose. "No matter how much I push myself, it's never good enough for him."

My eyes are still on the ceiling, but Jasper is watching me.

"Maybe it's not about you, Z?"

I glance at him. "What do you mean?"

He shrugs, leaning back into his seat. "Sometimes it feels like he's trying to make up for something, like he needs you to make it not just for you, but for him, too."

Make up for what?

The question settles in my chest, like parts of me already know something that I don't.

I shake the thoughts off, sliding my hand over my jaw. "He's just obsessed with the Aldenhurst legacy and control."

The silence stretches in the room before I pull myself off the bed, needing a shower to wash off the sweat and tension from practice. I cross the room toward the bathroom, leaving Jasper to himself.

The hot water helps with my sore muscles, but it does nothing to drown out my thoughts. I brace my hands against the tile and let the water spray over me, trying to wash off everything, practice, my father's voice, Jasper's words. Closing my eyes, I let the water do what it can.

Once I'm finished, I return to my room, lie on my bed, close my eyes, and will my body to let go. The moonlight bleeds through the tall windows, casting pale shadows across the floor.

I put on my earbuds and hit play on my playlist. Soft piano melody, no words. It's supposed to help me sleep, but not tonight. I count the seconds between each breath and pretend the pressure behind my ribs isn't there, coiling like wire.

My body is exhausted, but my brain won't shut off. It's like too many emotions are trying to break through at once, all crashing into each other. But I can't let them in. I shove them down like I always do. My chest aches from holding it all in, and I can't breathe through the pain.

I sit up, grab my skates by the bed, and pull my hoodie on before walking out. I stop at Jasper's door, but the light is off. He's probably asleep, but I send him a text anyway.

> Me: Going out for some fresh air.

A few seconds pass.
Then three dots blink across the screen.
A reply comes in.

> Jasper: Done. Go.

I don't smile, but something in my chest eases.
He knows to cover the feed in the cameras so no one notices

me sneaking around. I put my phone back in my pocket and quietly slip out into the hallway.

It's past eleven, and the campus is mostly quiet, except for a few students sneaking between dorms.

I keep my hood up and my head down, cutting across the bridge and past the east buildings. The trees bend around me like they're watching.

No one sees me.

Ten minutes later, I slip through the rusted door of the old athletics wing and head down the dark stairs.

And there it is.

The Shadow Rink.

They don't talk about it on campus anymore. Not officially. But everyone's heard something. That it was shut down after an accident. That someone got hurt. That it's cursed.

I make my way to the benches and lace up my skates. The moment I step onto the ice, everything else disappears.

No drills.

No shouting.

No expectations. Which means no disappointments.

Just me and the ice.

The weight in my chest loosens. My legs move on instinct, muscle memory taking over. One hard push, and I'm gliding. I pick up speed, starting with crossovers, leaning into the turns, before launching into a left forward inside twizzle that rotates clockwise. My mind clears with every rotation.

Here, I don't have to be the coach's son. Or the Aldenhurst legacy. Or anything at all. I can just skate until my legs burn, not because I have to, but because I want to.

Picking up speed, I glide into a forward spiral, stretching my legs behind me and letting the ice carry me. Each jump, each spin, each push of my blades carves away the tension from earlier, bringing back a sliver of that joy, that freedom I used to feel when skating with mum.

My father was away most of the time with the national team before his accident. Mum and I would spend hours skating on the frozen lake at our mansion. She'd laugh as I tried spins I couldn't fully control yet. Her laughter would fill me with warmth even though it was freezing outside. Then she'd help me, telling me I could do it. I remember the pride I felt when I finally landed a spin perfectly, the way her eyes would sparkle like I'd done something magical.

The memory stings because she left.

I push myself harder, trying to outrun the anger, the ache, and the longing in my chest. Until my legs burn, my mind numbs, and the ice is all that exists.

CHAPTER 8

LUNA

"Again," Coach yells from the side of the rink.

Nico glides in a slow circle before getting into position, but he doesn't even look at me.

I bite back my own frustration as I meet him in the center, ignoring the pain in my ribs from that last lift. We go for the lift again, but I land off-balance, and Nico's grip on my waist slips just enough to throw the whole thing off. We stumble apart.

"Stop." Coach's voice cuts through the rink like a blade. "This isn't working." She points between me and Nico. "You two have zero trust and zero chemistry."

I open my mouth, but nothing comes out. She's not wrong.

Her eyes land on me.

"You're talented, Luna. Both of you have potential. But if you don't trust your partner, this ain't going to work."

Even though we've been training together for almost two weeks, it still feels like we're strangers on the ice.

"You want to make it through qualifiers?" she barks. "Then start acting like a pair. Spend less time on the ice and more time getting to know each other. Talk. Get lunch. Bond with each other. Or we'll have to find you both a new partner."

There's no guarantee I'll find another partner this semester.

Qualifiers. She's not talking about some friendly campus performance. She means the Continental Ice Pair Qualifier, the one that decides who competes at the European Winter Elite Circuit in December.

The one being hosted here, at Valcérre.

Where every scout, sponsor, and Olympic development rep in Europe will be watching from the stands. And if Nico and I can't figure it out in time? We'll be benched until we find new partners. I can't let that happen.

I glance at Nico, but he's already skating toward the edge of the rink.

"Hey." I follow him to the benches that run along the glass. "Do you want to hang out later?"

"Not today," he mutters, reaching for his bag.

"Okay, maybe tomorrow then—"

"I've got plans." He cuts me off, sliding his guards over his blades, then walks away. He disappears through the locker room doors, towel slung over his shoulder, like none of this matters.

And maybe to him, it doesn't.

Nico comes from a family of skaters, Olympians, sponsors, legacy ties. He doesn't need to care. He doesn't need this the way I do.

He's here because his parents want him here. I'm here because I fought for this. This is all I've ever wanted.

My fingers grip the edge of the cold metal bench. I press my lips together, forcing the sting in my eyes to stay right where it is.

Not here.

Not where anyone can see.

I blink hard, pulling in a slow breath.

That's when I feel it, the prickle on my skin. I hate that my body knows who it is before I even look up.

I lift my head toward the balcony, and there he is.

Zayden. Leaning on the upper balcony railing, hoodie blocking his face behind the glass, but his eyes are already on me.

As if the day couldn't get any worse. Our eyes lock, and my

body reacts before my brain can. A pressure builds behind my eyes.

No, no. I blink, trying to hold it back, but a single tear escapes.

I swipe it away angrily, hoping he didn't notice. I drop my eyes, switch my skates for my boots, and push to my feet. Grabbing my bag, I storm toward the stairs, not looking back. Instead of heading toward the athlete lounge, I take the back exit. I always do on days like this when I don't want anyone to see me.

Practice ran late, and the little daylight we had is already gone. The sky in Valcérre never really turns blue, just shades of gray. My boots crunch over thick patches of snow as I pull my coat tighter around myself and head toward Wolfswood Hall. It's colder at dusk. The campus is mostly quiet, just a few students wandering between dorms.

I run through today's practice in my head.

You want to make it to qualifiers? Start acting like a pair.

The problem is, I'm the only one trying.

I inhale the cool air and release it through my nose before pushing open the heavy door to my dorm.

The lobby is empty. I climb up the stairs, and as I reach the last step to the second floor lounge, I smell cigars. Someone is always smoking.

A group of students sits near the fireplace, watching a black-and-white film on the projector, but everyone is listening through their headphones.

In the far corner, another group is having a silent party with their neon headphones, dancing to whatever music they're listening to.

There's a game of chess going by the window, now covered with blackout curtains. An empty bottle of whiskey sits on the floor next to them.

This is Valcérre; the students study hard but play harder.

I slip past them toward the hallway to my suite. I scan my card and push the door open. The smell hits me first, beef and seasonings. Kimbap. It's like sushi, except the meat is cooked.

Annika and Sophie are curled up on the couch. Sophie's chopsticks are halfway to her mouth. They both look up as the door closes softly behind me.

"Rough practice?" Sophie asks.

"You could say that." I drop my bag by the door, hang my coat, and kick off my boots.

Annika nods toward the coffee table. "We got kimbap." She smiles. She was so excited when she found out I love it as much as she does.

My chest tightens with a small, grateful ache.

I offer a tired smile. "Thanks. Let me shower first." I disappear into my room before they can read me any further.

My back leans against the door as I close it behind me, eyes closed. I just need a second before heading into the shower. The cold wood presses through my hoodie, and just like that, I'm ten again.

My back pressed against the cold metal bench at the bus stop as I tried to stay warm despite the cold air cutting through my jacket. My stomach ached from being hungry; I hadn't eaten anything since lunch.

I missed the bus by thirty seconds trying to nail a toe loop, and the next wouldn't come for another hour. The bus stop was across from the center, and I saw it as I was coming out.

"Wait!" I waved at the driver as I ran across the street, but I was too late. The driver didn't see me, and he pulled away, leaving me behind.

I was always the one who got left behind.

I stood there, knees already sore from practice, staring down at the empty street, praying the schedule was wrong, that maybe one would come early, just this once.

It was just after six p.m., and it was getting dark outside. The center was already closed and everyone else had been picked up.

My flip phone vibrated in my bag as I sat on the bench. It was a text message from Rylee.

> Rylee: Did you get on?

I hesitated then lied.

> Me: Yes, I'm on.

If I told her the truth, she would ask me to call a taxi and that would cost way more. She was already working full-time and juggling school, barely sleeping.

> Rylee: Okay. Good. Text me when you're home, okay?

> Me: Okay, love you.

> Rylee: Love you too.

I tried calling our mom, but it went straight to voicemail. I didn't know why I even bothered.
So I sat there and waited.
Telling myself that it was okay.
That everything was fine.
That I was fine.

I blink. The pressure creeps up my throat, but I swallow it down. I've learned to hold it in, to tuck it somewhere deep enough that you forget it exists.

Once I'm done taking a shower, I put on a hoodie with matching sweatpants and join Annika and Sophie in the living room.

I drop on the couch beside them, letting my body sink into

the velvet cushions. My plate is waiting for me on the coffee table. They're watching a K-drama with French subtitles.

Grabbing my sticks, I open my plate and bring one to my mouth. The flavor hits instantly—seaweed, steamy rice, with all the juicy stuff in the center.

The tension in my chest eases just a little.

My phone buzzes with a new notification. I reach for it, expecting a text from Rylee or a schedule alert from Coach. But it's neither of those.

It's a text message from an unknown number.

> Unknown number: Want to prove you're not just another ice princess? Come to this location at midnight and alone.

I stare at the screen, my body going still. A little part of me knows who this person might be.

Knows it's him.

CHAPTER 9

Luna

THE MESSAGE HASN'T LEFT my mind all night. I roll over and check the time, 23:42.

I sit up slowly, holding my breath as I read the message over and over, even though I know it by heart now.

Part of me is screaming that this is a bad idea. This is how people get murdered, Luna.

I should delete the message and block the number.

But the other curious and stubborn part of me says *go*.

It has to be Zayden who sent it. He's the one who called me an ice princess.

Throwing my blanket aside, I slide out of bed. My hoodie goes over my head, then I put on my coat and my gloves.

My skates are still by the door, and I grab them on my way out. When I step into the hallway, it's quiet. The campus is asleep, just a few students passed out in the lounge, probably too drunk or high to make it to their room.

I quietly make my way down the stairs and through the back exit. Snow drifts gently from the sky, lanterns glowing like ghosts in the distance, casting long shadows across the stone path.

I follow the pin location on my phone, my boots crunching over fresh snow. I still have no idea where I'm going. What's the saying? Curiosity killed the cat.

A few minutes later, I come to a stop at what looks like an old building no one uses anymore. This can't be right. I check the location again, and yes this is where this mysterious person wants me to meet them.

I reach for the door, and it opens. The air inside is somehow colder than outside. It's dark, except for faint light from down the stairs.

The sound of blades cutting across ice catches my attention, and I follow it down the stairs. That's when I see it.

An ice rink.

One that no one mentioned during my campus tour. I move closer, stepping through the bleachers as the skater jumps into a triple axel and lands clean. A fucking triple axel. It took me years to master that move.

Then I catch a glimpse of his face as he skates—more like flies—past me.

Zayden.

Part of me knew it was him who sent the messages, I just didn't expect to find him moving like this. He hasn't seen me yet, and I continue watching him from behind the glass.

A sense of deja vu washes over me, like I've seen those movements before. The tension in the way he moves, like he's trying to outrun something. Every spin, every push paints his pain, frustration, and the need to escape it all. I can almost feel it like it's bleeding through the glass and straight into me. He makes every motion looks like poetry.

Even though I'm in awe, I'm still mad that he thinks he knows me. He wants me to prove that I'm not another ice princess? Fine.

I drop my bag on the floor and switch out my boots for my skates. He still hasn't stopped.

Once I'm done, I step onto the ice, and the moment I do, he slows to a stop. Like he felt me before my blades even made a sound. Our eyes lock from across the rink.

No words, no smirks. Just…tension.

Show me what you got, hockey boy. Let's see if you can keep up.

One foot crosses over the other, I lean into a curve as I push off the ice. I stretch my arms for balance, letting my skates guides me. With my right skate digging into the ice while the left toe pick drives upward, I launch into toe loop jump. I land clean on the back outside edge of my right skate, knees absorbing the impact. I flow into a spiral with my leg stretching behind me before bringing my skates together and steadying myself. I glance over my shoulder, and he's mirroring my movements, like we've trained together.

Seriously?

I grit my teeth, pick up speed, and pour everything into my stride. He stays with me, and somehow, we start moving together.

Our skates cut clean lines across the ice, matching each other step for step, breath for breath. I shift into a turn—he mirrors me. I cross over to switch direction—he's already there.

It's infuriating.

And seamless.

I don't even realize I'm drifting toward him until our arms brush. Something sparks beneath my skin. He reaches out for me, and I let him.

His hands find my waist, and my body reacts before my brain can. The next thing I know, he's lifting me. No hesitation. No flinch. Just trust and chemistry.

When did I start trusting him?

I'm above him, and his hands are exactly where they should be. It doesn't feel like a lift. It feels like I'm flying, that sweet, perfect second of weightlessness.

And for the first time since I got here, I feel free.

No pressure.

No judges.

I land back on the ice, breath catching in my throat. His

hands linger at my waist. His scent, something icy and citrus, fills my head, and I forget everything.

Why I hate him.

Why I shouldn't be here.

Why I thought I needed to prove anything at all.

I pull back, breathless, skating a few feet away just to give myself space. My heart's still racing, too fast and too loud.

What the fuck was that? I have so many questions. He's a hockey player and should know how to skate, but no hockey player moves like that.

"How the hell do you know how to skate like that, Zayden?"

He doesn't respond, and that makes it worse.

"Say something," I bite out.

Still nothing.

Finally, his lip part. "Why are you even here, Luna?"

"What?" I blink.

He skates slowly toward the bench, where his jacket and bag are waiting.

"Are you stalking me now?" he asks without looking at me.

"Seriously? You texted me," I snap.

He stops and turns to face me. "No, I didn't."

"If you didn't, then who did?" I grab my phone off the bench to show him, and it vibrates with a new message.

Unknown number: You two were cute together. But do you even know where you are? Or what happened here?

I look up slowly to find Zayden's eye glancing between his phone and me. The screen lights up his face, and his brows pull together. So, he got the same message.

I don't know who sent it, or what it means. But the chill that runs through me has nothing to do with the ice.

"Zayden…"

"Go back to your dorm." He slides his phone into his pocket.

My head snaps back. "Are you serious?"

"You shouldn't be here." He sits on the bench to remove his skates and switch them for his sneakers.

"Why not? You're here."

He doesn't say anything, instead, he grabs his bag, heading for the exit.

I want to yell at him, demand answers, but I figure now is probably not the right time. I grab my things, too, my skates off and over my shoulders as I follow him.

Whatever this place is…it's hiding something.

And I'm going to find out what.

CHAPTER 10

Zayden

I don't hear her footsteps at first, but I can feel her following me. Just like as I felt her the second she stepped onto the ice.

We climb back to the first floor, and I push the door open, holding it just long enough for her to catch up.

Outside, the cold hits again—harder this time.

She hugs her coat tighter. Doesn't say a word.

I glance at her as we start toward the dorms. "You shouldn't be sneaking out like that," I say quietly. "It's not safe."

She doesn't argue. Just walks beside me, silently.

Luna slows as we reach Wolfswood Hall. She looks up at the dark windows then at me. Her expression is unreadable. A mix of confusion, frustration, and something that looks a lot like fear.

"You're not going to let the message go, are you?

She lifts her chin. "Are you?"

I don't answer, holding her gaze for one beat too long. "Get inside."

She scoffs. "Don't boss me around, Hockey Boy."

The corner of my mouth twitches into an almost-smirk as she disappears through the door. But I shut it down before it forms. I wait until the light above her entry blinks green and the lock clicks.

Then I turn and walk back into the dark. I try to forget how natural that lift felt. The way her body remembered mine, but she doesn't seem like she remembers me. Maybe that's a good thing. I can't get caught up in her right now.

Ravensbourne is quiet as I make it inside, except for a few students still drinking and playing poker at the student lounge.

I scan my card and step into my suite. The living room is empty; everyone must be asleep. Instead of going straight to my room, I knock on Jasper's door.

It opens just a little, and Jasper squints at me with his messy hair that still looks effortless. "It's two in the morning, Aldenhurst. What do you want?"

"I need a favor."

He mumbles something under his breath and steps aside to let me in. He sighs, moving to the desk in the corner of his room and flipping his laptop open. "It's always a favor with you."

I know he's not mad, just groggy because I woke him up, but I don't want to risk it by waiting until tomorrow.

I stay standing. "I need you to wipe the camera feeds from earlier."

That wakes him up a little.

"Which ones?"

"Between Ravensbourne and Wolfswood. Exterior and hallway angles. From around 11:30 to 1:30."

"All right. What am I scrubbing?" He starts typing, his fingers moving rapidly despite the hour. But then he stops. "Okay, what the hell is this?"

"What?"

He turns the screen slightly. "First, you sneak out alone, around 11:40."

Click.

"Then twenty minutes later, Luna."

Click.

"And guess who walked her back to her dorm?"

I say nothing.

Jasper leans back slowly, arms crossing over his chest. "What the hell is going on ?" he asks, quieter now.

I ignore his question. "Did you see anyone follow her or me?"

He shoots me sideways glance but doesn't push. "Not that I can see in the feed."

"Good," I mutter, stepping back toward the door.

Jasper turns in his chair. "That's it? You're not gonna tell me what you were doing with Luna?"

I pause, hand on the knob. "Go back to sleep, Jasper," I say over my shoulder. Then I walk out, the door clicking shut behind me. I need to figure out who the hell sent the messages.

If my instinct is right, this thing's bigger than just us. I think whatever's coming started long before either of us showed up at that rink. And I'm not dragging Jasper into it until I know what we're really up against.

CHAPTER 11

Luna

IT'S BEEN A FEW WEEKS, and I still don't belong here. Not on the ice. Not in class. Not even in my room, where the silence is always waiting to swallow me whole.

I need out of my head tonight.

That's the only reason I said yes when Sophie invited me to a party. "Just something low-key," she said, at a place called The Vault.

Low-key, my ass. Nothing is low-key when it comes to Valcérre.

The Vault is an old building at the far edge of campus. During the day, it looks abandoned. Dark stones, ivy-covered walls, and boarded windows.

But right now, it looks like something haunted, barely visible in the dark.

"This is it?" I look over at Sophie.

"Pretty cool, right?" Sophie grins.

Cool isn't the word I'd use to describe it, but sure.

We climb the steps slowly, with Sophie leading the way and Annika and I following her.

Sophie stops at the door and reaches for the small panel in the center. She knocks three times then leans in and whispers, "Nel gelo, arde ancora il fuoco (In the frost, the fire still burns)."

"Was that Italian?" I blink.

"Welcome to the Vault." She smirks over her shoulder as the door slides open.

I hesitate before following her and Annika inside and down the worn stairs.

We reach the bottom of the narrow stone stairwell, and Sophie pushes open a tall, black door. The heat and noises hit me all at once, totally different vibes compared to the outside of the building. Bass-heavy music, laughter, too many voices blending together.

It smells like whiskey, musk, and chaos. It's barely lit with chandeliers hanging from arched ceilings. To the right, two guys with matching hockey jackets are playing at a pool table. Another one is making out with two girls in a velvet booth.

"Welcome to Valcérre's night life." Sophie nudges my shoulder.

I follow them deeper inside, toward a dimly lit corner with a velvet semi-circle booth. Three guys are already sitting there. The first one is Asian. He has a sharp jaw, messy dark hair, and a cocky grin that tells me he's fully aware of how good-looking he is. And next to him is another guy I've seen around campus. Tan skin, dark tousled hair, and brown jacket over a black T-shirt. He has that quiet confidence that screams hockey player and rich boy.

And the third one, I recognize instantly.

Zayden.

He leans back in the shadows. Every inch of him is calm and unreadable, until his eyes lift and land on me.

I grab Sophie's wrist before we reach them. "What is he doing here? You didn't tell me he was gonna be here or that you guys knew each other."

"Would you have come if I did?" she counters then tugs me forward before I can answer.

"Luna, this is Jasper." She gestures to the one with the smirk in the middle. "And that's Cameron." She points to the one on the right. Then a pointed glance toward the one pretending not to care. "You've already met Zayden."

I stiffen slightly, ignoring how my pulse kicks.

She loops her arm around my shoulders. "And this is my sister. Luna."

Cameron sits up straighter. "Wait! Ice Princess is your sister?"

"Don't call me that. I'm not an ice princess or just another pretty face on the ice. I've worked hard to be here." I narrow my eyes at them.

Jasper taps Cameron on his shoulder. "Knock it off." He turns back to me, his smirk gone now. "I'm sorry about that. He didn't mean anything bad by it, but I'm sorry if we offended you in any way. That goes for Zayden, too. We shouldn't have called you that."

I nod, surprised by how sincere he sounds. "Thanks."

Sophie turns to Cameron and elbows him hard in the ribs.

He makes a face. "Ow—okay, okay." He looks at me, one hand over his chest dramatically. "Apologies, Ice Princess—I mean Luna."

I roll my eyes as I slide into the booth beside Zayden, since that's the only seat left, trying not to react from how close our arms are.

Everyone turns to Zayden.

He doesn't move, or even blink. Just stares straight ahead like if he holds still long enough, the moment will pass. But it doesn't.

Jasper crosses his arms.

Sophie raises an eyebrow.

Even Cameron's watching him now.

"Sorry," Zayden mutters, so quiet I barely hear it, like it physically hurts to say it. I glance over at him, and he holds my gaze. His eyes soften a little, and there's something there that feels like regret. My heart does something stupid, part relief, part frustration.

"Next time y'all talk about her like that, I won't be so nice," Annika says, her voice deadly as she looks at each of them.

Cameron clears his throat and sinks a little deeper into the booth. "Noted."

Jasper just stares. "Fuck, that was so hot." Then he leans toward her. "Will you marry me?"

"No," she says dryly.

He presses a hand to his chest. "Ouch. Straight to the heart."

"You'll survive," she says trying to suppress a smile.

Sophie snorts into her drink. I try not to smile, but it's impossible.

I glance between them, arms crossed. "How do you all even know each other?"

Sophie shrugs. "Jasper and I have class together. He introduced me to Cameron, and Z is my cousin."

"Your cousin?" I blink, hoping she's not talking about who I think. Even though there's no one else at the table whose name starts with Z.

"Zayden is my cousin on my mom's side," she adds like it's not a big deal.

"And you didn't think to tell me that, like two weeks ago?" I give her a death stare.

"You mean like when you were going off about how much you hated him?" *Yes, exactly then.*

I hate you right now, I mouth at her.

"Je m'en fiche que ce soit ton cousin—c'est un connard et je le déteste (I don't care if he's your cousin, he's an asshole and I hate him)."

Sophie smiles into her drink. "He speaks French, you know."

I nearly choke on my own oxygen, if that's even possible. I'm going to kill Sophie slowly. I look over at Zayden. No smirk, no comment, just that unreadable look. Which is somehow worse.

"That was kind of harsh." Jasper snorts.

"I knew I liked you," Cameron adds.

"Wait. You all speak French?" My eyes go wide.

They all nod.

I huff. "Of course, you all speak multiple languages." I lean back in my seat. "Traidores. Necesito nuevos amigos (Traitors. I need new friends)," I add under my breath.

"Sorry, babe. You're stuck with us." Sophie laughs.

Jasper leans over the table toward me. "Welcome to the circus."

I lift a brow. "Is that what this is?"

"Only when Sophie's involved," he teases, nudging her with his elbow.

"Wow. Rude," Annika says.

"Hey, I didn't say it was a bad thing," he says, looking at her now.

Annika rolls her eyes, but there's a small smile pulling at her lips. "You're so full of it."

"Yeah, but I'm charming." He grins.

Jasper and Annika are going back and forth about something. Sophie is watching me like she's waiting for a confession. Zayden hasn't said a word.

Then Annika leans in and smirks. "Look whose girlfriend just showed up." She nods toward Zayden.

I look up as Anastasia walks toward our booth, short black dress, designer boots, and eyes as sharp as ice.

"She's not his girlfriend," Sophie whispers. "She just wants to be."

I watch Zayden out of the corner of my eye. He doesn't move. I hate the tightness that creeps into my chest.

Annika grins. "She's been trying for, what, two years now?"

Jasper lets out a low whistle. "Persistent. Gotta respect it."

I'm suddenly very aware of how close I'm sitting to Zayden. How he hasn't moved away, and how the heat of his body seeping into my skin.

Anastasia stops at the edge of the booth, her gaze shifting back and forth between Zayden and me, and I swear her mouth twitches slightly.

"Didn't know you'd be here," she whispers to him.

Zayden ignores her, eyes on his phone.

The girl can't take a hint. Her smile falters, but she recovers fast. "Well, it was nice seeing you." Then she's gone.

I take a long sip of my drink. "You two are kind of perfect for each other."

"She's not my type." His eyes are on me when he says it. My stomach flips for some stupid reason.

"So, what is your type?" Sophie leans in and asks.

Zayden doesn't answer.

Sophie groans. "Why do I even bother?"

Cameron pulls her closer to him, one hand casually finding her waist as he whispers something in her ear. Whatever he says makes her laugh.

"Cameron!" She swats his chest slightly.

"Come on." He stands, tugging her gently. "Let's dance."

Sophie glances back at me before she lets him pull her into the crowd. *Talk to him*, she mouths to me.

I roll my eyes at her.

Jasper and Annika are gone, too. It's just me now, and Zayden. Despite the music pounding and the party in full swing, the silence between us is suffocating. Every breath feels too loud and every second heavier than the last.

Screw this.

I push off my seat and slip through the crowd, toward the stairs. The music fades behind me, and by the time I reach the main floor, everything is quieter and I can finally breathe.

Instead of going for the exit, I keep walking. There's an archway leading to a balcony that I somehow missed when we came in. The view out here is beautiful. Snowy mountains stretch like shadows in the distance. A full moon hangs above them, casting silver light across everything. The sky is clear for once, no clouds, just stars—thousands of them.

"Are you following me now?" I ask when I feel him behind me. Then something warm settles over my shoulders. I didn't realize I left my coat.

"You forgot this." His voice brushes the air beside me.

"Thanks."

He leans against the wall.

How can someone be so quiet but his presence so loud?

"You okay?" he asks.

"I wish people would stop asking me that."

I glance at him, and he's just standing there, hand in his pocket like he's letting me decide if I want to say something more or not.

So, I talk, even though I shouldn't, especially not to him. "I just feel like I'm falling behind," I admit. "I don't know how to be part of this world. Everything feels like a test and if I mess up once, I lose everything."

I don't expect him to say anything back, but it's nice to have someone listen.

"I spent years trying to prove I belonged here. To them. To my dad. To the team." He looks away then back to me. "It doesn't matter. You could be perfect, and they'd still try to find some way to tear you down."

The silence stretches between us.

"So what, I'm just supposed to stop caring?"

"No." He shrugs. "You just stop letting them decide who you are."

A breath escapes me in a half laugh, half something else. "Why are you even telling me this?"

He doesn't answer.

I shake my head. "For someone who doesn't usually talk. You have a lot to say."

His lips twitch like he might smile, but he doesn't.

I huff out a laugh. It comes out a little more breathless than I want it to. "You're a weird guy, you know that?"

He raises an eyebrow.

"One minute, you're insulting me in front of your whole team, and the next, you're out here giving me some emotionally repressed pep talk like you're my therapist."

"Is it helping?"

I narrow my eyes. "Unfortunately. Still hate you, though."

The silence stretches between us again, but this time, it's not heavy.

"So, are we gonna talk about it, the rink, the messages?"

He closes the space between us before I even finish. He's so close that his breath is warm on my skin when he says, "There's nothing to talk about. And don't go back there again." Then he turns and leaves.

That's it? God, I'm such an idiot. I hate him. I seriously, honestly, hate him. He doesn't want to talk about it? Fine. I'll figure it out myself. I turn toward the stairs to find Sophie and Annika when I slam right into someone.

"Whoa! Careful," a pitchy voice says.

I step back, blinking up at the person.

Anastasia.

Of course.

"Harsh. Even for him." She looks over her shoulder to where Zayden disappears then back to me.

I roll my eyes and try to move past her, but she sidesteps, blocking my path.

"Don't take it personally," she adds with a teasing smile that doesn't reach her eyes. "Zayden doesn't like anyone."

I say nothing.

"Still—kind of cute of you, thinking he cares."

I finally meet her gaze. "Are you done?"

She smiles. "Just…be careful. This place has a way of chewing up girls like you." Then she walks away the same way she came.

Girls like me? What's that supposed to mean?

Okay, I hate her too!

Her and Zayden really are perfect for each other.

CHAPTER 12

Luna

I sit across from Nico at a little café tucked near the edge of campus. It's surrounded by arched floor-to-ceiling windows with wrought iron frames that are curved like cathedral frames. Snow clings to the glass outside, blurring the view of the trees beyond and making everything feel like it's happening inside a snow globe.

Coach wants us to bond, and I basically begged Nico to have breakfast with me.

"Look, I know we're not best friends or whatever, but I really need this to work."

He doesn't interrupt. Just watches me quietly.

"I've dreamed of this since I was eight. Competing. Nationals. The Olympics. All of it. This school…this program…it's everything to me."

I finally meet his eyes.

"And I can't do it alone. I'm trying, but if we don't figure this out, Coach will separate us. And there's no guarantee I'll get another partner or another shot."

There's a long pause before Nico exhales and nods.

"I get it," he says simply. "I didn't choose pairs. My parents did. They think it'll get me more visibility. But I'll try. Okay? I'll really try."

Relief softens something in my chest.

"Thanks," I whisper.

Something pulls my attention, and I glance over Nico's shoulder.

Zayden is sitting alone across the café at a table near the ivy-covered window. One arm draped over the back of his chair, his eyes already on me.

And when our gazes lock, it's like the room hushes. The memory rises before I can stop it. It's been a week since that night.

A week of pretending our bodies didn't move in sync with each other. Since he lifted me like it was instinct, my body trusting him like it never has anyone else before.

Stop staring at me. I glare at him.

He lifts his eyebrow. *You're the one looking at me.*

"I fucking hate him," I mutter under my breath, stabbing my fork into my chocolate chip protein pancake. I hate how he stares at me like he sees through the version of myself I've been pretending to be since I got to campus.

Nico glances up and lifts his eyebrows. "Strong words."

I blink at him and chuckle. "So, why figure skating?" I ask Nico, ignoring the big elephant across from me.

"My parents were Olympic figure skaters," he says without looking at me.

That gets my attention. "Seriously?"

He nods. "They fell in love on the ice. The whole fairytale ending."

"Damn," I whisper, eyebrows lifting. "No pressure or anything."

A small smile tugs at his mouth. "Yeah. It's a lot." He hesitates again then adds, "I'm sorry, by the way."

I blink. "For what?"

"For avoiding you. For being a dick to you."

It's not like I haven't noticed it, the silence, the distance, the way he disappears right after practice like I'm invisible.

"I'm not great at the whole social thing." He takes a sip of his coffee.

The corner of my mouth curves into a smile. "It's okay. I'm kind of bad at people, too. I just fake it better."

Nico laughs under his breath. "Noted."

And for the first time since all this started, something shifts between us. Not a friendship. Not yet. But something.

When I look up again, Zayden is gone, and that shouldn't disappoint me the way it does. I turn back to my tray, my appetite suddenly gone with him.

I glance up at Nico. "Hey, do you know anything about an old rink at the far edge of campus?"

His body goes still, and he doesn't answer right away. Then finally, he says, "You mean the Shadow Rink?"

"Shadow Rink?"

He shifts in his seat, looking uneasy. "Yeah, that's what they call it now."

"What was it called before?"

"I think the Ice Arena D. It was a private rink used mostly by star athletes and legacies students."

"What happened?"

"I don't know." The lie is written all over his face. He knows more. "Just...stay away from it."

"But, why? What is it you're not telling me?"

He leans back in his chair, shaking his head like he's already said too much. "Just leave it alone."

"It sounds like you're warning me."

"Maybe I am."

There's something tight in his voice now, like fear, but before I can push further, he stands and grabs his tray, his croissant untouched. "Thanks for breakfast. I meant it. I'll try."

And with that, he walks off. My skin crawls with questions.

I leave right after him, heading over the bridge toward the academic building, Nico's voice is still replaying in my head.

My head's spiraling with so many questions as I make my way toward my psychology class.

"You okay?" The question comes from behind me. I glance over my shoulder.

Serene.

She's holding her book to her chest, offering a gentle smile. Her red curls frame her face perfectly. Serene sits next to me in psychology class.

I exhale. "Just tired."

"Uh huh. What did Nico or Zayden do now?"

Geez, am I that easy to read?

"They didn't do anything," I say as we walk together.

Well, that's not the whole truth.

"Have you heard of the Shadow Rink?" I whisper.

Serene pauses, tilting her head up. "That place was closed years ago. No one talks about it."

I didn't even know it existed until last week.

"Do you know why?"

She shakes her head as we resume our walk, changing the subject to something else, but all I can think about is the Shadow Rink. The messages Zayden and I received that night. His face when he saw it, like he knew something.

My phone buzzes, and I grab it; it's a reminder of my virtual therapy with my mom.

I stop walking, just for a second. A cold presses in through my blazer like it wants to crawl under my skin and stay there.

I should be relieved. Things with my mom have been...fine. The anger that used to burn a hole in my chest is gone. The resentments faded away like an old bruise, and all that left is emptiness, no warmth, no affection, just nothing. I don't know how to fix our relationship. I know she's been trying, but I don't think any amount of therapy can fix this.

I keep moving and slide into a seat near the back of the

lecture hall just as the professor starts rambling about cognitive frameworks.

When the lecture ends, I have no freaking idea what he talked about. I'm not even sure I was there. My notes are a mess. Half-sentences I don't remember writing. Something about burnout and peak performance. The irony isn't lost on me.

Back at the dorms, the girls are already there. Annika is sitting with a face mask, watching another K-drama. Sophie is holding a tablet, probably sketching something for athletic benefits.

The smell of a vanilla candle on the coffee table hits me instantly, and it reminds me of Rylee. She's obsessed with that scent. The idea of calling her crosses my mind, but I can't keep calling her every time I spiral.

Annika glances at me as I walk in. "You good?"

"Yeah," I lie, tossing my bag on the floor. "Just tired."

Sophie looks up briefly, catching something in my expression. Her eyes linger, like she wants to ask more, but she doesn't. Just gives me a quiet nod and goes back to sketching.

I head to my room before she decides to say anything.

Therapy starts a few minutes later. I sit at my desk, headphones in, webcam on. Dr. Andrea greets us. My mom smiles from the other side of the screen, says she misses me, says she's proud. I nod. Say I'm fine. We both pretend that's enough.

The call ends, and I stare at the screen until it fades to black. My reflection looks exhausted.

After my shower, I sit with Annika on the couch in the living room. Sophie went out earlier. I curl up next to her with a mug of tea I barely drink as we watch a K-drama series. She talks at the screen, laughs at a line I missed. I nod when I'm supposed to, offer a small smile when she looks over at me.

We watch a few episodes—well, Annika does. I'm there, but not really. My thoughts keep drifting. Back to the Shadow Rink.

"All right, I'm going to bed." She yawns.

"Me too."

We turn off the TV and head to our rooms.

"Night," I say before stepping into mine. I close the door behind me and exhale into the silence.

I lie on my bed, staring at the ceiling, but sleep doesn't come. My body is tired from my training with Nico, but my mind won't let go. We're doing better, and Coach didn't look at us like she wants to murder us. The woman is scary.

It's almost midnight when I finally give in. I pull on a pair of sweatpants, a hoodie, and my favorite sneakers.

I grab my bag from beside the door and tuck my skates inside. I'm outside before I can change my mind.

The cold hits my face like a slap as I cut across campus, the air sharp with frost, the snow crunching beneath each step. Valcérre is asleep, windows dark, lights glowing faintly along the stone walkways like ghosts keeping watch.

I'm not sure what I'm expecting from the Shadow Rink.

Answers?

A sign?

I know I shouldn't go back there.

It's reckless. It's stupid. It's exactly the kind of thing people whisper about after something goes wrong.

But I don't care. The truth is that night I skated with him was the first time I felt free since I got here. Even though I would never admit this out loud, I'm hoping he's there again.

CHAPTER 13

Zayden

I knew she'd come again.

Did I ask Jasper to let me know if he saw her sneaking out again? Maybe.

She doesn't see me as she laces her skates and then steps onto the ice. Then she moves, not the way she usually does during training.

She's faster, freer. There's this fire to her movement, sharp, elegant, and a little wild. I stay in the shadows for a while, watching her.

Just her and the ice.

Something about the way she moves feels like a secret no one else was meant to witness.

She's good.

Really good.

Not like Anastasia.

Luna is something else entirely.

Where Anastasia is poise, Luna is power.

Where Anastasia floats, Luna flies.

There's nothing soft about the way she moves. She's not an ice princess, she's an ice storm. Unpredictable. Dangerous. Beautiful in the way lightning is right before it strikes. But I already knew that. She's better than she was three years ago, when I saw her skating for the first time.

Before I can think about what I'm doing, I'm moving. Pulled

in by a gravity I can't fight. My skates hit the ice, and her head snaps up.

She sees me, but she doesn't stop or ask why I'm here, just keeps skating, so I join her. Not close at first. Just enough to find her rhythm. Let it pull me in.

She's not holding back. Her spins are quick, tight, dangerous. As she passes me, I catch her by the waist. She jumps, and I throw her with no hesitation. She lands perfectly.

Then she laughs. The sound catches me off guard for a second, because I've never heard anything more beautiful, especially coming from her. I've gotten used to her icy glare. I didn't know she had that in her.

She charges toward me again, and I lift her higher this time, spinning faster. These are not movements you would see in a competition; they are ones that would get us disqualified if we were competing.

She skates across the rink and then back to me. I don't back away this time. She slows just enough to stop a breath away from me. Her laugh fades into a soft, quiet smile.

And God—she's beautiful. I've known that since the first time I saw her on the ice. But having her this close, seeing the curve of her lips, the glow in her cheeks, the softness that replaces all her fight, and when she looks at me like this, it's different.

She's still breathing hard from skating, chest rising and falling between us, and I'm sure she can hear my heartbeat. Hell, I can feel it in my throat.

Her eyes flick to my lips, and I swear we both stop breathing. My hand twitches like it wants to reach for her, to touch her face, her waist, anything.

But I don't.

Then she exhales and steps back, and I let her. I turn away before I do something stupid, like kissing those fucking lips. I skate toward the far end of the rink, eyes on the ice, not her.

It was the adrenaline.

That's all it was.

"Zayden…" I like the way my name sounds on her lips.

I look back, but she's frowning down at her phone. I pull out mine, too, seeing the message.

> Unknown number: There are more secrets buried here than you two dancing around each other.

CHAPTER 14

Luna

I'VE BEEN PUSHING myself all week as Nico and I get ready for the showcase tomorrow. My legs burn, my lungs are tight, but I don't stop. Not with the continental qualifier on the line. Not when every single person in this program is just waiting for me to slip.

Nico holds out his hands, and I step into them. Something about us has started to sync, not just physically, but rhythmically.

We go for another lift, and it goes smoothly, no wobble. It's perfect, but not the same as when I do it with Zayden.

I shake the thought away like it's sweat.

Focus, Luna. Stay sharp.

We land the sequence. Nico lets go. I take a deep breath.

"Again!" Coach yells from across the rink.

I nod, even though my whole body wants to scream *no*.

We keep going. Over and over. Jumps. Spins. Lifts. Corrections. Adjustments.

We've been perfecting our routine, and Coach gives us a nod of approval.

"You're both done for today." She claps her hands once. "Rest tonight," she adds. "Be ready tomorrow."

Then her gaze narrows on me.

"Whatever's in your head, Del Sol, get rid of it before you step on the ice tomorrow."

I freeze for a beat.

Then nod.

"Yes, Coach."

She walks off without another word.

Nico skates away toward the benches. I follow slowly and drop down on the bench.

My phone buzzes.

My heart leaps before I can stop it, but it's just a weather alert. I sigh, dragging a towel across the back of my neck.

Still no message.

No location.

No explanation.

No Zayden.

After we both received the message again last time, I demanded he tell me what he knows. He took my number and promised he would send me a location for us to meet and talk. He hasn't, but we've both been busy, me getting ready for my showcase and him getting ready for his first game of the season.

"You okay?" Nico asks.

"Yeah," I lie. "Just…tired."

He nods once, like he gets it. "You were great today," he says. "We've got this."

I want to believe him. I really do.

"Thanks," I say, forcing a small smile. "You too."

He nudges my shoulder gently as he stands. "Go rest. Tomorrow, we'll destroy them."

I huff out a quiet laugh, even though my chest is tight. Because no matter how many hours I train, no matter how perfect I get the routine, there's still this quiet part of me that whispers, *You don't belong here.*

You're just pretending.

And one wrong step will prove them all right.

I head back to my dorm and take a quick shower. I sit on my bed, barely feeling the heat from the radiator in the corner.

Everything aches.

I stare at my phone for a long second. Then I tap the call button.

It's late in Paris, but she picks up on the second ring.

"Luna." Rylee's face fills the screen.

"Hi." Seeing her face brings a small mile to mine and warmth into my chest.

"You okay?" she asks, already frowning.

"I'm fine. I'm just…tired."

Her smile fades. "You've been saying that for a week."

"The showcase is tomorrow, and I need to qualify for the continental round." I look down at my knees, picking at the edge of my blanket.

"You will. You've been training like a maniac. And you're amazing, Luna."

I close my eyes. "I don't feel good enough. Not here. Not lately."

"Listen, baby girl, I could go on all night about how amazing you are, how talented, how driven, but you need to start believing it for yourself. Because you're incredible."

I just nod, because if I open my mouth, I might cry, and I don't want to cry.

"Now, go make yourself some chamomile tea and rest. Because tomorrow? You're gonna be amazing. I already know it."

"Thank you." I smile.

"Love you, sis."

"Love you, too."

We hang up, and I sit there in the quiet, phone still in my hand, blanket bunched in my lap. Talking to my sister usually helps. But tonight, I need more.

That familiar tightness is still there, just under my ribs, where all the doubt lives. The ache that even Rylee's voice can't quiet.

So I stand, pull on my boots, and grab my skates before slipping out of the dorm. The reasonable part of my brain tells me it's a bad idea, but I ignore it.

The second I step inside the Shadow Rink, the air goes still. Like it knows something I don't.

I shouldn't be here. The messages and the warnings should scare me, but somehow, it's the only place I can breathe.

Dropping my bag on the floor, I sit

"You shouldn't be here." The familiar voice comes from behind me.

I turn to find Zayden standing there.

"I couldn't sleep and needed something to clear my head. I didn't know I had a stalker."

He watches me with that guarded expression, like he's deciding whether saying something is worth the effort.

"It's not safe here," he finally says.

"So why are you here, then?" I narrow my eyes at him.

"Because I knew you'd be here." He looks away quickly, rubbing the back of his neck like he didn't mean to say it.

"No more games, Zayden. You know something, and you're going to tell me." I step closer to him; his broody, guarded expression doesn't scare me.

He exhales through his nose. "Not here."

"Then where? Last time you said you were gonna send me a location, but you never did."

"Come with me."

"Where are we going?" I grab my bag and follow him outside.

And of course, he doesn't answer.

Ugh, I fucking hate this guy.

I follow him to an underground parking lot, and we stop in front of his Jeep. He grabs my bag and throws it in the back before opening the door for me to get in.

The drive is quiet. Outside, the road winds higher into the

snowy mountain. It's dark, the only light coming from the high beams of his car. Snow swirls in front of the dashboard.

Zayden is quiet, eyes fixed on the road, one hand on the wheel and the other holding the gear shift.

No music, just the occasional *swish...swish* of the wipers and the soft hum of the engine. He's completely at home in the silence, like it's a part of him.

I fucking hate it.

Growing up, I never liked the quiet; it just reminded me how alone I was. I'd leave the TV on, or music, or anything with voices, just to feel like someone else was there. Something to fill the empty spaces.

I try not to stare, but the dashboard lights are soft, and they hit him just right. His locs are pulled back, a few strands slipping free, brushing against his cheekbone. His lips are pressed together as he focuses on the road, and I hate how I notice it. I hate the guy, but he's fucking beautiful.

"You better not be kidnapping me," I mutter, mostly to myself. "If you're planning on murdering me before my showcase, I'll haunt your ass forever."

I glance at him out of the corner of my eye again, and the corner of his mouth twitches slightly.

Still ridiculously attractive.

I frown at the window and tell myself I'm just bored. It's dark, and I'm tired. And yeah, maybe I'm noticing how his hands look on the steering wheel, but that doesn't mean anything.

He glances at me just once, and the amused look in his eyes sends butterflies to my stomach.

About twenty minutes into the drive, we pull into a clearing tucked between snow-covered pine trees.

The headlights catch a stone and timber cabin in front of us. Zayden kills the engine. Neither of us moves at first.

"Wait here," he says before getting out.

Of course, I ignore him, pushing the door open and stepping out of the car. The cold punches straight through my hoodie.

"I told you to wait." He shakes his head as we walk toward the porch, my boots sinking into the snow.

"Since when do I take orders from you?"

He glances at me over his shoulder with an exasperated look before keying in a code and pushing the door open, stepping aside to let me walk in first.

I slowly spin around as I take it in. Vaulted ceilings, exposed beams, and a massive stone fireplace. Black-and-white framed photos line the walls, and there's a shelf full of trophies and medals.

The inside of the cabin is beautiful, but it's freezing.

"Is this your cabin?"

Zayden crouches in front of the fireplace, stacks a few logs, and lights a match. The wood cracks as the fire catches. Flames curl upward, throwing long shadows against the stone as the heat builds slowly.

"It was my family's," he says, glancing up at me. "But it's been passed down to me. Now it's mine."

I raise an eyebrow. "So, is this where you bring all the girls?"

Slowly, he rises from the floor, his eyes never leaving mine as he takes a small step toward me. "I've never brought anyone up here, not even Jasper."

I shift my weight slightly, trying to appear casual and like the fact that I'm the first girl he brought up here doesn't make me feel kinda special.

He's still looking at me, and the intensity in his eyes causes my cheeks to turn hot.

After a moment, he nods toward a dark hallway. And I stupidly follow him. For all I know, he's taking me to his dungeon.

We reach a door, and he opens it. There's a stone staircase that leads down into darkness. I wait for my fight or flight instinct to kick in, but it never comes. For some crazy reason I don't understand, I trust this guy. If I'm wrong and I die tonight, I'll be so pissed at myself for trusting my instinct.

The deeper we go, the colder it gets. This should be a clue right? That there's a freezer down here where he keeps his dead bodies. Then I see it, and I stop breathing.

A rink.

CHAPTER 15

Zayden

"You have a cabin with an ice rink in the basement?" Her eyes light up like a kid seeing candy.

I lean against the wall, watching her.

She takes a seat on the bench as she switches her boots for her skates. Slowly, she glides onto the ice, turning to face me. "Coming?"

I raise an eyebrow.

"You brought me here. You either skate or talk." She circles once, turning back to face me, again. Her eyes lock on me, and I can't look away.

So I walk to the locker on the wall, pull it open, and grab a pair of skates. I lace them up in silence then step onto the ice. The second I do, it's like the air changes. It always feels different being on the ice with her, like something just clicks in place.

She watches me for a second, her eyes unreadable. Then we move, and I stay a few feet behind her. She circles wide at first, testing the rink, owning it.

She glides backward, eyes flicking over her shoulder to find me, and I follow without hesitation. Our paths overlap and intertwine naturally.

We mirror each other without trying. We turn at the same time. Lean in the same direction. Like this is instinct, not effort.

She turns again, skates past me, close enough that her shoulder brushes mine. I feel it all the way down to my spine.

She slows, pulling into a soft glide beside me. "How do you know how to skate like that?"

I don't answer at first.

"Hockey players don't skate like that," she adds.

"I didn't start with hockey."

She turns her head, and her eyes land on me.

"I used to just skate." My voice drops a little. "Back then, it was just me and the ice. Before the games, before the pressure."

She watches me with that soft expression.

"My mum was a figure skater before she gave everything up when she had me. She taught me how to skate before my dad handed me a hockey stick."

"So what happened?"

I glance away. "My dad happened."

When I turned ten years old, figure skating became off-limits. *That's not what gets you drafted. That's not what Aldenhursts do.* My dad made it all about the game. Drills, speed, checking, points.

But I couldn't give it up completely. I would sneak out to where no one could see me and skate in secret. I taught myself jumps, spins, and crossovers. When I first moved to campus, I found the Shadow Rink. At night, when I couldn't sleep because of my nightmares, I would sneak up there and just skate.

She moves again, slower this time. "So you're self-taught?" She glances over her shoulder. "You're really good." She gives me a soft, and unexpected, smile.

My chest does this weird thing it's never done before, twisting and tightening, like it forgot how to function for a second.

She's always frowning and glaring at me. I don't know how to react or what to feel when she's not.

"So are you," I say, quieter than I mean to.

She bursts out laughing, her voice bouncing off the empty rink.

"So, I'm not just another ice princess anymore?" she asks casually, but there's something vulnerable underneath it.

"You were never just that," I say, watching her skate around me.

"Yeah right," she mutters under her breath, like she doesn't believe me.

I hate myself for putting that look on her face. For making her feel small when she's anything but.

Before I know what I'm doing, I reach out for her, pulling her closer. My hands find her waist, and she doesn't pull away.

Her eyes lock on mine, and I get lost on them. I didn't realize they had gold flecks in them before.

I swallow, my mouth suddenly dry. "I shouldn't have said that," I murmur. "I was just trying—" I shake my head. "I was being stupid."

She studies me like she's trying to figure me out. I have a feeling she sees more than others do. Her chest rises and falls rapidly. Her mouth parts like she wants to say something, but forgot what.

She blinks and steps back. "You're not very good at saying sorry," she teases, skating backward.

And I'm left standing in the middle of the rink with every nerve lit up.

She skates a slow circle around the edge, dragging her hand along the boards like she's thinking. "I started skating when I was eight. It was the only place where I felt free and in control at the same time. The only place that felt like home."

I know exactly what that feels like.

"But lately, it's just been pressure. Pressure to be better. To prove something. It hasn't felt like mine anymore…"

She hesitates then glances at me.

"Except the few times I was on the ice with you." The words slip out too fast, and she immediately stiffens like she didn't mean to say them.

"I mean—not like that. I just meant…" She looks away and clears her throat. "It felt…easier. That's all."

She spins away before I can say anything, gliding backward across the rink. "Anyway. The Shadow Rink?" Luna quickly changes the subject.

My spine straightens. If she knows the name, that means she's been digging. I was hoping she would forget about it and let it go. But I should've known better.

"I want the truth." She glances at me over her shoulder, her brows pulling in slightly.

She steps in closer. "You knew the second we got those texts. I think you knew what the place was before I ever stepped foot on that ice."

I keep my mouth shut, because if I start talking, I'll tell her too much.

She keeps going. "I need to know who's sending me those messages and why. So if you know something, Zayden, say it."

She deserves to know the truth, but I also know what happens when people dig too deep around here. I don't want her in this any deeper than she already is. Not until I figure out why she received the message or why someone wanted her at the rink.

"Zayden." Her voice sharpens.

I look up, and she's staring at me, demanding the truth. Besides my dad, no one has ever dared to demand anything from me. They talk behind my back, they murmur things when they think I'm not listening.

Not Luna.

"You brought me here and said we'd talk. So talk. I deserve to know what the hell we're getting pulled into."

My hands clench at my sides, because I do know. Not everything, but enough to know about the Midnight Challenge. That someone died there. That my family has been tied to this school and its secrets for a long time.

But I can't tell her any of this, because if I do, I might put her in danger. If anything happens to her…

"I'm trying to protect you," I blurt out.

She laughs. "I don't need your protection, Zayden. I've been taking care of myself since I was eight years old."

What is that supposed to mean?

"Why the fuck did you bring me here if you weren't plannin' on telling me anything?"

She's still talking, but I can't hear her words anymore. My eyes are drawn to her, the rise and fall of her chest, the tilt of her head, the fire in her gaze. She's fucking radiant, in the way a wildfire glows before it consumes everything. And I'm standing there watching it burn, unable to breathe. I don't even think, I just move. Her voice dies mid-sentence as I take her face in my hands, crushing my lips to hers, letting out everything I've been holding back since the first time she confronted me in the athlete lounge, or all the times she glared at me from across a room. The need, the heat, tension, desires, all spill out into that one motion.

She gasps into my mouth, hands curling into my chest like she doesn't know whether to push me away or pull me closer.

Then she kisses me back like she's angry that it feels this good, like she's cursing me with her mouth.

Her hands fist my shirt. My fingers thread through her braids. We move like we're fighting and falling at the same time.

Then she presses her teeth into my bottom lips, not hard enough to break the skin, but enough for me to feel the sting. Just enough to make me lose it for a second.

"Fuck." I groan into her mouth. Because it feels too good, and she's too fucking much.

Then she pulls back, breathless and eyes wide.

"That didn't mean anything," she says quickly, skating away, and it didn't. She was talking too much, and I needed a way to make her stop.

I'm grateful when she bends down to swap out her skates for her boots, taking the opportunity to adjust my pants.

"Can we go?" she asks without looking at me.

I skate over to the bench and sit beside her. I pull my skates off one at a time and switch them for my boots.

She follows me up the stairs without a word, the tension heavy in the air.

We don't speak the whole drive down, and that shouldn't bother me. Usually, I like the quiet, crave it, need it. Growing up, when my father's voice was too loud and impossible to escape, silence was my safe place. He didn't yell because he was angry. Not always. Sometimes it was about training, my stats, my footwork. Whether I was too soft on the ice, or if I was ever going to be the kind of player "an Aldenhurst should be."

Every correction came louder than the last. So I learned to be quiet. And over time, I started needing it. In locker rooms, on buses. In my head, silence meant control.

But right now, I hate it, because it's too loud.

Loud with everything I didn't say.

Loud with the way her lips felt against mine.

I shove the thought away and drown out all the noises. I welcome the quiet back as I watch her stepping out of the car and into her dorm without a glance back at me.

CHAPTER 16

Luna

Nico and I stand behind the glass as we wait for our names to be called. He says something, but I barely register the words. All I can hear is the pounding of my heart and the blood rushing through my ears.

I shouldn't be nervous. We've nailed this routine in practice over and over.

To make matters worse, I can't stop thinking about that stupid kiss. It was just a kiss and didn't mean anything. I'm more upset that I let it happen.

A round of applause breaks me out of my thoughts as the pair before us finishes.

We're next.

Nico and I step onto the ice, and everything else disappears.

Except for *him*. Even in a room full of people, I feel him.

My eyes scan the stands until they land on Zayden near the back. His eyes are locked on me like I'm the only one here.

He's not cheering, clapping, or smiling. Just watching me, and that's what calms my nerves.

Not the deep breath I took in the locker room.

Not Nico's steady hand or the hundreds of hours of practice.

Just him.

I look away first, because if I don't, I won't move at all.

The music starts, and we glide to our starting position. I bring my necklace to my lips and kiss it, like I always do before every showcase or competition.

I close my eyes for a second, blocking out everything. The lights, the crowds, the judges. When I open them, I'm at the Shadow Rink, skating with Zayden. I move the way I do when it's just the two of us. Free, no holding back, not trying to prove anything to anyone.

Nico's hands rest on my waist, and we go for the final lift. He pushes me upward until I'm balancing on his palms, arms extended, one leg stretched upward. And he spins me through the air like I'm weightless.

Then he lowers me. I touch down on one blade, and we glide into our final position as the music comes to an end.

The arena is quiet before the applause begins. I look up to find Sophie and Annika in the audience, clapping and jumping. I smile and wave at them.

Nico squeezes my hand and leads me aside. We stop near the corner of the rink with the rest of the skaters and coaches as we wait for the results.

He bumps his shoulder against mine, and I glance up at him. He gives me one of his boyish smiles. His brown hair is a mess from the routine, falling in loose waves across his forehead. His fair skin is pinkish from all the movement. He's kinda cute, but definitely not my type. I don't think I'm his type either.

Then the announcer's voice cuts through the arena. "Ladies and gentlemen, thank you for your patience. The results are in for the Valcérre Ice Pair Showcase."

The room stills. Every sound fades, except the pounding in my ears.

"In third place..."

Names I don't fully register. Applause.

"In second place..."

A pause.

My lungs lock.

"Luna Del Sol and Nicholas Morriseau."

It takes a second for it to sink in, like my brain can't process what I just heard. Until Nico turns to me, grinning, and throws both arms around me.

"We did it."

My breath finally releases on a laugh as I grip him back, squeezing tightly.

Second.

We qualified. We're going to the Continentals.

I can hear Sophie and Annika screaming my name across the stands. I wave and smile at them.

The noise, the lights, the congratulations, they all start to blur. I mumble something to Nico about needing air and slip out of the group. I stop at the bench outside the rink where my bag is. I grab my skates guards and put them on the blades before heading to my locker to change.

The sound of the arena fades into the background as I swap my skates for my boots. I don't bother changing out of my costume, just pull my coat over it.

I sling the bag over my shoulder and push open the side door, the cold hitting me instantly.

It's dark outside, except for the light coming from the single street lamp from across the building.

I haven't even looked yet, but I know he's here. My body senses him before my brain can catch up—like it always does.

I fucking hate it.

He's leaning against the stone wall of the arena, a few feet away from the exit, half-wrapped in shadow. His black puffer jacket makes him look broader, his hands shoved in his pockets.

"What are you doing out here?" I ask.

His eyes lock on me like he's trying to decide whether to answer or not.

"Seriously, are you stalking me now?" I snap.

He lifts an eyebrow, telling me that he was here first.

Okay, he has a point there. Even though I never agreed to speak fluent Zayden Aldenhurst.

"Second place. Not bad for an ice princess, right?"

Before I have time to see his reaction…

Buzz.

My phone vibrates, and I pull it out of my coat.

> Unknown Number: You've been invited to the Midnight Challenge. Shadow Rink. At midnight. Be there.

My throat goes dry.

I look up.

Zayden's already staring at me. "What is it?"

"It's another anonymous message."

"Let me see." He grabs the phone from my hand, reading the message before he gives it back to me. "You're not going."

Not a suggestion, but an order. Who the fuck does he think he is?

"Excuse me?" I blink at him.

He steps toward me. "I'm not letting you go back there."

I straighten my back and adjust my bag over my shoulder. "You don't tell me what to do, Zayden."

"This isn't a joke, Luna."

"Then maybe start telling me what's going on. What the hell is a Midnight Challenge?" I glare at him. This time, I'm not letting him dodge the question.

"Not here," he exhales, like he's already tired of this argument.

"Then where?"

"The cabin, I'll explain everything there," he says, already walking away.

"No." I stand my ground. "You keep saying you'll explain everything, but you never do. I'm not moving until you tell me what you know."

"Don't make me carry you to the car." He steps forward, closing the space between us. We stare at each other, neither of us moving. And for one wild second, I think he might actually do it.

"You better not lie to me again," I mutter as I shove past him.

Did I mention I loathe him?

I fucking do.

THE INSIDE of the cabin is colder and darker than last time. Zayden tosses wood in the pit, starting the fire like it's just another normal night and we're just here to hang out.

It catches quickly, and the orange flames light up the sharp lines of his face, making it hard to look away.

I cross my arms over my chest and wait. When it seems like he's not going to talk first, I snap. "You said you'd tell me. I'm here, so fucking tell me. What's a Midnight Challenge, and why am I getting invited to it?"

He doesn't answer or even look at me.

And I'm getting fucking tired of being ignored.

I move toward him, my fists clenched at my sides. "Zayden."

He finally looks at me, and something in his expression shifts, like whatever he's been holding back is heavy. Like saying it out loud will cost him something.

He tosses the last log onto the fire and stands slowly, dusting off his hands. "It used to be a secret competition."

"Used to be?" I ask.

He nods. "Back when the Shadow Rink was open. Invitation only. No coaches. No rules. Just the best athletes, underground bets, and a shit ton of pressure."

"And?" I whisper. "What happened?"

His eyes meet mine. "Someone got hurt. Afterward, the rink was shut down."

I take a step back. "And you knew all that and didn't say

anything until now?" The words cut through the space between us.

Zayden flinches. "It's not that simple, Luna."

"Bullshit."

"You don't understand how things work around here." He looks tired and frustrated. Like this conversation is taking everything left in him.

I scoff. "Right. Because I'm not a legacy like y'all. Got it."

"That's not what I meant." He runs a hand over his mouth like he's trying to shut himself up.

"There are things we don't talk about. Not without consequences. The Midnight Challenge is one of them." He's closer now, eyes locked on mine, so many emotions swirling in them. "This is why you can't go. Whoever sent that message is messing with you."

"You don't get to decide that." I've been making my own decisions for as long as I can remember. Besides, no one messes with me and gets away with it. Maybe if I go, I'll find out who's behind it.

He starts pacing then stops to look at me again. "You don't get it. It's not safe for you to go back there."

I shake my head furiously. Funny of him to act like he cares now. "Why do you even care? You don't even like me." I laugh bitterly. "I'm just another ice princess, remember?"

That wall he always keeps up? It cracks. Just a little.

"Well, guess what? I'm going."

His nostrils flare. "God damn it. Stop being so fucking stubborn."

"Fuck you, Zayden." I shove him hard in the chest, and he grabs my wrists. Not rough. But enough to stop me. "Let go of me."

Neither of us moves. We're breathing hard now. Close enough to feel the heat rising off each other like the fire behind us.

And then he's kissing me. I should push him off, but the second our lips meet, every part of me lights up, and all I feel is him.

And I want more of him.

His hands are already on my thighs, lifting me like I weigh nothing. My legs wrap around his waist on instinct, and then my back hits the wall, hard, but I barely register it.

I grab his hoodie, dragging him closer, even though there's no space left between us. Every line of his body is pressed against me. But I need him closer.

I gasp when his hips shift, pressure slamming into the ache that's been pulsing low in my belly. I grind against him without meaning to, needing friction, needing something more.

He groans, deep in his throat, and bites my bottom lip. I moan into his mouth, and he kisses me harder, like that sound ruined him.

His kisses trail down my jaw, my neck, up to my ear. Zayden's hands are everywhere, on my waist, my thighs. His mouth finds mine once more, this time deeper, slower. The fire has burned through us, leaving something softer behind.

Our foreheads press together, and the world goes still as his thumb brushes across my cheek.

"Please," he whispers. "Promise me you won't go back there."

Something opens in my chest.

Because I wasn't expecting this. Not from him.

And that scares me more.

"Zayden…What is it you're not telling me?" My voice shakes.

He brings his eyes to mine, and for a second, I think he's gonna tell me, but instead, he lets go slowly. I slide down until my feet find the floor again.

He takes a step back, but I still feel him like a ghost pressed against my skin. "Come on. I'll take you back."

Seriously!?

I stare at him, hoping for something, but he gives me nothing.

"Fine." I move past him without another word and head for the door.

CHAPTER 17

Zayden

She's still catching her breath when I pull back. Her eyes wide with too many emotions to name. She's waiting for me to say something, but I don't want to drag her further into this.

"Come on, I'll take you back." I step back and let her go.

"Fine." She moves past me toward the door, but not before I see the hurt across her face.

I follow her, grabbing my coat and keys. We're both quiet as I open the door, and I stop dead in my tracks.

Snow falls so thick we can't see anything ahead. The path, the trees, the road, and my Jeep, have all disappeared.

"We can't drive in that," I say. "It's coming down too hard."

"Then I'll walk." She walks past me. "I'm not staying here with you," she mumbles.

"Are you insane?" I catch up to her outside. "You really think you can make it back down a mountain road in a blizzard?"

She keeps walking. "I've handled worse." That makes my heart aches a little.

"Yeah?" I step in front of her. "You've handled hypothermia before?"

She tries to shove past me. "Move, Zayden."

"Luna." I grit my teeth. "If you don't come back inside, I swear to God, I will carry you."

She glares up at me, furious, freezing, and so goddamn stubborn.

I take a step closer. "Please, come inside."

Her face is still sharp with anger, her shoulders shaking a little—whether from cold or something else, I'm not sure.

"Fine." She turns around.

By the time we're back inside, she's dripping wet. Snow melting into her hair and clothes.

"You need to shower." I point toward the first bedroom down the hallway. "Towels are in the bathroom closet, and I have some spare clothes you can use in the bedroom, top drawer."

She doesn't argue this time, just disappears down the hallway. By the time she comes back, I've already taken a shower in the other bedroom, made some chicken noodle soup, and added more logs to the fire.

She's wearing one of my old Valcérre jerseys and a pair of gray sweatpants with the legs rolled up a little. Her braids are still damps, hanging loose around her face. Fuck, she's beautiful.

Her eyes flick to where I'm sitting on the couch in matching gray sweatpants and hoodie before she looks away.

She looks down at her phone. "No signal."

I watch her from the couch, trying not to stare too hard, but it's impossible when she looks this good in my shirt.

"My friends are going to freak out," she mutters under breath. "They were probably waiting for me after the showcase."

She still staring at the screen like the bars will appear magically.

"I'm sure they'll figure out we're together." I lean back into my seat. "Jasper knows I have a cabin up here, anyway."

She groans. "Great. So they'll think I'm in some cabin hooking up with you."

I tilt my head, watching her. She looks half horrified, half flustered. "I mean... Would that be bad?"

She glares.

I smirk.

"Come sit." I pat the spot beside me.

There's a blanket waiting for her and a bowl of soup on the coffee table. She hesitates before taking a seat at the far end of the couch like I'm contagious or something.

"I don't bite."

"You kidnapped me." She glares at me again.

I lift an eyebrow. "You tried to walk into a blizzard."

"Because I didn't want to be stuck here with you."

Ouch.

"I don't care if you're mad at me," I mutter. "Just need you to eat this and stay warm." Because I know underneath all that fire, she's cold and hungry.

She eats in silence, her eyes fixated on the fireplace as she finishes her soup slowly.

"Why don't you like to talk?" She breaks the silence as she puts her spoon back in the bowl. "Are you shy or something?"

"Not shy," I say, letting my head fall against the couch.

She lifts a brow. "Then what is it?"

"Talking wastes energy. People say too much, and most of it's bullshit."

She turns toward me more fully. "So, you think you're better than everyone?"

I shake my head. "No. I just learned early on it's safer to keep my mouth shut. The more people know, the more they can use against you."

She watches me, quieter now. And something in her eyes pushes me to keep going.

"People can be fake. They say whatever they need to be liked, to feel safe or in control." I meet her eyes. "But you're different."

She blinks. "Different how?"

"You're real and don't try to be anything but yourself."

It's quiet again, but her thoughts are so loud, I can almost hear them.

"I hate the silence." She says it as if she's talking to herself, or the flame. "When I was little, I used to be home alone a lot. My sister had just gone to college, and my mom wasn't really around."

She looks down at the now-empty bowl and whispers, "I used to turn on cartoons and leave them running all night, just to pretend someone else was there."

My chest tightens. It's funny how different we are. Where she hates the quiet, I crave it. I reach for my phone and pull up one of my downloaded playlist.

I untangle my wired earbuds and hold out one of the buds to her. She narrows her eyes at me suspiciously. "It's just music to help fill the silence."

Her eyes soften, then she scoots closer and takes the earbud from my hand. She puts it in her ear, and the cord tugs between us as a soft exhale escapes her lips, like the music relaxes something inside her.

Slowly, her head tips against my shoulder.

"I didn't take you for a Billie fan." Luna glances at me sideways.

"She gets it." I shrug.

"Good taste." She chuckles.

I try not to smile but fail miserably.

She shifts a little closer, and her head moves to my chest. My other hand comes up around her waist under the blanket. Her body fits so easily against mine; it's stupidly dangerous.

She hasn't moved in a while, and when I glance down, she has her eyes closed, breathing slow and even. I take in her features. Her face is soft now, calm. One of her braids falls across her cheeks, and I brush it gently behind her ear. She stirs slightly, fingers curling into the front of my hoodie like she doesn't want to let go.

God, I'm so fucked.

It's too easy, how calm I feel around her, that I don't mind when her voice fills the silence.

She looks so peaceful that I'm afraid to wake her up, but I know she'll be sore in the morning if she stays like this.

I carefully slide my arms beneath her knees and back.

She murmurs against my chest, half-asleep. "Mm... Zay..."

I shift slowly, standing to carry her to the guest room. The fire's low now, shadows dancing across the floor as I cross the cabin.

"Zay'n..., put me down..." Her brows pinch together even as her eyes stay closed.

"Shh," I whisper, adjusting my grip. "It's okay. Go back to sleep."

Her body softens at the sound of my voice. I carry her the rest of the way down the hall, nudging the bedroom door open with my foot.

I lay her down gently, and she curls instinctively toward the pillow, dragging the blanket up with one sleepy hand.

I stand there watching her like a creep.

"You don't always have to fight, you know." I lean in and whisper to her sleepy form, "Good night, Luna."

CHAPTER 18

LUNA

I THINK I'M DREAMING.

Or dead.

Or dreaming while dead?

Do dead people dream? Wait never mind.

Whatever I'm lying on right now feels like actual heaven. It's so soft and warm, I'm pretty sure my soul has melted into it. Don't get me wrong, the mattress at school is nice, but this is magical.

I stretch slowly, toes curling under the blanket. Every muscle in my body is loose, like I've been floating. God, can I stay here forever? No early practice. No pressure. Just this bed and maybe some chocolate pancakes. A soft moan slips out before I can stop it. My brain barely remembers where I am until someone clears their throat.

My eyes snap open.

Zayden's leaning against the doorway. His locs are loose, falling messily around his face.

"Morning." His voice is raspy, like he hasn't used it yet this morning. It's illegal how good-looking he looks this early in the morning. I probably look like a hot mess.

I sit up way too fast, and the blanket falls off one shoulder. I blink at him like I just got caught doing something inappropriate.

Which I guess I kind of did.

"Morning."

A beat of silence stretches between us as I remember the soup, the couch, the blanket, and the jersey I'm still wearing. How I fell asleep with my head on his chest and he carried me to bed.

I glance at him, and he's watching me like he's remembering last night, too.

"We should probably head back," he says finally, pulling away from the doorway. "Heated ground's kicked in. Roads should be good." He turns to leave. "We leave in five minutes. I'll warm up the car."

He disappears down the hall, and I faceplant back into the mattress and groan. I reach for my phone on the nightstand, and the battery is dead.

By the time I've put my clothes back on and brushed my teeth, he's already waiting for me by the door.

"Ready?" he asks.

I nod as he opens the door, and the cold hits the second we step out. Above us, the sky is gray with thick clouds. Valcérre mornings don't come with golden sunrises or soft pastel skies.

The snow is mostly gone now, melted into wet streaks. A fucking underground heating system, so genius.

Zayden walks ahead, opens the passenger door, and waits. The Jeep is also cleared, steam rising from the exhaust.

I slide in without a word, and the door shuts gently behind me. The heat is already running, and the seat is warm beneath me as I fasten my seatbelt. Zayden gets in and buckles his seatbelt.

"Do you mind if I use your charger? Phone's dead." I hold my phone up at him.

He nods toward the extra charger cord, and I plug it in.

"Do you like pop music?" He glances over at me.

I nod, a little surprised that he asked.

Zayden scrolls through his phone, tapping on something before putting it in the cup holder.

A few seconds later, a soft beat fills the car, and it takes me less than a second to recognize the song.

"August" by Taylor Swift.

I blink then laugh.

He glances over at me. He's not laughing or smiling, but his expression has softened a little.

"I just didn't take you for a Taylor Swift fan," I say, still smiling.

He lifts an eyebrow. "God forbid a guy have good taste."

I laugh again. "You're a weird guy, Zayden Aldenhurst."

"We've established that already." The corner of his mouth twitches slightly, like he's fighting back a smile.

My phone takes a few minutes to power on, but when it does, everything starts pouring in.

Buzz. Buzz. Buzz.

Dozens of notifications flood my screen, texts, group chats, Instagram tags.

LAS chat:

> Sophie: Luna, where tf are u?
>
> Annika: pick up your phone.
>
> Sophie: Why am I going to voicemail?
>
> Annika: OMG are you ok?
>
> Sophie: Please, tell me you're okay.
>
> Sophie: Have you seen the video? Is this from tonight?
>
> Sophie: Call me, plz.

@valcerreskating reposted a video
@valcerregossip: New couple alert or something else?
@MidnightIce tagged you in a video

I click on the page, and there's only one post, and the caption says:

Hockey Boy vs Ice Princess.

There we are, me and Zayden, skating together at the Shadow Rink. The camera's far off, but the video is clear enough to know it's us. The way we move, the way we look at each other, it's not subtle.

I go still. "Zayden…"

His phone lights up, too. "Shit," he mutters, pulling over to the side of the road.

We sit in silence for a second while the video plays between us again, looping like a carousel.

16,021 views.

5,728 likes.

403 comments.

I click on the comments.

Wait… since when does Zayden Aldenhurst SKATE like that?

Bro's not just a hockey player. That footwork? That's figure skating precision.

Tell me I'm not the only one who felt the tension in this.

Hockey Boy got moves. Who knew?

Look at the way she hits that toe spin like she's flying.

She's not just good, she's olympic good.

They're so in sync it's lowkey terrifying.

Okay but how long have they been skating together and why did no one know??

Are they secretly dating?

I thought they hated each other.

I look over at him. "Who filmed this? And why?"

He doesn't answer, just stares at the screen.

Then another notification pops on my screen from the anonymous sender.

Unknown Number: Ellias Vaughn.

I stare at the words, heart suddenly pounding in my ears. I look over at Zayden again, and he received it, too.

"Zayden," I whisper. "Who the hell is Ellias?"

"We'll talk later," he says, pulling away from the side of the road.

"Later, when?"

He finally looks at me. "Find me after practice behind the athletic building."

I nod as I stare at the window, watching the snow-covered trees blur past us.

We pull up in front of my dorm, and Zayden puts the car in park. Neither of us says anything for a while. I glance over at him. His hands are on the wheel, and he's staring ahead.

I go to open the door, but before I can step out, his hand grabs mine across the console.

When I turn to look at him, his gaze is already on me. His eyes say a thousand things he doesn't say out loud.

I'm sorry you've been dragged into this.

I don't know how to protect you from what's happening.

And mine tell him that I don't want to leave, that I don't want to step out into the chaos waiting for me outside of the car. I want to go back to the cabin. Back to listening to Billie together, to falling asleep on his chest, back to that moment that felt like a little piece of home.

His fingers tighten around mine.

You'll be okay.

I step out of the car, and when I turn around, he's already gone.

I don't even register the walk up the stairs, or the stares, as I make it through the students' lounge area. But as I scan my key card, stepping into my suite, a voice breaks through my foggy brain.

"Where were you?" Sophie storms toward me, panic written all over her face, and my stomach sinks. "You disappeared after the showcase. Nico thought you were dead in a ditch somewhere. I almost called Rylee to tell her something bad happened to you."

"I'm fine," I say quickly. "I just needed to clear my head."

"For almost twelve hours?" Annika says gently, stepping forward. "Without telling anyone?"

I open my mouth then close it. My throat is dry, and my heart's still trying to catch up with everything.

"And the video?" Sophie thrusts her phone at me.

The video.

Zayden and I skating together like we know each other.

"You've been sneaking out with Zayden after you repeatedly told us you hated him," Annika adds.

"It's not what it looks like."

"You're literally in his jersey." Sophie gestures at my chest like it's a betrayal. "What the hell, Luna?"

I shake my head. "Nothing happened."

"You expect us to believe that?" Sophie stares at me.

I look at both of them, their eyes full of questions, and I feel like the worst friend in the world.

"I was with Zayden, okay? But I swear…it's not what you think. I'll explain after practice."

Sophie stares at me.

Annika's brows pinch together. "You're okay, though?" she asks softly. "Really?"

I nod, even though I'm not. "Yeah… Can we talk after practice? Please?"

Sophie looks like she wants to keep grilling me because she knows I'm holding back. But then her expression softens. "You scared the hell out of us, babe." She steps forward and wraps her arms around my shoulders. Annika joins in from the side, and suddenly I'm wrapped up in both of them.

For a second, I just let myself breathe. Let myself feel it, even if I still can't tell them everything.

"I'm fine," I whisper. "I promise."

They pull back, studying me like they don't believe me, but they're letting it go, for now. I'm so thankful for that, because I don't want to drag them into something I don't understand myself.

"Practice," Sophie says again, wiping under her eye like she's not emotional. "After that, I want answers."

"Yeah," I say. "Okay."

But the truth? I don't even know what the answers are yet.

CHAPTER 19

Zayden

The door shuts behind me as I step out of my dad's office. He wanted to see me after the video of me and Luna went viral. I expected the conversation, but I definitely wasn't ready for the one that followed.

I walk past the athlete lounge, toward the locker room. No one says anything about the video, or maybe they do and I just don't hear them.

The locker room is loud as always when I get there. The usual laughter, some of the guys joking around. They look up when I walk in, but no one says anything; they know better. Jasper gives me a look from across the bench. I didn't even have a chance to talk to him when I got back this morning.

Then he walks in as I change into my gear.

The coach, that's what he's always been, even off the ice.

The room goes quiet.

"First game of the season is in few days," he says. "This is where it starts."

Everyone is alert now. Some of the guys nod.

"There's no room for distractions, drama, or mistakes." He looks at me, long enough for the entire room to feel it. "Keep your priorities straight, and if you can't keep your head in the game, you don't belong out there."

He turns toward the exit, and the team follows him.

The second my blades hit the ice, I'm gone. I push faster, harder, and more recklessly than I should. My body moves on instinct as I try to outrun the noises in my head. The conversation dad and I had in his office earlier, Luna's laugh from the car ride, the video, the text message.

"Where the hell is your head?" my dad yells at me from the boards, but I can barely hear him.

Cameron skates pass me. "Didn't know hockey players could move like this." He says it loud enough for me to hear. "You and Ice Princess make a cute pair, though. If hockey doesn't work out, you can absolutely be a figure skater."

I drop my gloves without thinking, grab him by the collar, and slam him into the boards.

"Zayden!" Jasper yells from behind me. "Let him go."

My fist curls for a punch, but I don't hit him. I push him off and skate to the far side of the rink, but not before catching the look on my dad's face.

Control yourself. Remember what's at stake. Don't forget who's watching.

My helmet is off before I reach the bench. I snap my blades guard onto my skates and keep moving. My gear feels heavy with every step.

By the time I reach the locker room, the noise is gone, but I can't outrun the storm building in my chest.

I peel off my gear piece by piece, gloves, elbow pads, jersey soaked with sweat and frustration.

My skates go into my bag. I pull my hoodie over my head and shut the locker behind me harder than I mean it to. Still not hard enough to silence the voice in my head. Not hard enough to forget her face.

I turn toward the exit. The usual one that leads through the lounge, where I'll have to see people and hear jokes I don't have the patience for.

Turning around, I take the back way down the narrow hall, instead, toward the back exit.

I push the door open, and that's when I see her. Waiting for me to explain everything like promised.

Her face lights up for a second when she sees me, and my cold heart does that little thing it does whenever she's around. Like it knows her.

For a second, I want to cross the space between us. But I can't, not after what my dad said. So I look down and walk right past her, even as my body is screaming to reach out for her.

She's probably gonna hate me, but it's better this way.

CHAPTER 20

Luna

He walks past me like I'm invisible, like he didn't promise we'd talk.

"Are you fucking serious right now?" I snap, spinning around. "You don't see me?"

He stops but doesn't turn around.

"You said we'd talk," I say, louder this time. "You promised." I take a step closer, my voice shaking from anger.

"There's nothing to talk about," he says, still not turning to look at me.

"Wow." I laugh bitterly. "Now I see why everyone stays the hell away from you."

"Maybe you should stay away, too," he says over his shoulder.

My throat burns, but not from the cold air. I thought things would be different. Just because he made me soup and we listened to Billie together.

"Maybe I will, but I'm not stupid, Zayden. There's something going on here, and I'm gonna find out the truth with or without your help."

I turn to walk away, but before I can take a step, Zayden is in front of me. He backs me up against the wall, not hard enough to hurt me, but just enough to trap me. "You need to stop." His eyes are stormy and something close to being scared. Scared for him or for me?

"Stop what?" I snap.

"Stop digging into things that don't concern you." He's so close I can feel his breath on my skin.

"Or what, Zayden?"

"You don't know what you're getting into." His fingers twitch on my arm like he doesn't know whether to push me away or pull me closer.

"So tell me."

My chest rises and falls rapidly, so does his.

Neither of us moves.

For a second, there's only the sound of our breathing and the pulse pounding in my throat.

I hate him.

I want him to kiss me.

I hate that I want that.

His eyes drop to my mouth, and mine lift to his. The space between us could be shattered with one breath.

"Stay out of this, Luna. Focus on your skating, that's what you're here for, right?"

A little too late for that.

He lets go of my arm, but I don't move. I don't even breathe.

"I hate you," I yell at him, furious, and aching in ways I don't even understand.

"Yeah?" He leans closer. "I hate you, too."

But he doesn't stop.

"I hate that you're so fucking stubborn."

A little closer.

"I hate that I know what your laugh sounds like. And I hate that I like hearing it."

He's breathing hard now—so am I.

"I fucking hate that I want to kiss you right now." He stares at my lips then lifts his eyes to meet my gaze.

I should shove him away and tell him he doesn't get to kiss

me after all of this. That he doesn't get to hate me and want me at the same time. But my body doesn't move. Instead, a small exhale escapes my lips.

That's all it takes for his mouth to crash to mine. Then he's kissing me like he hates me and can't get enough of me at the same time. Like he's drowning, and I'm the only thing keeping him afloat. And I kiss him back just as hard. Because I hate him. Hate him for making me want this. Hate that I have no fucking idea what this even is.

His tongue searches for mine, and my lips part, letting him in. He tastes like adrenaline and cold air. I grab a handful of his locs, dragging him closer, and the sound from his throat sends heat curling through my core.

It's all lips and tongues and gasps and too much and not enough and—

God, I'm dizzy.

Zayden's hold tightens on my waist like he's afraid I'll disappear if he lets go. He shifts the angle, kissing me deeper, and we consume each other.

I'm fucking lost in him.

Just like last time, the kiss softens. His lips move slower, tongue grazing against mine in one last lingering stroke before he slowly pulls away.

His lips hover over mine like he wants to kiss me again. Eyes closed, chest rising and falling so fast I can almost feel his body shaking.

Then his forehead presses to mine, and he exhales like it hurts. "Just let it go, Luna," he says quietly, breathing me in one last time before pulling away. His whole body is tense, like it's killing him to do this.

And then he walks off. No explanation, no glance back, just gone. Leaving me wrecked, angry, and so goddamn confused I want to scream.

Instead, I take a deep breath, fix my clothes, and shove

everything down. I don't have time for Zayden Aldenhurst and his fucking hot and cold games. He's right. I came here to skate, not to get caught up in his storm.

He wants me to stay away from him? That's exactly what I'm gonna do.

I don't remember walking away. One second he's kissing me, and the next I'm in the library. I didn't want to go back to my dorm just yet. I'm not ready to face Sophie and Annika. I promised them we'd talk later, but how do I explain something I don't understand myself?

The library is quiet, just a few early birds. I take a seat near the back and open one of the library laptops. A pressure builds behind my eyes as the screen powers on.

I open a new page, and type *Ellias Vaughn*. A single article pops up from five years ago.

> **First-year hockey player found dead in Valcérre Arena.**
>
> *Valcérre University officials confirmed the death of first-year hockey player Ellias Vaughn, 18, who was found unresponsive on the ice in Ice Arena D early Monday morning.*
>
> *Staff preparing the facility for training reportedly discovered Vaughn's body shortly before 5:30 a.m. They believe Vaughn may have sneaked into the rink sometime after midnight for a solo training session.*
>
> *No official autopsy has been released. As of now, authorities are treating it as an accident. The university has not commented on whether unauthorized access to Arena D will lead to further investigation.*
>
> *A memorial is expected to be held after the holiday break. The university has asked the press to respect the family's privacy.*

That's it. No autopsy report, no investigation, or quotes from anyone who saw what happened. That doesn't add up.

Zayden mentioned they ended the Midnight Challenge after an accident. Could this be related?

My head throbs harder, and I rub my temple, trying to breathe through it. I'm used to my migraines by now, and this one is manageable.

I type *Shadow Rink* next, and nothing comes up. *Valcérre Midnight Challenge.* Still nothing. What the fuck? Even the video of me and Zayden skating together is gone. Erased like it was never real, deleted from every account, and every repost.

I reload again, and again. Still nothing. Panic rises in my chest as I swallow against the rising nausea in my stomach.

"Hey," a voice says.

I look up as Serene slides into the seat across from me and drops her book on the table. Her red hair is twisted up into a messy bun that looks effortless.

"Hey," I say with a small smile, trying to sound normal.

"Working on something for class?" She nods at the laptop.

"Something like that," I lie.

She studies me for a few seconds, like she doesn't believe me. I look down at my phone again, trying to find the video, maybe a repost, but nothing. How is that even possible?

"You okay?" Serene's voice breaks through my thoughts again. I almost forgot she was here.

"Yeah, I just have a lot going on." I hesitate before adding, "Have you heard of the Midnight Challenge?"

Serene takes a sip of her coffee before answering. "I've heard the name before." She leans a little closer, like she's whispering a secret. "It's one of those things people don't really talk about. If it did exist, it doesn't anymore. Someone must have buried it."

"So, you think it was real?"

"Maybe. If it was, someone definitely doesn't want people to find out about it."

"You saw the video, right?" I ask before I can stop myself. "The one with me and Zayden."

"Yeah, then it was gone, like someone wiped it."

Every hair on my arms rises. "Right, like, who would even do that?"

"Whoever did it has reach. Real reach."

How deep does this thing go?

"Are you and Zayden…like, together?"

"What? No."

"Could have fooled me." She gives me a soft smile.

"I— It's complicated."

She sips her coffee silently, but her eyes are still on me.

"What?"

"I saw how he looked at you. Your chemistry was obvious even through the video. That connection is rare."

What do I even say to that?

"And whoever's sending those messages clearly wants the truth out."

My blood goes cold.

"I didn't tell you that…"

Serene blinks. "You didn't tell me what?"

"About the messages."

I didn't.

I *know* I didn't.

She tilts her head, a soft frown tugging between her brows. "Yeah, you did. At your locker when you asked me about the Shadow Rink."

Maybe I did and forgot.

I nod. "I probably did. My brain gets foggy when I'm stressed."

She smiles at me. "I get it. I'll see you in class." She stands, grabbing her book and coffee from the table. "And if you want information about the Midnight Challenge. You won't find it online."

"So, where should I look?"

She leans down and whispers, "Try the archives."

"The archives?"

"Yes, it's in the basement level of the library, and you probably need a key to get in there. But if you want the truth, that is a good place to start." She gives me one last smile before walking away.

As soon as she's out of sight, my phone buzzes.

I glance down.

> Unknown Number: Ellias Vaughn. It wasn't an accident.

I stare at the screen, hands suddenly cold.

> Me: Who are you?

No response.

> Me: Why are you telling me this?

Nothing, but I know this isn't some prank. Someone wants the truth out.

> Me: Why me?

I send the text, not expecting a reply, but the three dots appear.

> Unknown number: Because of how he looks at you.

What does that even mean?

> Unknown number: He knows more than he lets on.

Who? Zayden.

I know he's holding something back, but the question is why?

> Me: Who?

I wait for a response that never comes, but I already know the answer.

CHAPTER 21

Zayden

I don't remember the walk back to my dorm. One second, I was pulling away from her even when every cell in my body screamed at me to kiss her again, and the next, I'm here.

Lying flat on my bed, staring at the ceiling like it might erase everything, but it doesn't. My lips still burn from how I kissed her like she was my oxygen. The way her body felt against mine, the way she pulled my locs, the sound she made.

Fuck!

That's always been the problem. My emotions never come in neat, manageable pieces. They crash over me like waves that don't stop breaking. Anger, guilt, want, fear. They don't knock politely; they rip through me like they own the place.

This is why I shut everyone out. Why I keep my head down, keep my fists clenched, keep my heart locked away. Because when I feel, I feel like I'm going to drown in it.

And Luna? She's the goddamn storm I never prepared for.

I press a hand over my chest, feeling the rapid rhythm of my heart. It's beating too fucking fast because of her. Not in the same way it does after practice, not from adrenaline, not from rage or pressure. This feels different, like she infused it with a little more blood.

Then the memory hits, and I'm twelve again.

I sat in the corner of my room with my knees pulled to my chest. My shoulders were shaking, and my throat ached from trying to hold it in, but the tears came anyway. I fucking hated it.

Another bad practice with my dad. I'd messed up on the ice, and he yelled at me the whole drive home.

"Aldenhursts don't make mistakes," he'd said, and if I couldn't handle pressure, I'd never make it. He called me soft, said I needed to toughen up.

The door creaked open, and someone walked in. I didn't look up, but I knew it was her. She took a seat beside me.

"You feel that?" my mum finally said after a while, pressing her palm against my chest. My heart was pounding so hard, like it was begging to come out. "It means you're still good. Feeling this much is not a weakness, baby. It's your gift. Don't let anyone take this away from you. Not even your dad."

He wasn't always like that, but after the accident, when he couldn't play anymore, he poured every ounce of his rage into me. I absorbed it all, but it hit ten times heavier than it should have, like his anger multiplied the moment it landed on me. Sometimes all I wanted was to disappear, to stop existing, just to escape the weight of it.

"I'll always be here to remind you," she said, wrapping her arms around my shoulders.

Then she left.

She fucking lied.

The door swings open, and Jasper steps in. He shuts it behind him. "What the hell was that at practice?"

From the corner of my eyes, I can see him leaning against the doorframe, arms crossed over his chest as he waits for my answer.

"What happened at your dad's office?" he asks after a while. "I saw you leaving earlier."

The memory of our meeting claws its way back before I can shove it down.

He sent me a text to come to his office after I dropped Luna off.

"Close the door," he said as I walked in. I did.

He tossed a tablet on his desk. The video of Luna and I skating together played on the screen.

"You think this is a joke?" he snapped. "Skating with her at that rink, and letting the video get out?"

"I didn't know someone was recording us," I said through gritted teeth.

"It doesn't matter. You're in it. You're a hockey player, not some goddamn ice princess." He glared at me like I'd ruined everything. Like I'd embarrassed his precious Aldenhurst legacy. "I told you to stay away from that rink, and you brought her there."

"I didn't bring her. Someone led her there. Because someone wants the truth out." I stepped closer to the desk.

His face went pale, something like fear spreading across it. It vanished a second later, but I saw it.

"It wasn't an accident, was it?" My voice dropped lower, afraid of the answer. "You were there that night, you know what happened."

Silence.

"You don't have any idea what you're talking about," he muttered. "Stay away from the rink, and that little girl."

I flinched. "You don't get to decide—"

"I do when it puts everything we've built at risk. She's a distraction. You want to make it to the national team? Stay the hell away from her."

"My personal life is not your problem."

"That's where you're wrong. She became a problem the moment she stepped foot in the Shadow Rink. And if you keep pushing, Zayden, she might end up like Ellias."

"Did you just threaten her?" My fists clenched at my sides.

He turned away, already moving on like that should be the end of it. "The video's already gone. I made sure of it."

"If something happens to her..." I growled.

He lifted a brow, daring me to finish.

"I will burn the whole damn school to the ground."

His eyes darkened.

"I know Ellias didn't die by accident. And I will find the truth and bring you down with it."

His face tightened, and fear flickered across it. If I had doubt before, not anymore.

I turned toward the door.

"You think I'm bluffing?" I said without looking back. "Try me, Coach."

"Z." A voice cuts through my fog.

I blink hard as the room comes into focus. My fists are still clenched at my sides.

"Where'd you go?"

I don't answer right away. My heart's still racing.

"You gonna tell me what the hell happened in your dad's office?" He's standing in front of me now.

"He saw the video of me and Luna."

"Let me guess, he wasn't too happy about it." Jasper waits.

"He threatened her." I barely get the words out, still trying to control my breathing. The anger settles deeper in my chest.

"What?" His whole body goes still. "Because of the video?"

I sit up slowly. My elbows rest on my knees as I stare at the floor. "The video, the Shadow Rink, Ellias, all of it. I think he's scared."

"Of what?"

"That someone's dragging the truth out."

"What truth?" Jasper takes a seat at my desk.

"You've heard of the Midnight Challenge?" I look up at him.

He nods.

"It's not just rumors. It was real and people got hurt. Ellias didn't die skating alone. He died on the ice during one of the challenges."

"And you know this, how?"

The air in my lungs freezes as I think about the conversation I heard a few months before my mum left. "I overheard my parents fighting about it."

My mum was crying. I'd never heard her cry like that before. Not like she was sad, but furious and heartbroken at the same time.

"A kid is dead, Zayn. Is that what this place does to people? That damn Midnight Challenge should have been shut down years ago," she snapped.

"Ellias wasn't supposed to die. We just needed him to lose," he said, quieter now.

"They need to shut it down, or I will take them down myself."

"You think you can take them down? Do you even know how deep this goes?"

"Watch me. I'll burn the whole school to the ground if I have to. I'll go public, talk to the press, the families, the Federation—everyone. I will tear down every name tied to this school—including yours." Her fury was shaking the wall.

"You can't go against them. These people are powerful. You'll get yourself killed." Panic and fear crept into his voice.

"Maybe," she said, softer now. "But I won't stay quiet. Not when a child is dead."

"And you think your dad had something to do with Ellias?"

"I think so," I say. "Or at least he knows what happened. He was there that night."

"Jesus, Zayden."

"There's something else," I say quietly. "I've been getting anonymous messages. Luna, too."

"Messages?"

"About the Shadow Rink, the Midnight Challenge, Ellias, and they're the ones who led Luna to the rink. I think they leaked the video, too."

"You've been getting those messages for how long?"

"A few weeks now."

Jasper pulls away from his seat. His sneakers scuff the floor as he paces back and forth. "Weeks, Zayden? Why the hell didn't you tell me sooner?"

"I didn't want to drag you into this." I look up at him.

He stops pacing now as he stares back at me. The look on his face is not anger but worry.

"I need your help," I say. "Can you trace the messages and find out where they came from, who's sending them?"

"I need my laptop. Be right back." He heads out.

He comes back a couple minutes later with his laptop.

"Let's trace who's been messing with you." He sets it down at my desk and glances at me. "Still got the texts?"

I hand him my phone, and he connects it with a cable.

"This might take a while." He cracks his knuckles as he begins typing.

There's no turning back now. I'll find the truth, even if it means blowing up everything, my draft spot, the fucking Aldenhurst name.

"Whoever is sending those messages is smart enough to cover their trails. This is gonna take longer than I thought." He closes the laptop. "I'll finish later, or we'll be late for class." Grabbing his laptop, he heads for the door.

"Keep this between us," I call after him.

He nods and shuts the door behind him.

I'm left alone again with the silence that I love and crave. Except this time, it's filled with thoughts of her.

I drag my hands over my face and lean forward.

When did she start mattering so much?

Maybe it was the first time I saw her on the ice, or the night she challenged me at the Shadow Rink. Maybe it was every second after that when I couldn't stop noticing her. Or maybe it was long before that. Three years ago on a frozen lake when she didn't even know my name. She's always been there, living between my thoughts.

I push up from the edge of the bed and head toward the bathroom. I need a fucking shower.

By the time I'm done and my uniform is on, Jasper is already waiting for me in the living area. Cameron is also there, leaning against the door frame with his arms crossed over his chest.

Jasper gives me a look that says, *Don't screw this up.*

"Hey," I say, clearing my throat. "About earlier..."

Cameron nods before I can finish. "Yeah, same. We're cool."

I nod back. "Cool."

We head out, and Cameron walks ahead, flirting with some girls in the hallway. Jasper walks quietly beside me, no teasing or poking, like he knows I'm barely keeping it together.

Then my body freezes, and of course, it's her.

Luna is coming out of the library. She squints at the light, rubbing her temple like she's trying to ease something.

She scans the hallway before her eyes land on me. Everything stills, and we stare at each other for a second. Then she looks away like I'm part of the wall. No fire, not even one of those cold glares she used to throw at me.

I told her to stay away. So, why does it hurt like hell that she's actually doing it?

"You might need to make it a little less obvious that you're obsessed with her," Jasper teases.

I ignore his comment and keep moving, even when my body screams to go after her. I breathe through the pressure in my chest and remind myself to focus on the game this weekend. I'm doing this to protect her.

CHAPTER 22

Luna

I SLOWLY PUSH the door open, hoping to avoid Sophie and Annika, but I should have known better.

Sophie is sitting cross-legged in front of the TV with a controller in her hands, but she's not playing. Her eyes lock onto me. Annika's on the floor in a perfect midsplit, mindlessly scrolling on her phone like she wasn't waiting for me.

"Look who finally showed up. You've been avoiding us all day," Sophie says.

She's kinda right. But I also have been looking into Ellias and how to get into the archives like Serene suggested. Maybe I'm being paranoid, but I have a feeling she knows more than she's telling me.

I drop my bag by the door and head toward the kitchen for some water. The light from the fridge hits my vision, and I close my eyes against the pressure behind them.

"I just had a lot on my mind." I swallow.

I want to tell them everything, but it might not be a good idea to bring them into this.

"You promised we'd talk later. We want to know why you were skating with Zayden at the Shadow Rink."

I freeze. "You know about that place?"

"Just the rumors. That it was a secret rink but got closed down. People don't really talk about it anymore, and some students say that place is haunted."

I blink. I didn't expect her to know about it. How much do they know?

"A few weeks ago, I received a text, no name, just a location to show up to if I wanted to prove I wasn't an ice princess."

"And you went? What if they were some kind of serial killer or kidnapper?"

Trust me, I know.

"I thought maybe it was a prank. Or some weird initiation thing. But when I showed up…he was already there."

"Zayden?" Sophie asks.

I nod, leaning against the fridge. My head's still pounding.

"I was pissed, so I challenged him. We skated, and he was stupidly good. It was intense and weirdly in sync. Didn't think much of it until the video showed up."

"So, it was Zayden, then, the texts and the video?" Annika asks, turning to face me.

"I don't know."

"And last night?" Sophie asks. I was hoping we didn't have to talk about last night. "Did something happen? Like, happen, happen."

"I don't want to talk about that right now."

Sophie and Annika exchange a glance. "We all saw that chemistry in the video, and the sexual tension you two have had since day one," Sophie says.

"Can we not? At least not tonight." The pulse in my temple throbs harder. I press my fingers there, like that will make it stop. I can't do this right now. "I have a migraine, and if I don't shower and go to bed right now, I'm gonna vomit."

"Okay," Annika says quietly.

"You don't have to talk about him, but we're here if you want to," Sophie adds, her tone softer.

"I know." I give them a smile before disappearing down the hallway.

After my shower, I walk back into my room. I smell chamomile and honey. Sophie sits at my desk, holding a mug.

"I made you tea." She holds it out to me.

I take the mug from her, taking a seat at the edge of the bed. "Thank you." I smile softly at her.

She moves from the desk and sits beside me on the bed. "Annika and I are going out for a bit, will you be okay by yourself?"

"Yeah, I'll be fine." *I'm used to being alone.*

She wraps one arm gently around my shoulder. "Okay. Get some rest. And text me if you need anything."

I nod.

She walks toward the door to leave then stops. "Love you."

"Love you, too."

The door closes softly behind her, and I'm left alone again. My eyes drift to the window, and out there in the distance, I can see Ravensbourne Hall. I close my eyes for a second, the memory from earlier playing behind my eyelids.

He told me to stay away, and yet he still looks at me like he cares. But he doesn't. No one has ever cared before, not even my sperm donor because that's all he ever was. The last time I heard from him was the time I was desperate and naive enough to call him. Rylee had moved to Paris, and things were getting bad with my mom's new boyfriend. He used to hit me when he got angry. So I called and begged him to let me come live with him.

You know what he said?

Some bullshit about how it wasn't a good time.

Rylee was the only one who gave a shit about me, but she left anyway. I know she had to, but I was still left alone.

I finish my tea and set the mug on the nightstand. Lying down in the bed, I pull the blanket up to my chin. My body is tired, and my head is killing me. But my mind won't let me rest, even with the white noise playing from my phone.

I flip onto my stomach, hoping that helps, but nothing. I hate that I'm thinking about him, the kiss, the night at the cabin.

I hate him.

That's what I tell myself every night when I can't sleep. Every time I replay the way he kissed me in my head.

I didn't come here to get distracted by the broody hockey player. I came here to skate. To earn my place and make it to the Olympics, not to get caught up in whatever storm is Zayden Aldenhurst.

CHAPTER 23

Luna

For the next couple days, I avoid everyone, even Sophie and Annika. I push harder during training. My migraines keep getting worse and nothing seems to help, but that doesn't stop me. It never did before. This is what it takes to get to the top.

After practice, I spend most of my time at the library, trying to find anything about Ellias, but I still have nothing. Just a locked archives room and a name everyone's too afraid to say out loud.

But I know someone who might be able to help.

Jasper.

I've heard the whispers that he's kinda like a tech genius and can hack into almost anything.

I find Jasper by the east rink exit after my practice, and thankfully, he's alone.

"Hey," I say, stepping into his path.

He blinks, like I caught him off guard, taking out one earbud. "Heyyy." He gives me one of his boyish smiles.

"Can I talk to you for a second?"

"Is this about Zayden? Because you guys need to figure out whatever fuck is going between you two. He's been acting like he's fine but barely holding it together."

"What? No. This isn't about him." Not entirely.

"Oh. I mean you two have been avoiding each other…but we can all see how miserable you are."

I raise an eyebrow.

"Never mind. What do you want to talk about?"

"I need a favor."

He narrows his eyes at me. "What kind of favor?"

"I need to get into the restricted archive room," I say quietly.

He pulls me aside. "You want to break into the archives? The ones locked behind a coded door."

I nod once.

"Luna, it's restricted for a reason."

"I know."

"Do I want to know why?"

"Probably not."

He exhales, scratching the back of his neck. "Does Zayden know about this?"

"No, I don't owe him anything."

"Then it's definitely a no." He starts walking away.

"Please, Jasper."

He stops and looks at me over his shoulder.

"I wouldn't ask if it wasn't important."

He groans. "You're not gonna tell me what this is about, are you?"

"No."

"You're gonna do it with or without me?"

"Absolutely."

He mutters something under his breath. "Midnight. South stairwell. Bring gloves. And Luna?"

"Yeah?"

"This never happened."

"Thank you."

"Don't thank me yet. If we get caught, we're dead, and if Zayden finds out I put you in danger, I'm dead, too."

Then he disappears down the hallway.

I try not to think about what his last comment about Zayden means.

❄

I WAIT until I know Annika and Sophie are asleep and then sneak out. I stay out of view of the cameras, like Jasper suggested. The campus is quiet, but I'm used to it by now. When I make it to the side entrance of the library, Jasper is already there, leaning against the wall in a black hoodie, arms crossed over his chest.

"You're late."

"Sorry, I had to wait until the girls were asleep."

He pulls the door open, and I follow him inside. The library is dark, except for Jasper's phone's flashlight. Long shadows stretch between the shelves, and my imagination fills them with faces.

We reach a door at the back of the library that says *Staff Only*.

Jasper pulls a small device from his bag and crouches in front of the keypad outside the archive door. He taps the device to the digital lock, and we wait a few tense seconds before a green light flashes and the door clicks open.

Impressive.

He swings the door open, and cold air spills out—so cold it fogs the edges of his flashlight. "After you, Nancy Drew."

I stare at the narrow stairwell that disappears into the shadows.

We start descending the stairs with Jasper's flashlight lighting the way. The deeper we get, the colder it is. Then there's another door.

What the fuck?

Jasper steps closer to it and squints at the lock and then exhales slowly.

"Please don't tell me we came here for nothing."

"This lock is not connected to the school system."

"Meaning?"

"This requires a more sophisticated device." He pulls out another device that looks like a mini laptop with something that looks like an antenna, just like the old phone I used to have.

"How many of those do you have?"

"Enough."

I watch him working on the device. His expression is calm and focused, like he could do this in his sleep. "How do you know how to do all this?"

"My dad designed the system."

"Wait, what?"

"All tech at Valcérre is created by Virex, my dad's company and one of the largest tech companies in the world. Sports, military, government-grade systems."

The lock beeps, and he smirks but doesn't open it yet.

"You're serious?"

"Dead serious. The only reason he lets me play hockey here is because I agreed to study sports tech, and I can beta test some of his gadgets. He expects me to take over the company once he retires."

"Wow, that's…"

He shrugs. "I learned how to code before I even know how to read." He tucks the device back in his bag.

"Remind me not to mess with you."

He laughs before pushing the door open. I step inside, and it's even darker than the stairs.

"There should be a light switch." I reach for the wall.

"Don't. The school's security system is tied to motion-activated electricity. If anyone's monitoring grid activity, they'll know someone was down here."

I lower my hand. "Right. Of course, you'd know that."

He finds a desk lamp and switches it on, giving us enough light to see the rows of long shelves with files cabinets. "Manual light. No motion sensor, and low voltage. It won't trigger anything."

I nod and then look around.

This place is set up like a library.

Each cabinet drawer is labeled.

Students Files:
Last names A-H
Last names I-Q
Last names R-Z
Athletic Records
Hockey Players
Figure Skaters
Scholarships Recipients and Reviews
Academic Misconduct
Injury/Medical Incidents
Sports Incidents and Injuries

"If a player died while skating alone, it should be in here, right?" I point toward the cabinet labeled **Sport Incidents and Injuries**.

"It should be."

I tug it, but it's locked. "Can you open it?" I look over at Jasper.

He gives me a look that says *Is that even a question?*

Of course, he can.

"So," he says quietly. "This is about Ellias, isn't it?"

"No..."

"Luna, don't lie to me."

I glance at him, and his face isn't judgmental. "I just need to know what happened," I whisper. "No one talks about him. There's nothing online. But something feels off. And the more I look...the more wrong everything feels."

He looks at me. "Why do you care so much?" he asks. "You didn't even know him," he adds, softer now. "Why are you doing all this?"

And for a second, something raw swells in my chest—grief

for someone I never met. Because the truth is, it's not just about Ellias.

It's also about me.

"I was ten years old when I tried to run away. I just wanted to see if my mother would notice. When I came home hours later, she didn't even know I was gone." I breathe through the pressure in my chest. "Ellias is already a ghost, but someone should still care. We should know exactly what happened to him."

"Okay." He pulls a pin out of his pocket and opens the file drawer.

I flick through the tabs. So many names, so many dates, but nothing says Ellias.

"Why isn't his name here?" But I already know the answer.

He didn't die skating alone that night.

"If it's not here...then it has to be somewhere." I search the other cabinets. There has to be something here that can tell me what happened to him.

That's when I see it.

All the way in the bottom of a filing cabinet. **Midnight Challenge - Restricted**.

This one is not like the others. There's a small rectangular panel embedded in the front. "Is that a key card reader? "

"Worse. It's a dual-layer system. Key card and biometric."

"Can you open it?"

Jasper crouches beside me, inspecting the lock. His mouth twists. "I don't have the tools with me."

"Can we come back?"

He hesitates. "If we don't get caught first."

CHAPTER 24

Luna

I ALWAYS HATE THE SILENCE, but tonight, it's worse. It wraps around my throat and squeezes. The kind that makes every thought louder, every memory sharper, and every doubt impossible to ignore. It creeps into my chest and settles there.

The silence I remember from when I was little—lying in bed, waiting to hear the front door open, knowing no one was coming to check if I was okay.

On top of that, nothing helps with my headaches, not my meds, not lying down in the dark, not when I'm this stressed. I keep thinking about the locked cabinet, the missing files, and everything else related to Ellias.

I curl deeper under my blanket, but it doesn't help. I feel… wired. Cold. Restless. And there it is again—that pull toward the Shadow Rink.

I shouldn't go, but it's the only place here where I can breathe. Even if there's a chance of him being there. I push the blanket off and sit up with a quiet groan. *I just need to skate.*

I pull on my fleece-lined jumpsuit, tugging the hood over my ears, and lace up my boots. I grab my gym bag with my skates and head out.

The walk to the Shadow Rink is a blur until I'm sitting on the bench, switching out my boots for my skates. Next thing I know, I'm pushing off the ice, and for a few minutes, everything is okay.

My blades glide across the surface as I breathe in through my nose. A pain presses behind my left eye, but I keep going.

Then I hear the sound of another set of blades hitting the ice, coming toward me. I don't have to turn around to know it's him, and I hate the way my heart stutters.

The low sound that comes from him tells me he's pissed.

I ignore him, taking a slow, wide curve, but I'm getting dizzy now, white spots swimming behind my eyes. I stop, bringing my hands to my knees.

"Luna?" he finally says.

"Go away, Zayden." I try to skate away from him, but I barely make it to the benches before I throw up.

This is so embarrassing.

"Shit, Luna." He skates toward me.

"I'm fine. Just leave me alone." I try to get up. I don't want him seeing me like this. But my knees buckle, and my head throbs like someone hit me with a hammer. Everything fades, like I'm falling in slow motion. Strong arms catch me and lower me gently onto the bench.

A cool hand presses against my forehead. "Fuck. You're burning up."

He kneels in front of me, not even caring about the mess a few feet away from him. His hands brush against my ankle as he switches out my skates. Then I feel him beside me. He shifts me until my head is leaning against his shoulder. "I got you. Just stay like that for me for two seconds so I can switch out my skates."

"I don't need you—" I try to argue with him, but my head falls into his shoulder anyway.

He finishes and turns toward me. One arm wraps around my knees as he lifts me off the bench.

"Put me down... I can..." I shove at his chest, but he's already moving.

"I don't need you…" I say again, the words barely making it out.

"Damn it, baby, just stop fighting me for a sec." He exhales hard through his nose.

Baby?

Great, now I'm hallucinating.

I close my eyes and rest my head against his shoulder as he carries me the rest of the way. I don't have the strength to fight anymore tonight. I can fight him in the morning.

CHAPTER 25

ZAYDEN

She's asleep in my arms when I make it to my dorm, all the fight gone from her body. I scan my key card and kick the door open with my foot. Thank God, the guys aren't here.

Once inside my room, I lay her on my bed. She stirs and mumbles something I can't make out.

"Okay, think, Zayden." I pace around the room before opening one of my drawers and grabbing a cotton T-shirt. I run to the bathroom and wet a small towel.

Back at the bed, I set the towel down and gently unzip her jumpsuit. Underneath, she's wearing a baby-blue pajama set. I pull the jumpsuit off the rest of the way and toss it aside, leaving her in her PJs.

"I don't…need your…" she says faintly before her eyes close again.

"You don't know how to stop fighting, do you, Luna Del Sol?" I stare at the girl who crashed into my life like a storm, whose wreckage I want to be caught in.

I press the cold towel to her neck and then her forehead. "You're okay." I stare at her face. "What were you thinking going back there like this?"

"Rylee…" Her voice is so quiet, I almost don't hear it. "Please don't go—please don't leave me." She sounds so young, like she's a kid again. My chest splinters open for her, and that little girl. The little boy in me knows how it felt when my mom walked out of our home and never came back.

She's quiet again, and her body is still warm. I run to the bathroom and wet the towel again.

"Sissy... sing me...lullaby, please?" she slurs, still half asleep.

"Your sister is not here, Tempestina Mia (my little storm)," I whisper to her.

"Lullaby...please," she pleads again. She's not asking me. I don't think she even knows I'm here, and I don't really know any lullabies or how to sing. But before I know it, my mouth is moving, and the words slip out.

Brilla, brilla, una stellina,
Su nel cielo, Piccolina.
(Twinkle, twinkle little star.
So small up in the sky.)

She exhales slowly, sinking deeper into the bed. Her body relaxes inch by inch, like the sound is pulling her deeper into sleep.

She's fully asleep now, and her skin is not burning up. I slide down on the floor with my back against the bed, but my chest still aches.

"Zayden?" She tries to get up, but I stop her, and she doesn't fight me.

"Hey, I'm here. How you feeling?" I grab the water bottle from the nightstand. "Can you drink a little?"

I bring the cap to her lips, and she takes a small sip before lying back down. "What's going on?"

"Just a migraine..." Her voice is barely above a whisper.

Just. Like it's no big deal. What would have happened if I wasn't there?

"Do you get those often?"

She turns over onto her stomach, cheek pressed against my

pillow, and she's asleep again. I brush her braids back, hand lingering longer than it should. Fever is finally gone.

Don't scare me like that again, baby.

"Z, where were—" Jasper walks in holding a drink and freezes when he sees Luna.

"Shhh, she's sleeping."

"Oh, sorry man." He turns around to leave.

"Jasper." I motion for him to come in, and he closes the door behind him. "She was at the Shadow Rink. Almost passed out, and said it's just a migraine."

"Shit. Did you call the nurse or something?" He leans against the desk.

I shake my head. "Couldn't."

He watches me for a second as the reason why I couldn't clicks in.

"You think he's watching?"

Probably.

I glance over at Luna. She's curled in on herself now.

"I need you to delete the footage from tonight. From Wolfswood Hall and Ravensbourne. The Shadow Rink. All of it."

He nods before leaving the room and coming back with his laptop. Jasper sits at the desk as he types away, but I can feel his eyes on me and Luna.

I drag a hand down my face. "Tomorrow is the first game of the season. Scouts'll be watching. My dad expects me to lead and win, and I can't screw this up. But then I'm here with her, and if he finds out, I don't know what he'll do."

"He's not gonna find out." Jasper glances up from his screen.

"Zayden..." My name escapes her lips.

I pull up from the floor. "I'm here, baby." I smooth my hand over her shoulder. "Shhh. Go back to sleep."

"Yeah, you're screwed." Jasper chuckles.

I know.

"Any updates on who's been sending me those messages?"

"Not yet, but I'm working on it. They're smart, using VPNs to mask their locations and rerouting through dead servers."

"So, dead end." I swear under my breath.

"No, you know I love a good challenge." He smirks.

The last time I saw him this excited, he hacked into the school database and stole the answers for the final exams.

"They think they're smart, but not smarter than me." He turns serious now. "I'll find them."

I have no doubt he will. This is Jasper we're talking about.

CHAPTER 26

Zayden

"Aldenhurst! Aldenhurst!" My name is being chanted from the stands. I look up at the balcony where the scouts and sponsors are watching.

This is the first game of the season. First chance to prove that I'd earned the captain spot, that it wasn't handed to me because of my legacy and last name.

I scan the stands, looking for her face even when I have no right to, but she's not here. When I woke up this morning, she was gone, but my sheets still smelled like her.

"Now entering the ice, your Valcérre Tigre Blanca," they announce over the loud speakers.

"Let's wreck them." Jasper hits me with his stick.

My skates glide on the ice as I take my position at the center. Jasper follows on the right wing, and Cameron takes his defense position. Knees bent and sticks ready for face-off.

Across from me, their captain smirks. Leon fucking Marceau. Saint-Aulaire's golden boy. We've been rivals for as long as I can remember. He applied for a scholarship at Valcérre but didn't get in, and he blamed me. His family can't afford to send him here.

"Didn't think you'd show up. I thought you switched sports." He grins. "Figure skating suits you better, and that video with you and your little ice princess was really cute."

I know exactly what he's doing.

My grip tightens on my stick, but my expression remains calm.

"How does Coach Aldenhurst feel about his golden boy twirling on the ice?" Leon's still grinning like he's already gotten under my skin.

The ref raises the puck, and I inhale through my nose. The puck drops, and before Leon even blinks, I stride past him with it. I pass it to Jasper, who's already flying with it.

Nice try, Leon.

I shove off the ice with two defenders following me, keeping the Saint-Aulaire team out of Jasper's way. Cameron skates to his right in case he needs the extra pass, but Jasper is not slowing down.

For a moment, it looks like Jasper's going to take the shot. But he waits for a second too long to confuse the goalie just like we practiced a hundred times before. Then he passes the puck right to my stick.

I don't think, just shoot. Glove sides, top corner. The puck hits the back of the net before the goalie has time to react.

The horn screams through the arena, and so does the crowd. First score in less than three minutes. I skate backward as the team swarms me. Jasper slams into me first, yelling something I can't hear as we skate toward the benches.

My dad is standing behind the plexiglass, unimpressed.

"Your dad is not impressed," Jasper jokes.

"That's his happy face," I mutter.

Then everything fades, because I feel it again, that fucking shift in the air.

Luna.

I glance up without meaning to, and my eyes find her in the crowd. Third row, hoodie up, and her arms crossed over her chest. Even in a crowded room, my eyes will find her. Annika sits beside her, whispering something, but her eyes are on me.

She shouldn't be here, not with how pale she looked last

night. My heart kicks against my ribs, and I rip my gaze away from her. It doesn't matter that my lungs don't feel so tight anymore. She's not here for me.

Everything snaps back into focus as Jasper hits me in the back with a knowing smirk. This guy never misses a beat. He's about to say something, but the ref whistles, calling us back to the center.

Saved by the whistle.

The puck drops again, and Leon snatches it this time. He's moving across the ice before I can catch up to him. Stupidly fast. I push up harder, but he's ahead by a breath. That's all he needs to snap off a shot straight into the net.

The Saint-Aulaire crowd goes crazy.

Leon skates by me, smirking.

I glance toward the bench again, where my dad is watching with a look that says *Get your fucking head in the game. No distractions.*

We end the first round 1–1.

Second round.

I win the face-off this time and move with the puck. I pass it to Cameron, who drags it wide then passes to Jasper, who scoops effortlessly.

One shot straight into the net.

Valcérre 2, Saint-Aulaire 1.

Things are getting more intense, and the Saint-Aulaire team is getting more aggressive. Leon gets the puck again this time, but I slam into him, forcing the puck loose. Jasper scoops it up then passes it to another player, who sends it flying across the ice to where Cameron is already waiting.

A Saint-Aulaire player tries to scoop it, but I'm faster. They are still fighting over Cameron, giving me an opening, and I shoot.

The buzzer screams, and the crowd goes wild.

Valcérre 3, Saint-Aulaire 1.

Cameron skates beside me. "That was nice, Cap."

Jasper smirks. "I told you not to let this clown get into your head."

My eyes flick toward the crowd for a second, and she's still there. I look away quickly.

"Didn't think Captain Ice Princess still had it," Leon says loud enough for me to hear.

Jasper huffs. "Ignore him. He's just trying to provoke you."

I don't say anything.

We're moving again. Leon has the puck, and I shove him hard into the board and steal it. He stumbles and snarls but recovers quickly.

He's behind me with two of his defenses on his sides. He hits me hard enough to earn a whistle.

"Is the ice princess as good in bed as she is on the ice?" Leon says loud enough for us to hear before we make it to the benches.

"What the fuck did you say?" Jasper launches at him. He tackles Leon mid-ice, slamming him to the ground.

The crowd loses its mind. Players from both teams move in. Refs dive in, whistles going off. Jasper's already landed two hits on Leon's jaw. Blood spatters on the ice, but the fucker is laughing.

"Oh, shit! I didn't know you guys share girls, too." That earns him another punch. Leon fights back, grabbing Jasper by the collar. The refs pull them away from each other.

I take the opportunity to grab Leon by his jersey. "You talk about her like that again, I'll break your fucking jaw."

Cameron pulls me away from him. "Come on, Cap. Jasper took care of it."

The refs point us toward the benches, yelling something I can barely make out. My dad is yelling, too. Leon and Jasper are being pulled away to the penalty boxes.

I fight the urge to look up, but I can feel her eyes on me,

pulling without permission. My eyes find hers in the stand, and she's already looking at me. Something in her gaze makes my heart squeeze. That silent question in her eyes that I feel in my chest. *Are you okay?* My breath catches in a way I'll never admit.

Then she glances to the left. I follow her gaze to where Leon is looking at her, too, with that smug look on his face. Jasper notices. Then Cameron. We're all looking at her now.

Fuck! Very subtle.

"Zayden!" my dad yells from the bench. "Bench. Now," he commands.

His eyes flick between us and the stands.

He fucking saw everything.

CHAPTER 27

Luna

"So, you weren't in your room when we got home last night," Annika says from beside me on the bench.

I pretend to focus on the game. Zayden has just scored and they're moving faster now, and more brutal.

"Zayden wasn't at the hangout spot, either, I wonder why," Sophie adds.

They both are watching me a little too closely.

I have no freaking idea what's going on. I didn't plan to go to the rink, or for him to be there. I didn't plan to wake up in his bed with his arms wrapped around me.

Damn it, baby, just stop fighting me for a sec. His voice replays in my head. I keep telling myself it was the migraine and I hallucinated the whole thing. But it sounded so real.

"Luna, are you even here with us?" Annika nudges me with her elbow.

I take a sip of my drink to buy me some time. Then the crowd is screaming, and when I look down at the ice, Jasper is on top of a guy, the captain of the other team. Ref whistles blare through the arena. Players from both teams are being pulled apart.

"Holy shit!" Annika grabs my arm.

"Oh my God, Jasper! Is he okay?" Sophie leans forward like she wants to go down there and check.

They pull Jasper away from the other guy—I think his name

is Leon. But Zayden is grabbing him by the collar before Cameron pulls him away from him.

Zayden's head turns toward me, and our eyes meet. He looks furious, and my breath catches in my throat for a second. The noises fade, and the only sound is the thud of my pulse in my ears.

Are you okay? I whisper in my chest, like he can hear me.

Jasper and Leon are being taken away to the penalty boxes. Leon is looking at me with that infuriating smirk, like he enjoyed every second of it.

Then Jasper and Cameron. They're all looking at me now.

Shit!

"What the hell was that?" Sophie leans in.

"I don't know," I say as Zayden's dad yells something at him.

"Were they fighting about you?" Sophie asks.

"I don't—" I shake my head, but I can still feel Zayden's eyes on me like the sun on a cloudless day. "They weren't."

My heart is beating faster, and I'm back there again. Listening to my mom and her boyfriend yelling and fighting because of me. Luna did this, and Luna did that. Because I existed.

I need air.

I stand quickly and squeeze through the row of students.

"Luna?" Sophie calls after me.

"I—just need to go." I don't wait for a response.

I mutter, "Excuse me," and, "Sorry," as I continue making my way out of the arena. My head begins to throb again.

I make it to the far hallway near the vending machine where it's mostly empty and quiet.

My back slides down the wall. I close my eyes for a second, bringing my knees to my chest.

"Hey, babe. You okay?" Sophie's quiet voice reaches me.

"Yeah, just needed a minute."

They walk toward the vending machine.

Annika hands me a bottle of water.

Sophie tosses a bag of plantain chips onto my lap. "For the queen of pretending she's okay."

"Thanks." I smile at her.

She sits beside me and passes a bag of BBQ potato chips to Annika. Then she opens a bag of cheese crackers for herself. I don't really want to eat, but it's plantain chips, my favorite. I open the bag and pop one into my mouth.

They let me sit in the quiet until I can't take it anymore.

"I hate him."

"Zayden? You already established that." Sophie turns to face me.

"You don't get it. I hate him, hate him. I know he's your cousin and all, but the guy is confusing. He told me to stay away from him, then he looked at me like he actually cares." I play with one of my loose braids.

Sophie pats my back, grinning. "Oh, babe. You don't hate him. You just hate that you like him. I get it. The guy is objectively hot."

"Sophie! He's your cousin."

"That's why he's so hot. And it's not my fault the Del Sol girls have a thing for men in my family."

I gasp and bury my face in my hands. "Sophie!"

"It's okay. He likes you, too. He just sucks at human emotion." She grins wider.

I groan, dragging my hands down my face. "I hate that I can't stop thinking about him, and how much space he takes up in my head."

Sophie bumps her shoulder against mine "Have you two… like hooked up?"

"No. We just…kissed," I say a little too quickly.

Sophie shrugs. "Maybe you guys just need to have sex and get it out of your systems."

"*Sophie!*" My eyes go wide, heat crawling up my neck.

Annika nearly chokes on her chips. "Subtle."

"I'm just saying. The sexual tension between you two is unbearable."

I press the water bottle to my forehead.

"Seriously, what are you so afraid of?" Sophie asks.

"I've never done that…before…with anyone." I stare ahead.

Sophie's expression softens. "Oh. I didn't know."

"It's not like I wear a sign. I'm probably the only nineteen-year-old virgin on the planet," I say quickly. "I've just never felt…ready." I never told them what it was like. The yelling, the fists, the way I used to flinch when footsteps got too loud. There was this one night. He didn't touch me, my mom's boyfriend, but I saw it in his eyes. If my mom hadn't walked in, something would've happened. I knew it. I felt it in my skin for weeks. Since then, I've never let anyone that close.

Sophie leans her head back against the wall. "That makes sense. Especially with everything you've been through."

I nod, but my throat feels tight.

"There's no rush, though. Whenever you're ready," Annika adds.

The truth is, Zayden Aldenhurst is not something I can just get out of my system. He's injected in my bloodstream, and everything that I am. He's stuck on me like a tattoo.

Sophie's phone vibrates, and she pulls it out. "The game is over, and we won 5–3."

Annika's already texting. "Cameron says everyone's heading to The Vault. Midnight party. Players get in first, but we're on the list."

I should say no. My head still hurts, and my feelings are a mess. I'm not ready to see him again.

Sophie turns to me. "Are you up for it? We don't have to go. We can go back to the dorm, make tea, and watch Korean drama."

That sounds amazing, and I almost say yes. But I don't want

to be the reason they miss the one thing everyone's been talking about all week.

"No, let's go."

"Are you sure?"

"Yes, I get to wear my little black dress." And my favorite pair of stockings.

Her eyes light up as she pulls to my feet. "Let's go, ladies. We have two hours to get ready."

"The code tonight is tigri blanca," Annika says as we make it out of the exit.

BY THE TIME we get ready and make it to the Vault, I regret it the second I walk in. The music is too loud.

The guys are already waiting at our usual booth. They are all wearing their Valcérre jackets. Zayden's jacket sleeves are rolled up to his elbows with his tattoo peeking out.

The second his eyes lock on mine, he gives me this look like he's mad at me for coming. He looks away like I'm exhausting him.

"You ladies made it." Cameron grins as we slide into the booth. "Celebratory shots." He set a small glass in front of each of us, and the liquid inside glows.

"What the hell is this?" I bring it to my nose.

"Valcerran Aurora shot." Jasper smirks. "The glow's from a special flower extract they infuse with it. It's legal. Mostly."

"To the first win of the season." Cameron raises his drink up before throwing it back.

Zayden grunts when I bring mine to my lips, and when I look over at him, he gives me that look again. Like, *What are you doing?*

Technically, I shouldn't be drinking, it usually makes my

migraines worse, but I take the shot anyway. It burns down my throat and settles somewhere beneath my ribs.

We all set our empty glasses on the table.

"Okay, now that we've got drinks, someone want to explain what the hell that fight was about?" Sophie asks the question we've all been thinking about.

Suddenly, the table is quiet. Even the music seems to fade away. Zayden shifts in his seat. Cameron scratches the back of his neck, and Jasper curses under his breath.

"Jasper!" Sophie leans closer. "What the fuck happened? You don't just go around punching people unless they do something."

Jasper looks at me before looking away. "He made a comment," he mutters. "About Luna."

I move uncomfortably in my seat.

"What kind of comment?" Sophie frowns.

Jasper looks at Zayden, who gives him a nod. He clears his throat before speaking. "He asked Zayden *is she as good in bed as she is on the ice?* I'm sorry, Luna."

Everything in me goes still, and I want to disappear. Zayden doesn't look at me, but his hand curls into a fist on the table.

"I'm gonna grab another drink." I slide out of the booth before they can say anything. The bar is open tonight, so I grab one of the bottles with the same drink Cameron gave us earlier and pour myself a shot. The heat spreads through my body, and if I stay still another second, I'm gonna explode.

So, I let the music pull me into the crowd, even if I have no idea what I'm doing. I've never been to a party before, and I don't dance unless it's on the ice. But I'm not thinking right now.

I close my eyes and let the music guide me. My shoulders roll back, my braids swaying with every roll of my hip. I let the beat drown out everything—except for him.

His gaze burns into my skin from across the room. And

that's why when some hockey guy with too much cologne steps behind me, I don't stop him. He leans down and says something in my ear with a laugh, but I have no idea what he said.

Then the air around me changes, and suddenly Zayden is here.

He grabs the guy by the collar and shoves him like he weighs nothing. The guy mutters something under his breath, ready to throw a punch, but one look at Zayden and he's backing off with his hands in the air, disappearing into the crowd.

Coward.

Then Zayden turns around to face me, and the look in his eyes pulls the air out of my lungs. Even in the low lighting, I can see it, the anger in his eyes, like he's mad I let that guy touch me.

His eyes drag over me from head to toe, as if he wants to devour me right here in the middle of the crowd.

God, I want him to.

I swallow hard, heat building between my thighs.

My chest rises faster. I look away first, forcing my legs to move. I head toward the bar, needing another drink. I'm about to pour myself a shot when someone grabs the bottle from my hands.

I spin around, ready to tell whoever it is to fuck off, only to find Zayden staring at me.

Of course, it's him.

"That'll make your headaches worse."

I scoff. "Why do you care?" I push past him and head upstairs.

I step out onto the balcony. The cold air bites into my skin, and I grab the railing, trying to breathe through the tightness in my chest.

And of course, he follows me.

"Seriously? Why are you following me?"

He takes another step closer, the heat of him brushing against my back despite the cold air. "You okay?"

"I'm fine," I lie.

"You shouldn't be here," he says, worry in his voice. "You should be in bed, resting."

I spin to face him. "Stop pretending you care."

"You think I don't care?" he whispers. "You think I don't fucking feel you every time you walk into a room?" His voice drops, ragged. "You're a fucking magnet, Luna. I feel you before I see you—your scent, your energy. I knew you were at the Shadow Rink last night, even though no one told me. I feel it when you're near, like gravity. Like a goddamn pull in my bones."

"Why do you keep pushing me away, then?" I hate how my voice comes out—quiet, tired, like I'm already breaking.

His voice lowers, like he's finally letting something slip. "I told myself staying away would protect you," he says. "That you'd be better off if I kept my distance. But that didn't last long, did it?" He huffs a breath that isn't quite a laugh, more like disbelief. "Not even a week."

We're too close now. Close enough that I can see the glint of something raw in his eyes. Close enough for him to kiss me. Which is the last thing I should want, and the only thing I do.

"Then I saw his hands on you, and I fucking lost it." His eyes drop briefly to my lips before finding mine. He's looking at me like he's trying to memorize every inch of my face in the moonlight.

"If you're gonna kiss me again," I murmur to break the tension, "kiss me somewhere that'll make me forget how much I hate you."

I expect him to walk away. But he studies me for a second before leaning even closer, so close that I can feel his breath on my face. "È questo che vuoi, Tempestina Mia (Is that what you want, my little storm)?"

"What?" I blink.

"Do you want me on my knees for you, Luna? Eating you out

so good that you forget every damn reason why you think you hate me."

Holy. Fucking. Shit.

The way he says it like a promise and a dare makes my thighs press together. My body turns into lava, even though it's freezing out here. Is that I want? I mean, no one has ever done that for me before.

Whatever was in that shot must have taken away all my resolve, because I hear myself say, "Yes."

That's all it takes for Zayden Aldenhurst to drop on his knees for me, right here on the cold balcony floor.

CHAPTER 28

ZAYDEN

THIS IS NOT what I expected when I came out tonight, but here I am, on my fucking knees.

My hands slide up her thighs over her black tights until I realize they're not tights.

Fucking hell.

She's wearing stockings—thigh highs, clipped to a garter that disappears under her dress.

I push the dress higher and find the straps connecting her stockings to the tiniest scrap of lace.

"Fuck, Luna..." I breathe out. "You wore this out?"

She looks down at me with wild eyes. "I didn't know you were gonna get on your knees for me."

I trace along the garter strap then dip my finger beneath the hem of her panties.

"You sure this is what you want?" I ask, giving her a chance to change her mind.

She nods, but that's not enough.

"Not good enough, Luna. I need to hear it."

"Are you gonna put that mouth to work and make me forget how much I hate you, or not?"

Fuck, I want to worship her and ruin her at the same time.

I hook my finger at the edge of her panties and slide the little piece of fabric down. She's already wet. Her scent hits me first, warm, sweet, and dangerous. I lower my mouth to her, tongue brushing against her heat, and the first taste is heaven, drawing a deep, guttural groan from my throat.

She arches toward me as I close my lips around her sweet spot, light at first, then harder. I drag my tongue along her center before pushing the tip against her entrance. Her muscle clenches around me, pulling me in. She's so warm and so wet.

"Oh my God, Zayden." She grabs the railing behind her.

I pause. "Be a good girl and stay quiet for me, yeah?"

I slide my hands under her thighs, lifting her slightly to angle her hips as lick her again. Then I give her nub a little pull, enough pressure to make her whimper. Her fingers thread into my locs, hips rolling against my mouth, chasing her climax.

That's my girl.

Dragging my tongue down her entrance again, I push in as deep as I can, curling it inside her, tasting the slick that's dripping down her thighs. My nose brushes her clit with every thrust, her thighs squeezing my head.

I pay attention to her reactions. She gasps when I lick, moans when I suck, and shudders when I push my tongue deep inside her entrance. I rotate between all three.

Lick.

Suck.

Thrust.

She's panting, moaning behind her palms, trying to stay quiet like the good girl that she is, but failing miserably. My dick is so fucking hard in my pants, pulsing with every sound that escapes her lips.

Her eyes are wide, glassy with pleasure, chest heaving, her body twitching with every stroke of my tongue. She's so fucking close.

That's it, baby. Come for me. I want her to come all over my face while I'm still hard as fuck for her.

I close my lips around her clit and suck, then I flick my tongue over the tip until she's squirming under my mouth.

Her head tips back, her hand still covering her mouth, but her moans spill through anyway—broken and beautiful and completely out of her control. I don't stop, not until her thighs are shaking and my name spills from her lips as she comes against my tongue. Her whole body trembles as she rides it out, hips twitching, slick pouring onto my tongue and into my bloodstream like a fucking drug.

She's still catching her breath when I stand up from the floor. My hands brace on either side of her hip. Her body is limp against the railing, legs still trembling like I just unraveled her.

I press my forehead to hers, breathing her in for a second. "Still hate me?"

"Ask me tomorrow." Her voice is a little raspy. "Right now, I don't know."

A chuckle escapes before I can stop it. The sound startles both of us.

"Fucking hell, Zayden Aldenhurst knows how to laugh."

I lean in, close enough to feel the heat of her lips. My hands graze the edge of the garter that's got me hanging on to my sanity by a thread. I want to fuck her right here against the railing. But I hold back. Not yet.

"You're going to ruin me, Ice Princess." The words come out a little hoarse from everything I'm holding in.

She lets out a shaky laugh. "Shouldn't you be doing the ruining?"

"Don't worry, I'm going to ruin you, too." Then I kiss her like I'll die if I don't. She kisses me back like she's been starving for it, too. I wrap my hands around her waist as I pull her to me.

Our mouths move fast, messy, and desperate against each other. It's freezing, but I'm burning. Her fingers are in my hair, pulling and tugging at my locs.

My lips trail down her jaw, across her throat, back to her mouth, like I can't get enough. Her lips part, and she opens for me. Our tongues tangle together, slow at first, then deeper. We kiss like nothing else exists besides the mountain behind us, the stars, and this balcony.

This is like nothing I've ever felt before, this all-consuming and addictive need. I chase the sound of her breath, the little sighs she makes when I suck her bottom lip.

My hands move up to either side of her face, and I brush my thumb along her jaw. Our lips are barely touching now. Her hands are under my shirt, nails dragging across my skin.

I brush my lips against hers. One more kiss. Then another. Like we're making up for lost time.

Then she pulls back just enough to look at me. Eyes shining under the stars. She's so fucking beautiful that I can't breathe.

"Can you get me out of here?" she asks quietly.

She probably doesn't know yet, but she could ask me for the stars and I'd find a way to bring them to her one by one.

I nod and pull out my phone.

> Me: Luna is with me. Tell Sophie only No one else. She can't tell anyone.

> Jasper: Okay, just be careful.

"Come on, let's go." I offer her my hand, and she takes it as we leave the Vault.

The drive to the cabin is quiet, but it's not awkward. She hasn't said anything since we left the Vault. Her head leans against the seat, knees tucked to her chest, eyes closed, and those fucking stockings. But I can tell she's not sleeping. There's a small crease between her brows.

When we reach the cabin, I step out first, round the car, and open the door for her.

"Wanna change into something more comfortable?" I ask as we make it inside the cabin. "I'll get started on the fire."

She nods before disappearing into the bedroom. I get the fire going and fill the kettle with water, letting it boil as I light the candle that's supposed to help her relax.

I'm pouring her tea in the mug when she steps out, wearing one of my T-shirts. She kept the stockings on. Those fucking stockings are going to be the death of me.

She takes a seat on the couch, and I hand her the tea—mint with a little bit of honey.

I sit on the other end of the couch. "Can I?" I gesture to her feet. "I read that foot massage helps with headaches sometimes."

Her foot goes to my lap.

"I'm gonna..." I clear my throat, nodding toward her leg. "Can I take them off? The stockings? I can't give you a proper massage with them on."

"Only if you're gentle," she teases.

"Promise."

I turn toward her and reach under the edge of the T-shirt. I find the first garter clasp and unclip it carefully, then the next. Her breath changes. So does mine.

"Wanna know why I wear them?"

I nod, because I can't form any words right now.

"They make me feel like a badass."

"Yeah?" I slowly roll it down her leg and toss it aside.

"I know they're just stockings, but they make me feel like I can walk into a room and own it."

I pause halfway to the second stocking. "You are badass, with or without the stockings." My knuckles skim the inside of her calf. I swear I feel her shiver. "And these stockings almost took me out."

She chuckles. "You're not so broody."

"No?" I remove the other stocking and set it aside.

"Yeah, you're secretly soft, like a teddy bear."

Soft.

My dad used to throw that word around a lot.

Stop being so soft, Zayden. Aldenhursts don't do soft. No one is going to respect you.

"Take it back." I glare at her.

"Nope." She just grins.

"I'm broody and cold." I narrow my eyes and lean back a little, trying to summon my signature broody face.

She fucking laughs. "You really think that's working right now?"

I glance at her, sighing dramatically. "Fine, but that stays between us."

She lifts her hand and drags an invisible zipper across her lips, locking it and throwing away the key.

I shake my head, smiling like an idiot because that was fucking cute.

She's so fucking cute.

Back to my mission. I reach for her feet and get to work. I start slowly, pressing into the arches then working my thumbs up toward the ball of her foot.

"You're really good at this," she murmurs, eyes half lidded and head falling back.

I shrug. "I might've googled it."

That gets a small smile out of her. "You googled how to give me a foot massage?"

"Feet pressure points for migraines," I add. "Went down a rabbit hole." She scared the shit out of me last night, and I wanted to be prepared.

She shifts a little, curling her toes when I hit the right spot. "Well, whatever you're doing, it's working."

I glance at her. "Feeling better?"

She hums. "Mhm. The orgasm helped, too."

My thumbs still, just for a second. "What?"

"Orgasms. They help with the pain sometimes. It's a release thing. Lowers the tension in my head, especially if I can come more than once. Get the blood flowing."

Jesus Christ. This is how I go.

But she doesn't stop there.

"I usually use my fingers," she says casually, like she's not completely ending me. "Sometimes the showerhead. I had this cheap bullet vibrator that broke in, like, three uses."

I shift slightly on the couch, subtly adjusting how I'm sitting. "When did the migraines start?" I ask, trying to change the subject to safer territory.

"I don't remember, maybe eight or nine. I know it was around when Rylee left. I'd be home alone most days. My mom worked late, and Rylee…was miles away. I didn't want to worry her. I told my mom once about the pain. She said it was just a headache. Told me to drink water and stop being dramatic."

"Where was your dad?" I can't imagine her just suffering through her migraines alone.

"Not in the picture." She exhales, like she's tired of answering that question. "I used to cry through the pain, which made it worse. So I started googling anything that might help. Cold compresses. Caffeine. Peppermint. White noise," she continues.

My chest tightens as I picture her crying alone in the dark.

"Sometimes they help a little. As I got older, I found that orgasms helped sometimes." She glances at me, her eyes softer than usual. "You're the first person I've ever done anything with. And with you, it wasn't about the migraines, or the relief, but it helped a lot. It felt good. Really good."

She's looking at me with those eyes that make my chest ache in a way I don't have words for yet.

"Come here, please." I pat my lap, needing to have her closer to me.

She studies me for a second before slowly climbing onto my lap. Her legs drape over mine, arms loosely looping around my shoulders, and my hands settle at her hips.

She fits perfectly.

I rest my forehead against hers for a second, just breathing her in. "You didn't have to tell me all of that," I say quietly.

She leans back just enough to look at me—eyes soft, honest. "I wanted to."

"You know that's not why you're here, right?" I tuck a loose braid behind her ear. "I didn't bring you here to have sex. Not that I'm saying I don't want you. Because, God, I do. So much it hurts."

Her eyes widen slightly.

I let my hand move gently across her back. "I brought you here because I wanted to give you space to breathe. To let someone take care of you for once. We don't have to do anything tonight. Or any night. You're not…expected to give me anything, unless that's what you really want."

She looks down for a second and then right back at me. Then she presses her lips to mine, barely there at first. No rush, no tongue, just lips to lips. And something about the gentleness of it all undoes me. I kiss her back just as softly, feeling the shape of her mouth, the warmth of her breath, and the softness of her lips.

When we pull back, she looks at me with a smile that could kill a man.

"I might have to keep you around," she says teasingly. "For medical purposes, of course."

I blink, trying to catch my breath. You never know what's going to come out of her mouth.

"That orgasm? Better than anything I've ever given myself. Even my rose couldn't compete."

I groan and let my head fall back against the couch. She's laughing, absolutely delighted with herself.

"I'm serious," she whispers between laughs, curling into me. "You're better than painkillers."

And yeah, I kind of hope she does keep me around, because her laugh is my medicine.

I wrap my arms around her without thinking. "I don't want you hurting alone anymore," I whisper into her hair. "Promise you'll let me know when it gets bad."

She's quiet for a few seconds, like she's thinking about it. But I wait. "I promise." She exhales into my neck.

CHAPTER 29

Luna

WHAT THE FUCK is happening here? I'm literally on his lap, head against his chest, his arms are wrapped around me like it's the most natural thing in the world.

Whatever this is, it feels good, safe, like I can breathe, like everything in me exhales. For once, I don't overthink it. Not what we're doing. What this means or what comes next. Instead, I let myself lean into him. His arms tighten around me slightly, like he felt that shift, too.

He hasn't said much, but I can tell something is weighting him down.

"How did it feel, winning tonight?"

Zayden doesn't answer right away. His hand stills on my back then slides down to rest at my waist.

"Felt good," he says eventually, but his voice sounds like it's coming from somewhere far away.

I lift my head just enough to see him. "Just good?"

"I love hockey," he admits. "The team. The rush. All of it. But... sometimes, after games like tonight..." He trails off, eyes distant. "I miss skating. No pressure or noise—just...moving on the ice for no one but myself. The quiet of it."

My heart squeezes.

"I sneak out to the Shadow Rink sometimes or I come to the cabin. It's the only place I feel like I can breathe. No yelling. No one's watching. Just the sound of my blades and the cold." He's staring at the fire like it holds all the answers. "Especially after fights with my dad. Or before games I know I can't afford to screw up."

I know exactly what he means.

"I get it," I say softly. "That feeling. The second the blades touch the ice and it's just…you. Your body. The music. Like everything else disappears and you finally have space to feel like you again."

He nods, his brow furrowed like he's trying not to let his emotion show too much. "The first time I saw you skate…you reminded me of me. Back before it all got so damn loud. And honestly? I was a little jealous."

"You're allowed to love both, you know," I whisper. "You don't have to choose."

He chuckles. "Tell that to my dad."

"You don't owe him, or anyone, anything. This is your life, Zayden."

Something soft and tired shifts in his eyes, and I see it. The boy behind the silence and the broody stares. Instead of replying, he leans forward and presses a soft kiss to my forehead. The kind that makes my chest ache in a way I can't explain.

"Come on," he murmurs, standing with me in his arms. "Let's get you to bed."

I wrinkle my nose, trying to lighten the mood. "I can walk, you know."

"I know. But I like taking care of you."

I stare up at him as he carries me down the short hallway.

"Is that your love language or something?" I tease.

A rare smile tugs at his mouth, the kind I don't think he gives to just anyone. "Maybe."

He pushes the door open with his shoulder and gently lays me down on the bed, tucking me in.

"Good night," he whispers, stepping back like he's about to leave.

But I catch his hand without thinking. "Stay?"

He gives me a small nod. "I usually sleep in shorts and no shirt. That okay?"

"Mhm."

My heart thuds a little faster as he turns toward the dresser and pulls his shirt over his head. His back flexes as he tosses the shirt aside. I didn't realize he had so many tattoos. I've seen glimpses along his forearms when he pushes up his sleeves. But this is different, and he has more than I expected.

Then he reaches for the waist of his sweatpants and pushes them down. His legs are long and toned with thick muscles. His shorts sit low on his hips. *God, he's beautiful.* I don't think I'm breathing properly right now.

He turns and catches me staring, and gives me that soft, crooked almost-smile that's been wrecking me all night.

Zayden climbs into the bed next to me, the mattress dipping beneath his weight, leaving space between us. Just far enough to let me decide how close I want him.

I crawl into him like it's instinct, pressing my cheek against the warm skin over his heart. He wraps his arms around my waist like we've done this a thousand times before. No matter how much I try to convince myself I hate him, there's something about him that feels like home. And right now, that feeling multiplies.

That aching, hollow part of me settles a little. It's been so long since I felt like this. Not since Rylee left when I was eight. Even after I moved with her to Paris when I was fifteen, things were different.

I was older then and didn't need her how I used to. She had her job, a new life, and later, the twins. But I've been quietly craving this feeling.

"This feels nice," I whisper.

"Yeah, it does." His arm tightens slightly around me. "Want me to sing you a lullaby?"

"What?" I glance up at him.

"You, uh…" He rubs the back of his neck with his free hand, suddenly shy. "Last night. You were talking in your sleep. You asked for one."

My heart stumbles. "I did?"

He nods. "You said something about your sister. And how you didn't want her to leave."

"Oh God," I groan, burying my face in his hard chest. "Please tell me that's all I said."

Zayden's chest rumbles, and he's laughing. "Well…now that you mention it."

I tilt my head at him suspiciously.

"You also confessed your undying love for me. Said I was the hottest hockey player alive and couldn't live without me."

"Zayden." I shove at his chest, heat rushing to my cheeks. "You're such a liar. I didn't say that."

"You'll never know for sure."

I roll my eyes at him. "You made that up."

"Did I?" He grins.

What is happening here?

Who is this Zayden?

"My sister used to sing to me when I was little. On the phone, after she moved away. It made me feel like…I wasn't completely alone."

"The offer's still open. I'm not the best singer, but I'll sing for you."

I smile faintly into his chest. "No song tonight."

This is enough!

CHAPTER 30

Luna

A SOFT THUD drifts in from the distance, like a cabinet being shut gently, and I blink. It takes me a second to realize where I am. Then a smile spreads across my lips as I remember last night and...Zayden.

I turn my head, expecting to see him still there beside me, but the space is empty, the blanket pulled back slightly. I sit up slowly, stretching my arms overhead. My muscles feel loose, lazy, like someone who had one of the best sleep of her life.

Pushing the blankets off, I swing my legs over the side of the bed and make my way toward the kitchen. Then I stop. Because standing in the kitchen with his back to me is Zayden. Shirtless, broad shoulders, barefoot, and gray sweatpants slung low on his hips.

The tattoos I barely got to see last night are completely visible now. One stands out. A skate and a hockey stick on his side.

He must sense my presence, because he turns to look at me. "Morning."

"Morning." I walk over and hop onto the counter beside him. "What's all this?" I ask, eyeing the pan.

"Quinoa bowl."

"You googled migraine-safe breakfasts, didn't you?" I ask, narrowing my eyes.

Zayden shrugs one shoulder. "You should stay the weekend," he says suddenly, without looking up. "Like a migraine retreat."

I blink. "A retreat?"

"Yeah. You. Me. Food. Sleep. No stress."

I tilt my head at him, pretending to consider. "Hmm. And does this retreat include...orgasms?"

Zayden chokes slightly then glances up at me like I've just short-circuited every brain cell he has. "That's...optional."

I grin, leaning back on my hands on the counter beside him. "Optional?"

He recovers fast. "Available upon request."

I hum. "That's good customer service."

"You're trouble," he mutters, but he's smiling now. The real kind—the one that softens his whole face and makes me want to kiss it off him.

I laugh, but it's quieter this time. My fingers curl around the edge of the counter.

I like us here. I like the way he smiles more. I like the quiet. I like that I don't feel like I have to keep proving I belong. But part of me already knows this won't last.

And once we get back to campus? The walls will go up again. The secrets and the silences. He'll start acting like I imagined all of this, and I still haven't told him about the archives.

I must go quiet, because Zayden turns toward me fully now, eyebrows drawing together. "What's going on in that head of yours, Ice Princess?"

I shake my head, but he already knows.

"You're thinking about what happens when we go back."

I nod.

"Luna," he says, stepping in front of me. "Whatever this is..." He hesitates for a breath. "We have to keep it between us." The moment the words leave his mouth, everything in me goes still.

I press both hands against his chest and slide off the counter and make my way toward the hallway. But before I have time to make it far, his hand curls gently around my wrist, pulling me back to him.

"Hey, talk to me, please."

"What do you want from me, Zayden?" I snap.

"I want you."

"Then why do I feel like some secret you don't want anyone to know about?"

"It's not like that."

"Isn't it?" I ask. "Are you ashamed of me?"

He shakes his head. "No. God, no." He looks wrecked, like that question hit something inside of him. "It's because Valcérre ruins anything that's good. You've seen it." He looks away for a second before looking back at me. "If they find out about us, they'll destroy it. They'll destroy you. And I can't let that happen."

I stare at him, every part of me begging to believe the way he's looking at me. But it's not enough. Not when he keeps pulling me in only to push me away.

"You don't get to do this." I motion between us. "The back and forth. One second, you act like you care, and the next, you're shutting me out like I imagined the whole damn thing."

Something burns behind my eyes, but I blink it back. I will not cry. Not here, and definitely not in front of him.

"I'm used to people not caring about me, I know how to be alone and how to take care of myself. I've done it my whole life." The words catch in my throat. "But if you care about me, I can't keep second-guessing it every time you push me away." A tear escapes before I can stop it, and I quickly turn around, hoping he didn't see it.

But of course, he did.

He gently turns me around to face him, and I look down at the floor, avoiding his eyes. "Look at me, Luna."

I don't.

I don't want him to see how much he affects me.

Then his fingers slip under my chin, and he gently brings my eyes up to meet his. "Don't hide from me," he says, catching a traitorous tear with his thumb. And I want to disappear. "I do care about you. So much it terrifies me." His eyes are full of something I can't describe. "Because I know the moment I let myself have this…have you, I won't survive if I lose you."

The words hit somewhere so deep that it hurts. I don't think anyone has ever been scared of losing me before. I want to say something, but the words are gone. Lost somewhere in the pressure behind my ribs, blocked by the way my throat's closing up.

Instead, I press my face into his chest and bury myself into the warmth of his skin. His arms tighten around me instantly, pulling me even closer.

"Promise you won't push me away again," I whisper. "Because if I open up to this, and you push me away again…" I swallow hard, my voice barely there. "I don't know what it'll do to me."

"I promise. I can't stay away from you even if I try."

"Okay, cool." And just like that, I'm crying. Tears spill down my cheeks, hot, stupid, and so not me. My whole chest trembles, and I'm trying to keep it in, trying to stay quiet, but it just keeps breaking through.

"God, this is so embarrassing. I don't do crying." I let out this half sob, half laugh that sounds completely unhinged. "Do you mind if I stay here forever?" I bury my face deeper into his chest.

A sound rumbles beneath my cheek that sounds like a laugh. "Come on. Let me see that pretty face." He tries to nudge me away, but I tighten my arms around him.

"Absolutely not."

He backs up slowly until he reaches the couch, lowering himself and bringing me with him. I'm still curled up on his chest, knees on either side of him.

"You can stay here for as long as you want," he whispers

against the top of my head. His fingers move in slow circles on my back. I could stay like this forever.

"So…" I tilt my head just enough to peek at him. "Is the migraine retreat offer still open?"

"Depends. You looking for the basic package or the premium one?"

"Hmm," I hum against him. "Does the premium one come with more of that breakfast I smelled…and, you know… orgasms?"

He groans into my hair, arms tightening slightly around my waist. "Jesus, Luna."

"What?" I ask, all innocence.

"You're gonna kill me." He closes his eyes.

We stay like that for a while, the silence stretching between us.

I shift slightly in his lap, and he sucks in a breath. I feel the way his body responds to mine, already hard beneath me.

"Shit, I'm sorry. Didn't mean to—"

"Get turned on?" I raise an eyebrow. "I'm pretty sure that's normal. And I would be offended if you didn't."

He exhales like he's been holding his breath. "I just can't help it with your body pressing against mine, but we don't have to do anything, okay?"

"Okay." I roll my hips slowly against him, and he chokes on a breath.

"Luna?"

"Yes?" I say sweetly, grinding harder this time, rolling my hips in a lazy circle against the thick bulge beneath me.

Zayden groans, head tipping back against the couch. "Fuck, Luna. What are you doing?"

I shift my angle, hitting a new spot. "Take a guess."

His hands grip my hips.

A whimper escapes me before I can swallow it. "This feels so good, Zayden." My panties are soaked now, clinging to me, catching the friction just right.

"That's it, pretty girl. Take what you need from me."

I ride him harder, dragging friction right where I need it. His cock twitches beneath me. "You like this?"

My moans get louder, more desperate. I can barely breathe through it.

"What do you think, Luna?" His voice drops to something darker, breathless. "Fuck, look at you. You look so fucking beautiful riding me like this."

I shudder, my body lighting up at his praise—thighs burning and heat building low in my stomach.

"Can I..." He looks down at my shirt where my nipples are already hard and begging for attention.

I nod.

Then he leans down, and his head disappears under my shirt. I gasp when I feel his mouth wrap around my nipple. He sucks, gently at first, then harder, before swirling his tongue around it. I love the way he moans low in his throat, like this feels as good to him as it does for me.

"Yes." My fingers find his locs where they are buried under my shirt, and I tug them just enough to make him groan against my skin.

His hand moves to my other nipple, giving her awaited attention. She was getting a little jealous. He runs his thumbs around the bud before pinching it gently, then a little harder. Just enough to make me gasp again.

He alternates between sucking one and rolling the other between his fingers, switching sides. And I feel every suck, every pull, straight to where I need him most. Like his mouth on my breast is directly connected to my pussy. The pressure deepens between my legs, and I'm so soaked; I'm pretty sure I'm leaking through his pants.

"Zayden...I'm so close," I breathe, hips grinding against his lap without thinking.

He lifts his head to look at me. Lips wet and slightly parted, and his eyes are heavy lidded like he's drunk on me. Then he fucking smiles, and I think I just got pregnant from that smile alone.

I grab his face and kiss it off him. He kisses me back, tongue sliding against mine like he needs this just as badly. His hands are still under my shirt, still playing with my nipples, and every time he flicks or tugs, it brings me a little closer.

I kiss him until I'm breathless, and then I pull away. I lean back slightly, palms bracing against his knees, arching my back as I roll my hips harder over him. The angle shifts—deeper, hotter, perfect.

"Fuck, Luna. That's it."

My eyes flutter closed as the pressure builds.

"Keep your eyes on me," he commands. "I want to see you when you come."

"Zayden, I'm gonna—"

"Come for me, Tempestina."

My whole body goes tight as pleasure crashes through me and steals my breath away. He pulls me against his chest, and I bury my face in his shoulder as my hips tremble through the last waves.

"Fuck, Luna." He lets out a guttural sound and grabs my hips, holding me down against him as his body shudders beneath mine.

Oh.

My eyes widen, and I lift my head slowly, blinking at him.

"Did you just..."

"Yep."

I smile and press a kiss to the corner of his mouth. "Well, I feel amazing," I say, still a little breathless. "But now I'm starving." I swing my leg off him, my thighs still trembling, and hop to my feet. I wander toward the counter where the bowl of quinoa is waiting.

"Damn," I say, taking a bite. "It tastes so good."

I look over at Zayden, who hasn't moved an inch. Head tilted back, eyes closed, mouth slightly parted, like he's still trying to recover.

Ruined.

I ruined him like he said I would, and I haven't even given him the real thing yet.

He finally pulls himself up. "I'm gonna go shower, you enjoy your breakfast."

I watch him walk away—barefoot, muscles shifting under his skin, the waistband of his ruined sweats sitting low on his hips.

Holy hell.

When did his ass get that good?

My eyes follow his ass down the hall before I shake my head. "God, I'm so screwed."

I finish my quinoa bowl, leaning back on the couch and smiling like an idiot. I feel lighter than I have in years.

The sound of water running in the bathroom down the hall makes it really hard not to think about him being wet and naked in there. Or the way his mouth felt on me.

I don't realize the water has stopped until the bathroom door opens and Zayden steps out. He appears in front of me wearing nothing but a new pair of gray sweatpants.

My eyes trace over his chest, past the sharp lines of his abs, to the V that disappears inside the waistband of his sweatpants.

Hmm.

There's definitely an imprint there.

I swallow hard, heart thudding like I just ran a marathon.

"Your bath is ready, so let me know when you're done ogling me," he teases.

"I was just admiring the view." I chuckle.

He closes the distance between us and lifts me off the couch.

"Zayden, what are you doing?" I laugh.

"What?" he murmurs, adjusting me against his chest. "Weekend of pampering. You don't get to walk."

"You keep spoiling me like this," I tease, nuzzling into his neck, "and I might not want to leave."

He doesn't respond as he carries me to the bathroom and sets me down gently in front of the tub. The room smells like peppermint and lavender.

"Enjoy your bath. I'll be outside the door if you need me." He turns around to leave.

"Don't go."

He stops at the door frame before turning around.

"Can you stay?"

He nods.

We stare at each other for a few seconds.

"Do you want me to turn around?"

"No," I murmur.

I hold his gaze as I pull the shirt over my head, but he doesn't look at my body at first. Then I hook my thumbs into the waist of my lace panties and slide them down, leaving me bare in front of him. I've never let anyone see me like this.

I don't hate my body. I guess I just never cared enough to pay attention except for the fact I was always taller than the boys at school and they didn't like that. But Zayden is looking at me like I'm the most precious thing he's ever seen.

His eyes slowly trail down my body, drinking in every inch of me, and I can feel the heat of it like a physical touch.

"God, you're so fucking beautiful."

The way he says it like it's ruining him does something to me, too. I step into the tub then sink down until the water wraps around me. I close my eyes as a soft, contented sigh escapes my lips.

He lowers himself against the door, but I can still feel him watching me.

"I'm thirsty," I murmur.

"I'll grab you some water." Zayden pushes off to his feet before I even have a chance to ask. The door closes behind him, leaving me alone in the water.

His footsteps fade down the hall, and I close my eyes as I let myself slide under the water. It reaches my shoulders first then my throat. Lower, over my chin, my mouth, and my nose.

Then everything goes quiet, familiar in a way I remember too well. I open my eyes, watching the water above me. I like it down here. It's not the same quiet as when my mom used to leave for days, or as loud as when she came back with a new boyfriend. She usually spent more time fighting with them than worrying about me.

Why am I even thinking about all that now? Maybe it's the lavender. Or maybe it's because Zayden's been making me feel things I'm not sure I'm allowed to want.

My lungs start to burn from holding my breath for too long. Long enough to wonder—what if I just stayed?

The door opens, but I barely register the sound, like it's happening far away—until strong hands plunge into the water and pull me up.

"Luna?" He's on his knees beside the tub, water dripping from his forearms. His chest's rising and falling too fast. "What the hell were you doing?"

My breath hitches as I blink the water out of my lashes. "I—I was just...thinking."

He grabs a towel and wraps it around me before lifting me out of the tub and pulling me down onto the floor with him. His whole body is shaking as he tightens his hold on me.

"Zayden, I'm okay," I whisper, tilting his head down so his eyes meet mine.

"You don't get to leave me too." His voice cracks against my temple.

Leave me too?

"That's not what I was doing," I say, softer now, threading my hands through his locs. "I used to do this when I was little. Went under the water and held my breath for as long as I could."

His fingers twitch on my waist, but he stays silent.

"I didn't know what else to do with the silence," I continue. "Rylee was gone, and my mom was never home much. Some nights she tied me to the bed so I wouldn't wander when she left. Said it was for my safety." I laugh, but it's the hollow kind. "She'd leave the ties loose, so if I got hungry enough, I could crawl to the kitchen."

Zayden goes rigid.

"I'd sit in the bath after and try not to cry, because it made my head hurt more. So I learned how to disappear under the water. I wasn't trying to die or anything—I just…wanted to feel nothing."

His glassy eyes locked on mine with a kind of haunted tenderness. "You scared me," he breathes out. "I walked back in and you were just…"

"I'm sorry," I whisper. "It's a habit. I didn't mean to scare you." My body's shaking now. Maybe from the cold creeping into my wet skin and hair or from the look in his eyes.

He closes his eyes, like that explanation isn't enough, but nods anyway. "You're shaking. Let's get you dressed."

CHAPTER 31

Zayden

I've never taken care of anyone before. Not a sibling, a friend, not even a pet. But taking care of Luna is as easy as breathing, and healing even.

I want to make her breakfast, run her a bath, and listen to her when she talks. Memorize the way her eyes soften when she's not in fighting mode.

We're lying on the couch with her body tucked into mine like she was made to fit there. Her head rests against my chest like it's the most natural thing in the world, like she didn't almost give me a fucking heart attack thirty minutes ago.

God, she has no idea how close I was to losing my fucking mind.

One second, I was grabbing a water bottle, and the next, my lungs forgot how to work properly. Something screamed at me to *go* as if my soul knew what my mind didn't.

I don't even remember entering the room, just the sound of water sloshing as I pulled her back up, shaking, terrified, my brain screaming *not you too*. Not her.

My feelings have always been too big, too loud, and too fucking much. I learned how to lock them down a long time ago. To keep my distance and not let anyone in too deep.

But with Luna, it's fucking impossible to do that. With her, it's like everything multiplies, until it's too much and still not enough.

And if she ever knew how she's already sunk into the deepest parts of me, she'd probably run.

I would.

But I can't turn it off. She's always been there, since that ski trip my cousin Luc invited me to three years ago.

Our family isn't close. They weren't exactly thrilled when my mum married my dad. Or that she got pregnant so young and quit skating, gave up everything, including the Olympics, while my dad still got to play pro.

My mum had just died a year before, and I was so angry at everything, my dad, the world, and mostly at my mum for leaving. So when Luc invited me, I said yes. At least to get away from my dad for a while.

I snuck out to the frozen lake behind the villa to skate one night, because that's the only place where I felt like I could breathe.

That's when I saw her, alone on the frozen lake, skating like it belonged to her. She didn't say anything when I started skating beside her. Never asked why I was there. And without thinking, we started skating together. Every single night, I waited for her like I needed her. And every single time, she showed up.

She wasn't afraid to skate on a frozen lake in the dark with a stranger. But the truth is—we never felt like strangers. She felt like peace, and I didn't know what to do with that.

After the trip, I never saw her again. Until that morning. When she looked at me through the glass and I felt it. And when I saw her skating, I knew there was something familiar about her.

She probably doesn't remember me, but I never forgot her. She was always in the back of my mind.

I'm still caught up in the moment, on those cold nights that felt anything but cold, on her, when she shifts against me.

She murmurs something I don't catch and moves on top of me. Her legs slide over my thighs, cheek pressed against my chest as small and contented sighs escape her lips. Then her whole body freezes like she just realized where she is. She jumps off my chest like I burned her and stands.

"Shit, sorry," she blurts, eyes wide. "I didn't mean to… I must've… God, what the hell is wrong with me?"

I sit up, propping an arm behind my head as I watch her unravel in front of me like a storm. Her braids are slipping loose from the bun she put them in, a few strands falling across her cheek.

She keeps pushing them back, and they keep falling forward, and I can't stop staring. The oversize T-shirt I gave her hangs off one shoulder, barely reaching her thighs. Honestly, it's driving me insane how fucking beautiful she is.

She finally pauses mid-rant and looks at me. "What?" she demands.

I don't say anything, because if I open my mouth right now, I might tell her too much.

She crosses her arms and meets my eyes, like she can hear every thought in my head. "Okay, yes, I know I fell asleep on your chest last night, but that was different." She glares at me like it's my fault.

I still don't know how she reads my fucking mind without me saying a single word. This isn't the first time.

"I had a migraine." She's pacing again. "Plus, I was still high on orgasm." Then she groans, dragging a hand down her face. "And this morning, I had a tiny meltdown, which obviously doesn't count either."

I lift an eyebrow.

"You're enjoying this." She pouts. "Say something!"

Instead of saying something, I tug her toward me and pull her back onto my chest where she belongs. She lets out the tiniest moan, like relief melted right through her bones.

"I hate you," she whispers, wrapping her arms around my neck.

"I know."

My lips find hers like a magnet, moving slowly against her mouth, saying all the things I know I shouldn't feel and still don't know how to say. She kisses me back like she already knows.

She's catching her breath when she pulls back, just enough to look at me. There's something different in her eyes now—less fire, more fear.

"Zay... Is it supposed to feel like this?"

Zay? I tense before I can stop it. My heart forgets how to beat.

"Like what?" Even though I already know.

She lets out a breathy laugh, the nervous kind, like she wants to take the question back before I can answer it. "I don't know," she mutters quickly. "Like it's fast, really fast. But...not at the same time." Her voice drops. "God, that sounds so stupid." She groans and buries her face in my chest. "What the hell is wrong with me?"

She tries to retreat—not physically, but into her mind. She's backpedaling, scrambling to cover up how real that just was.

But I get it. More than she knows.

I tighten my arms around her and press my lips to the top of her head. "There's nothing wrong with you," I murmur. "Some things aren't supposed to make sense. They just...are." She's been the *this* I couldn't explain for years.

"We're so fucked," she mumbles into my chest.

Actual, real laughter bubbles out of me before I can stop it.

Because she's right.

I've known this since the moment I saw her skating alone on that frozen lake.

She props her chin on her hands. "So what's next on the migraine retreat itinerary, Dr. Aldenhurst?"

"Lunch." I brush her stubborn braid away from her face. "Then a game, maybe yoga. How's your head?"

Her expression softens. "Better than I've felt in years."

"Yeah?" I study her face and the way eyes flutter shut for a second. "No headaches?"

She shakes her head. "No pain, no noise, and no pressure. Just..." Her voice softens, like she's talking to herself. "Quiet. I've never felt this free."

My heart beats a little faster at her words.

"Well, I guess your retreat is working." She chuckles.

"Yeah?" I laugh, something I've been doing more in the past few hours with her than I've done in years.

She nods, chin still propped on her hands. "Five stars, although there's room for improvement."

"Is that right?"

She bites her lip, eyes full of mischief. "No fluffy robe, no massage, no playlist."

"Noted." I play along.

"Also, I wouldn't mind another orgasm. Those are available upon request, right?" she says in that sweet, innocent voice, like she has no idea what she's asking for.

But she knows.

I flip her before she can even blink. She lets out a gasp as her back hits the couch. My thighs slide between her legs as they fall open for me instinctively.

Her hips leave the couch, grinding against the hard length of my dick, and I can feel the heat of her wet and bare pussy through the thin fabric of my sweats. She didn't put on any panties after her bath.

A low groan rips from my throat as I brace myself over her, every nerve in my body screaming to sink into her tight, sweet pussy.

"Is this what you want, Lunetta?"

She nods quickly, eyes wide, mouth parted.

My greedy baby.

"Say it." One hand braces by her head, the other dragging

slowly up her thigh, stopping just shy of the spot she wants me most.

"Zayden…"

I press my hips down just enough for her to feel how hard I am. She lets out a *desperate* moan, grinding to chase more friction.

"Fuck," I breathe, struggling to hold myself back. "You're so fucking wet for me."

"Please," she whispers.

"Please what, pretty girl?" I lower my mouth to her throat and let my lips brush against her skin.

Her brows pull together like she hates that she's actually going to say it. "Please make me come," she says in a soft moan, a plea.

I let the words settle. Then lean in close to her ear. "God, you sound so fucking pretty when you beg." Then I pull back, adjusting my pants as I stand. But I don't miss the wet stain in front of my sweats, and I'm not sure if it's hers, mine, or both.

Her eyes snap open. "Zayden, what the fuck!?"

"Lunch first. You're gonna need the energy." My heart's still pounding. My cock's still hard. My whole body wants to go back to her and bury myself so deep inside her she forgets her own name.

"You said orgasms were available upon request," she yells at me, still flushed.

"Processing times vary, sweetheart." I glance back at her over my shoulder.

"You're an asshole." She throws a pillow at me, and I catch it. "Say goodbye to your five stars. You're down to three."

I smirk. "I guess I'll have to earn them back."

"You better." She narrows her eyes at me.

"Oh, I will." I flash a grin. "By the time I'm done with you, you'll give me six."

Her mouth opens then closes. Her whole body stills, except for the way her thighs clench together. "I hate you!"

No you don't, baby.

I turn toward the kitchen like I'm still in control, which is very far from true. Grabbing a pot from the cabinet, I get started on lunch. I'm thinking of chicken soup, with fresh veggies and clean-cut meat. I had the cabin stocked yesterday morning with everything I need and everything google said was good for migraines.

I was relieved when she asked me to get her out of the Vault's party last night and she didn't fight me when I brought her here.

The truth is I was gonna bring her here no matter what. I'm not above a little kidnapping, not if it means making sure she's okay. I reach for the veggies, rinse them under the tap water, and set them on the cutting board.

"Oh God, Zayden." A soft moan comes from the couch.

I stop breathing.

Then I turn around.

What in the actual fuck?

She's still on the couch, legs wide open and one hand between her thighs. She stares at me, eyes half lidded and mouth open. Her finger is moving around her clit like she doesn't need me at all.

"Zayden," she moans again, back arching from the couch.

Fuck.

"Luna?" I take a step forward, dick already hard as fuck, ready to drop to my knees and take care of her.

"Don't," she commands. "You walked away, remember?"

Fucking hell!

I want to argue with her, crawl and begged her to let me do it. But watching her taking care of herself like this is fucking hot.

She moves faster now, and her moans get louder. My cock

throbs so hard it hurts. My hand slides beneath the waistband of my sweats. I just need something to relieve myself before I explode.

Her gaze sharpens instantly. "Don't you fucking dare touch yourself."

I freeze again and obey her.

She's grinding faster now, chasing her release.

"That's it, baby. Show me how you take care of that greedy pussy."

She gasps as another moan escapes her lips.

"Keep going, pretty girl. You look so fucking beautiful like this."

She moans again, a little louder.

She likes this.

My knees damn near give out as she slides one finger inside herself. She's so fucking wet, I can hear the sounds her pussy makes as she fucks herself.

"Please..." I hear myself say. I'm not even sure what I'm pleading for, her to let me take care of her or her to let me relieve myself.

She shakes her head before adding another finger. The sounds make me grit my teeth, nails digging into my palms.

"Oh God, Zayden... I'm gonna come," she whimpers, head tipping back and legs trembling.

"Come for me, let me see you fall apart."

Her fingers move faster, and it's the most beautiful, torturous thing I've ever seen. A moan rips from her throat, back leaving the couch as she chases her release.

"Zayden..." Her eyes roll back as she falls over the edge.

My cock jerks in my sweats, and it happens before I can stop it. The waves rip through me, every muscle in my body tightening as I come in my pants like a fucking teenager.

"Fuck... Luna," the sound tears out of my chest. I stumble backward and lean against the kitchen counter for support. The front of my sweats is soaked with my own release. I didn't even know this was possible. She didn't touch me, and I didn't touch myself.

Zayden 0, Luna 2.

Two ruined sweatpants in one day.

I watch as she pulls herself off the couch and walks toward me. She tilts her head to look up at me before lifting her fingers in front of me, glistening with her juices. "Think you can clean these for me, baby?"

I blink and nod.

"Open up." She brings them to my closed lips. I open my mouth, and she slides her fingers in. The taste of her hits my tongue, still warm, sweet, and a little salty. A groan rips out of my throat. Fucking heaven.

She smiles at me and pulls them out with a pop, dragging them across my bottom lip.

"Good boy," she says before turning and walking away.

The praise goes straight to my groin.

That's it, Luna Del Sol fucking owns me, has ruined me for anyone else.

CHAPTER 32

Luna

"Didn't your mom teach you it's rude to stare at people while they eat?" I tease as I finish the last spoon of my soup, aware of his eyes on me the whole time.

I expect him to give me one of his half smiles, but something shifts in his expression. The warmth from earlier leaves his eyes for a second, and I can see the pain behind them.

Shit.

Before I can say anything else, he gently grabs the bowl from my hand and brings it to the kitchen.

By the time he comes back, his face is unreadable again.

"Thank you for the soup." I smile at him. "Best I've ever had. It just earned you another star." I nudge him gently.

That gets me a small smile. "Still not the full five?"

"Not yet. But you're close." I stretch out on the couch. "What's next?"

"Game. Did you pick one?"

"Chess." I nod toward the chessboard on the coffee table that I found in the closet. "We get to ask one question per move."

He lifts an eyebrow as he grabs the chessboard and we move from the couch to the carpet on the floor, settling it between us.

"I go first." I fold my legs under me.

He smirks but doesn't argue.

I reach for my pawn and move it forward. "First question. What's your favorite childhood memory?"

He stares at the board for a few seconds. "When my mum

taught me how to skate," he says before moving his piece. His biceps flex with the motion, making it really hard to focus. His tattoos are distracting.

"Why figure skating?" he asks, like he didn't destroy my ability to form a sentence right now.

I shrug, pretending to think when I already know the answer. "Because it's the only place I ever felt free and in control at the same time."

He gives me a look that makes my whole body vibrate.

I slide my queen forward and take his bishop. "Ooops," I say, not sorry at all.

His eyes lift to meet mine across the board with the slightest smile he's trying not to show.

"Favorite color?"

"Storm gray." He narrows his eyes at the board, brows drawn together in concentration. Watching him think shouldn't make me this hot and bothered.

I must be ovulating, that would explain why I'm so wet right now. He leans forward again, reaching across the board with that annoyingly perfect arm, veins flexing as he moves his rook.

I don't even hear what he says, because I'm too focused on his arms.

"Luna?"

"Hmm?" I blink.

"I asked you a question."

"What was the question?"

"Favorite season?" He eyes me suspiciously.

"You didn't ask me what my favorite color is."

"Didn't have to. I already know it's blue."

I open my mouth then close it. Because he's right. "Winter. Not just for skating. I like how still everything is, and how sharp the air is. You can't fake through the winter, there's no room for pretending."

He smiles like he's tucking the answers away.

I study the board, trying to decide my next move, but it's hard to focus when his eyes haven't left my face. "You're not even paying attention."

"I'm paying attention, just not to the board." His gaze drags over to where my shirt keeps sliding over my thighs.

I move my rook and sit back, trying not to melt under his stare. "What scares you the most?"

He doesn't answer right away, like he's trying to decide how much to say. "You," he says, looking straight into my eyes.

"Me?" I blink.

"Yes, you. The reason I keep my walls up and don't let people in? It's not because I don't care. It's the opposite." He exhales like it hurts. "It's because when I let someone in…they get all of me. I don't do halfway. They get my focus, my loyalty, my fucking soul. And that kind of feeling? It's all-consuming and burns through everything else." He looks down at his clasped hands.

"I've learned to shut people out, because it's safer this way, but not with you." His eyes meet mine again. "You showed up like a storm and blew through every fucking wall I built. You're everywhere. In my head. My chest. Under my skin. I feel you in ways I can't even explain." He laughs like he can't believe he's saying all this out loud. "That's why you scare me, Luna."

I'm pretty sure I stopped breathing. What do I even say to that when he looks at me like this? I don't think and just move until I'm on his lap. Legs folding over his thighs as I straddle him.

I like this.

Being close to him, sitting on his lap, touching him. My body trusts him, and it calms the restless part of me.

"You scare me, too." I trace my finger across his chess without looking at him. "I've never let myself want this, or let myself feel like this, because it's easier not to want anything," I continue before I lose my nerves. "If you don't want anything, you can't get disappointed, right?" I laugh to break the tension. "If you don't feel, no one can hurt you."

His finger brushes my cheeks as he tilts my chin up to look at him, like he needs to see me like this.

"No one really cared before, except for my sister Rylee, but she still left."

He watches me like he sees me.

"Then you showed up and pissed me off and made me feel things I didn't ask for. And I hated you for it." My mouth forms a small pout before I can stop it. "Still kinda do."

His lips twitch into a smile, like he sees straight through me and likes what he finds anyway. "You're so cute when you're mad."

I look at him, and something about the way he's staring at me feels different, making it hard to maintain eye contact. So, I twist sideways, just enough to reach for the board behind us. I grab my bishop and slide it forward, knocking out his knight.

"Checkmate," I say innocently.

He laughs like he can't believe I just did that. "God, what am I gonna do with you?" He flips me onto my back. Chess pieces scatter in all directions, but neither of us care.

"That was a dirty move." He hovers about me, and I'm laughing so hard.

"Don't be a sore loser."

"You're trouble," he growls, dipping his head to brush his nose along my jaw. "And I'm so"—he kisses the corner of my mouth—"so"—the edge of my throat—"fucked."

Then his lips find mine as he kisses me like he's memorizing the shape of my mouth. My pulse races, and my body aches under his.

"Wanna play another game?" I grin against his lips.

He pulls back just enough to look at me suspiciously. "What kind of game?"

"Hide and seek," I say sweetly.

"You want to play hide and seek? Right now?"

I nod, trying to keep my face innocent, even though my heart's still racing from his kiss.

"What are the rules?" His eyes are darker now, like he already knows I'm up to something.

"If you find me..." I drag my finger lightly down his bare chest. "You can do whatever you want to me."

His whole body tenses above mine.

"Fuck, Lunetta." He doesn't move or even breathe for a second as he stares at me. "Why would I let you go when I already have you where I want you?"

I tilt my head, giving him my most innocent eyes, fingertips dragging down his chest. "Please." I add a little pout at the end. "I've never played it before."

"Jesus, Luna." A sound comes out of his chest that's half growl and half laugh.

I know exactly what his weak point is now, and I plan to use it.

He exhales hard and presses his forehead to mine. "Sixty seconds, little storm. Run before I change my mind." He pulls back just enough to give me room.

I slide out from under him and run.

I should be panicking, but all I can think about is the look in his eyes before he told me to run, like he wanted to devour me but was holding back for now.

Standing in the hallway, I scan my options. Master bedroom? Too obvious. Bathroom? No lock. The basement?

Perfect.

I take the stairs two at the time, careful not to make too much noise. My body's aching from the idea of him chasing me, and I'm so wet, it's dripping down my thighs.

The basement is dark, cold, and a little creepy. I walk past the rink toward the storage closet and open the door.

It's cluttered with old training gear. I close the door behind me and crouch between an old shoulder pad and a helmet.

Waiting.

Needing.

My pussy throbs, and I clench my thigh together. I press my fingers to my lips to keep myself from moaning.

What's he gonna do when he finds me like this? When he sees how wet I already am. How much I want this.

I've made myself come more times than I can count. But I've never craved someone else like this. Never wanted to be touched like this—stretched, filled, ruined.

The thought of Zayden finding me, dragging me out of hiding, and him doing whatever he wants to me…

Fuck, I'm making a mess on the floor.

And when he finally stretches me, when he's finally inside me for the first time…will it hurt?

God, maybe.

But maybe I'll like that it hurts. Maybe I want to feel it—that pressure, that fullness, that ache.

Come find me, baby.

CHAPTER 33

ZAYDEN

"...FIFTY-EIGHT. FIFTY-NINE. SIXTY." I open my eyes and scan the room.

Where would you hide, little storm?

"Ready or not, here I come, Tempestina Mia." A grin tugs at my mouth as I check the hallway closet, then the bathroom, the bedroom, knowing damn well she's not in any of them.

Oh, she's good at this, and I'm loving this too fucking much. The way she looked at me earlier with those wide eyes, sweet and manipulative as hell. She figured out my weak spot, and she's using it.

The anticipation, the satisfaction of hunting her, knowing I get to catch her and ruin her in the best way possible, is doing crazy things to me.

I'm hard as fuck, aching with it, but I am in no rush. Because the longer I wait, the more her anticipation builds. The more desperate she becomes. The wetter she gets. I know she wants this. She's probably hiding somewhere, soaked, just waiting for me to find her.

She's not upstairs, and I knew that the moment I opened my eyes. Because I always know when she's near. No matter where we are or how quiet or loud it is. I always feel her like a storm crashing in. But I still looked, still played her little game. Because what's the point of hide and seek if you don't actually seek?

I make my way down the stairs to the basement. The

temperature drops with every step, but I barely feel it, not when my body is burning. My heart beats a little faster, but it's not the adrenaline. It's her.

She's here, I know it.

"You're making this too easy, Lunetta." I smirk as I move toward the closet. "You know I can feel you, right?"

I lean back against the door, letting my head rest slightly against it. One foot crosses lazily over the other, like I have all the time in the world.

She wanted to play. Game on, baby.

"Luna, are you in there?"

No, answer, except for the smallest intake of breath.

"What are you thinking about in there?" I whisper. "Is it me?"

I lean back a little more, and the door makes a noise under the weight of my body. "You thinking about what I'll do to you when I open this door?"

Still nothing.

"How wet are you right now, baby? I bet you're soaked. Probably leaking down your thighs." I drag my knuckles across the door, imagining her flinching at the sound. My dick throbs at the idea.

"What do you want first, baby? My mouth, fingers." My voice dips. "You want this cock stretching your tight little pussy." Fuck, if I don't control myself, I'm gonna come in my pants again.

I wait, but nothing.

She's so stubborn.

"I need to hear you say it." I close my eyes, imagining her in there. My shirt barely covering her thighs, legs pressing together like it will stop the aching, dripping onto the floor.

"I can wait all day." That's a lie, the truth is I'm hanging by a fucking thread. "But the longer you make me wait, the worse it's gonna be when I do get my hands on you. Might have to fuck you right here on the closet floor." I smirk. "Maybe that's what you want. You want me to ruin you right where you're hiding, don't you?"

I tilt my head just enough to listen, and wait.

"Use your words, Luna, or I walk away right now."

My grip tightens on the knob as I wait for her answer.

"Everything," she finally says.

Fuck.

I turn the knob and open the door. And there she is on the floor, knees up as she stares at me. Lips slightly parted and her pupils blown so wide, like she's drowning in her need. And I've never seen anything more beautiful in my life. I wish I could take a picture of her right now and cherish it forever.

I drop to my stomach on the floor, hook my arms under her thighs, and pull her toward me. I don't wait another second before lowering my mouth to where she's soaked and aching.

"It's my turn to take care of this greedy pussy." I lick every drop of her arousal, like I've been starving for it for years. I drag my tongue up her slit before circling slowly around her clit.

"Zayden..." She whimpers my name when I hit the perfect spot, and I press her hips down when she tries to lift them off the floor. She's so sensitive, so needy, and I love it.

And God, that sound she makes, I'm getting addicted to it. I'm fucking addicted to her.

I suck her little bud into my mouth before sliding two fingers in, curling them until I find the spongy spot.

Her fingers fist into my hair as she lets out another gasp.

I slide my fingers deeper, and her walls clench around them. She's so fucking warm and tight. All I can think about is what it'll feel like when it's my cock inside her, stretching her. Making her mine.

I want to crawl inside the place where she hides all her hurt and make it mine. I want to be the reason she doesn't feel alone anymore.

I'm getting dizzy from it all. High on her.

My fingers move slowly inside her as I drag my tongue around her clit. She pulls my locs harder, and I groan against her skin.

I lift my eyes to look at her face, the way her eyes flutter and her lips part as she moans my name.

Her fingers tighten in my hair as she grinds against my tongue. I grin into her skin, dizzy on her scent, her taste, the heat of her wrapped around my fingers.

That's my girl. Take what you need from me.

She lets out this soft, stuttering moan that sounds like it comes from somewhere deeper than her throat.

Her thighs are trembling as I keep stroking inside her and my tongue circles gently around her sensitive nub. Then she goes quiet, her pussy gripping my fingers. But I don't stop. She's riding my face, grinding against my tongue like she can't help it.

Then she clenches around me as a shattering sound leaves her mouth. "Zayden, I...oh my God..."

She lets go, then something warm gushes against my mouth, soaking my fingers, my chin, and my chest.

Holy shit, my baby is a squirter.

"Fuck!"

"Oh my God," she gasps, panic flashing in her voice. "I didn't... Did I just—"

She tries to wriggle out of my grip, but I hold her down. I drag my tongue across her, catching every drop like it's the best fucking thing I've ever tasted—like I've been dying of thirst and she's the cure.

"Zayden, did I just pee on you... I'm—"

"Don't you dare apologize." I glance up at her, face soaked. "You squirted, baby, and it was the hottest thing I've ever seen," I say, licking her again, just to feel her shiver.

"You're not...grossed out?" She stares down at me, eyes wide with shock.

"Grossed out?" I grin, licking every last drop off my lips. "I want to make you do it again, and again."

She stares down at me like she doesn't know what to do with that. For a moment, I think she's gonna cry, then she says, "You're such a freak." She chuckles.

"Yeah? Then what's that makes you, little storm?" I raise an eyebrow at her.

I push up to my knees, slide my arms around her thighs, and lift her off the floor like she weighs nothing.

"What are you doing?"

"Taking you upstairs," I say against her temple, starting toward the stairs. "I'm not done with you yet. Not even close."

CHAPTER 34

Luna

Zayden carries me upstairs like I weigh nothing. Even though I'm not small. I'm tall, and I've always had some muscle on me, extra weight that makes lifts in pairs skating harder.

He sets me on the edge of the bed and just watches me for a second.

"Can I take this off?" He points toward the shirt.

I nod, and he reaches for it, lifting my arms so he can pull it over my head.

I'm bare in front of him. His eyes roam over my body like he's memorizing me. He pushes his pants down, leaving him in his boxers.

Holy shit!

He's so fucking hard and big.

My mouth goes dry. He's gonna destroy me. A little thrill dances up my spine at the thought. Nerves and need twist together in my belly as I crawl backward to the middle of the bed. The sheets are cool against my back, but I'm burning inside.

Zayden moves over me, the bed sinking under his weight. He's looking at me like I'm his whole sky. Like I'm his sun and his moon, just like my name. I've always felt like a contradiction, trying to be the sun, to shine, to smile, and burn through the cold. But sometimes the darkness wins, and I welcome it like the moon, disappearing into its shadows.

"You okay?" he whispers against my lips.

I nod.

"Are you sure you want this?" His hand trails down my arm.

"I've always wanted my first time to be with a hockey player." I drag my finger down his back. "They have the best hip movement." I smile up at him.

Zayden groans and drops his forehead to mine. Then he kisses me. His lips trail down my throat, leaving heat in their path. He kisses the spot just above my collarbone, then lower, down to my breasts. He takes one of my nipples into his mouth and sucks it, teasing me with his tongue. His fingers play with my other nipple, rolling it, adding just enough pressure to make me whimper.

"You're so sensitive," he murmurs, watching my reaction. Then he pulls back and reaches toward the nightstand. He grabs a condom and brings it to his mouth.

"Wait." I grab his hand before he can open it.

He freezes, eyes meeting mine. "Everything okay?"

"Do we have to use one?" I nod toward the condom in his hand.

His eyes search mine like he's trying to understand what I'm asking. "You don't want to?"

"I want to feel all of you," I say nervously. "I'm on the pill, and I've never been with anyone before."

He leans down, bringing his forehead to mine again. "I haven't been with anyone for a while either, and I've always used protection before. But do you know what you're asking?"

I nod, but he still doesn't move.

"I want you to come inside of me." I want him to fill every part of me, not just my body, but the ache I've been carrying for weeks. I want to feel him so deep I forget every doubt I've ever had. I want to wake up and still feel him there.

"You want me to fill you up, baby? Stay inside of you for days, so you never forget how this feels?" His mouth is so close to mine I can feel the warmth of his breath against my skin.

"Yes, please." I nod.

Zayden lifts his hips just enough to push his boxers down and off his legs.

Oh.

I knew he was big from the bulge in his boxers, but it's different seeing his full length. Whatever he sees on my face must betray me, because he smirks.

"What's the matter? Change your mind?"

The fucker!

"Nope." I shake my head, even though my mouth is dry.

He wraps his fingers around his length and strokes himself slowly. Then he leans down again, settling between my thighs. "Ready for me?"

I nod. My body is trembling with need.

He strokes once more before lining himself up at my entrance. Then he pushes in slowly, and I gasp at the pressure as he stretches me. He's not even halfway, and it's already too much.

"Jesus, Luna. You're so fucking tight." A groan escapes his throat as he stops, giving me a moment to adjust. "Breathe for me, nice and slow."

I suck in air, feeling the burn.

"I'm gonna move now, okay?"

I nod, already lost in the way he feels inside me. He brings his lips to mine, kissing me as he pushes in all the way. He's so deep that I feel him everywhere, and I can't help the gasp that slips out.

He pulls back slightly to look at me with a small crease between his eyes. "Luna, did I hurt you?"

I want to answer, but my body is too busy adjusting to him to form any words.

His eyes widen in panic. "Shit," he mutters. "I'm sorry, I went too fast, too deep." He pulls back a little.

"Zayden." I take his face in my hands. "I'm okay. I just needed a minute to adjust."

"Yeah?"

I nod, wrapping my legs around his waist. "More, please."

When he finally moves again, it's slow. Like he's afraid of hurting me, but I can tell he's barely holding himself back.

He pulls back what feels like an inch and thrusts back in. I arch into it, moaning as the pain turns into pleasure.

"Zayden..."

"I know, baby," he groans. "I know. You feel so fucking good." He lifts me slightly, angling my hips to take him even deeper.

I drag my nails across his back.

"Fuck—I'm sorry." His forehead presses to mine, and his mouth brushes against my lips. "I'm trying to go slow, but you feel like fucking heaven."

His next thrust knocks the air out of my lung as he pushes in deeper and rougher. And I love every second of it, the pressure mixing with the pleasure. I've never felt anything like it. The wet slap of skin against skin, the whimper that slips from my lips, the wrecked noise in his throat every time I clench around him.

"Fucking hell, Luna." He reaches for the headboard like he needs something to hold on to. I feel him everywhere, like our feelings are blending with each other.

He buries his face in the crook of my neck, fingers digging into my thighs, gripping me harder as he pounds into me. He shudders against me like he's falling apart. "Stop me if it's too much, baby."

But I don't want to stop him. He promised to ruin me, and that's exactly what he's doing.

"Please don't stop." I tighten my legs around him, fingers tugging at his locs and pulling his mouth to mine. I kiss him as he falls apart above me.

CHAPTER 35

Zayden

Her legs are wrapped around my waist, fingers in my hair as she brings my mouth to hers. I slide my hands under her thighs, pulling us up, until I'm sitting on the bed. She gasps as she settles on my lap, my cock still deep inside her, and her arms instinctively wrap around my neck.

My hands slide to her waist, guiding her hips slowly as we move together.

She buries her face in the crook of my neck. "Zayden..."

"Look at me, pretty girl. I need to see you," I whisper, rocking my hips up into her.

She lifts her gaze to meet mine, lips parted with those soft, little moans that are driving me crazy. She's so fucking beautiful that it's unreal.

This angle is better, deeper. And God, she feels so good like this. I've never experienced anything like this. I promised to ruin her, but she's the one ruining me.

My mouth drags down her throat to her breast, and she gasps as I take one nipple into my mouth. I roll the other nipple between my fingers, adding enough pressure to make her back arch.

She's moving faster now, chasing her fourth orgasm for the day. "Zayden, I'm—I'm coming..." she stutters against my ear. Her legs lock around my waist, arms wrap around my neck. Our slick bodies tangle together.

"Come for me, little storm. I'm right...right behind you." I grab her thighs, lifting them enough to give me more access as I use my hips to drive in deeper. She trembles in my arms, her whole body tightening around me as she falls apart for me.

"Last chance, baby. You sure you want me to come inside you?" The idea of my cum deep inside her—her carrying my baby, our baby, just the three of us, our own little family, far away from here—brings me closer to the edge.

"Yes, please."

Then she pulls me in with her like a goddamn tornado. My hips move on their own as I thrust in deeper, once, twice, before I'm coming harder than I ever have in my life. I tighten my arms around her waist, neck buried into her neck as I spill into her, and her body welcomes every drop.

I don't know for how long we stay like that before I pull back a little to study her face. "You okay?" I brush her cheek with my knuckle. "Did I hurt you?"

"No. Just ruined. You promised you'd ruin me, and you did." She chuckles.

I press my forehead to hers, closing my eyes as I breathe her in. "You ruined me, too," I whisper.

There's no coming back from this. She's fucking mine, and I'll burn the world down for her.

We still haven't moved. Her body is warm and relaxed against me. She lets out a soft exhale on my neck.

"You falling asleep on me, Lunetta?"

"Hmmm. Tired." She hums without lifting her head.

"I know, but you need a bath first. You're probably a little sore, yeah?"

She nods.

I shift slightly, trying to move us to the edge of the bed, and she winces at the movement. Her face scrunches the tiniest bit, like she's trying not to let me see how much it hurts, and guilt punches straight through my chest. "Shit, I'm sorry. I should've been gentler." I'm not proud of how deep I went, how hard I lost myself in her. Especially since this was her first time, but I haven't been with anyone for a while. Even then, it never felt this good, and I couldn't control myself.

"Don't apologize. I loved it. Loved that I was the one who made you lose control." Her mouth curves into that sweet, sleepy smile I'm starting to like a little too much.

I move us the rest of the way until I reach the edge of the bed before standing.

"Stop spoiling me," she says against my neck as I carry her to the bathroom.

I huff a laugh. "Sweetheart, you think you can walk right now?"

"Did I ever tell you how much I hate you?" She gives me a sleepy glare.

"Mmm." I muse, pushing the bathroom door open with my foot. "Didn't sound like it when you were screaming my name a few minutes ago."

She rolls her eyes.

I set her on the closed toilet lid, looking down at the mess we made glistening between her thighs and smeared across my stomach.

It's killing me how much I want to fuck her again, but I hold back. She's still sore.

I grab a small clean towel, wet it with some warm water, and kneel between her thighs to clean her up.

Her breath catches on the tiniest wince when I reach her sensitive part. I clean myself next before turning on the faucet and running the water, adding some lavender Epsom salt, hoping it'll help with the soreness.

I glance at her as the water fills the tub, and she looks like she's about to fall asleep.

"You gonna stay awake for the bath?"

"Hmm."

I help her in the tub, and her eyes flutter close as she sinks in the warm water, a contented sigh leaving her lips.

"Be right back. I'll grab you some water and snacks." I start to head for the door, but I freeze when I remember what happened earlier. Coming back to find her under the water, the split second when I thought she was gone.

"I'm not gonna go under. I promised," she says, eyes still closed.

Of course, she fucking knows what I'm thinking. She always does.

"Okay, don't fall asleep."

I force myself to move to the kitchen, grabbing a water bottle and some snacks. When I come back, she's still soaking in the tub with her eyes closed. I set the water and the snacks on the tray at the edge of the tub as I slide in behind her. She leans into me with a soft sigh, head lolling slightly against my shoulder.

"Hey, still with me?" I murmur in her ear.

She nods.

I reach for the water bottle, twist the cap open, and bring it to her lips. "Drink this for me."

She opens up and takes a few sips.

Then I pull the tray toward us so I can have access to the snacks, dark chocolate, slices of fruit, and a bowl of plantain chips.

"I got you snacks," I say, waiting for her reaction.

"Are those plantain chips?" She sounds a little too awake for someone who was half asleep thirty seconds ago.

"Mhm."

"Zayden…" She turns around to face me. "How…did you know…"

"That they're your favorite? Lucky guess." I lean back against the tub, watching the way her eyes widen.

"Zayden." She narrows them at me.

I shrug, trying to play it cool. "I might have seen you grab them from the vending machine in the athletic building near the back exit a few times."

She tilts her head, giving me one of those goofy looks. "So… you've been stalking me Aldenhurst?"

"Obviously." I grin.

She pops a piece of plantain into her mouth, like she's thinking it over. "I guess if you're gonna stalk and kidnap me, snacks and orgasms are a decent trade."

This woman. I let my head fall on the tile wall behind me, staring at the ceiling like it might help me.

She grins against my chest. "If you're looking for God, he can't help you."

I shake my head, chuckling under my breath, and tighten my arms around her. She's right, I'm already too far gone. No one can help me.

I feed her a piece of chocolate as she traces the tattoo over my chest. Her finger grazes the broken heart with a fractured wings above my chest.

"What's this one about?" she whispers.

"It's about my mom. She left when I was seventeen."

I don't tell her how my mother got in the car and drove herself into the icy lake. That she chose to leave me alone with him. Or that I spent months wishing she had taken me with her. I blamed myself for her leaving. Maybe we were too much, maybe I was too much, or I wasn't enough for her to stay.

"I'm sorry." She presses a soft kiss over the tattoo. "But it wasn't your fault."

My breath catches, and I stare past her. My throat is tight as I blink back the tears that threaten to spill. Until I feel her wet hand against my cheeks, gently bringing my eyes to hers.

"Whatever happened, it wasn't your fault." She presses a soft kiss to each of my eyelids.

My chest caves, heart kicking between my ribs. I don't know

what to do with all this warmth—with her. So I pull her to me, holding her tighter than I probably should. Burying my face in her damp hair as I breathe her in.

We stay like that for a while, just holding each other, until her breathing starts to even out.

"Falling asleep on me, baby?"

"Your chest is warm," she murmurs.

"All right, sleepy head, let's get you to bed." I help her out of the tub and wrap a towel around her.

She shivers a little as I dry her off before carrying her back to bed. She's out before I tuck the blanket around her, not bothering to put clothes on her.

God, she looks fucking beautiful. Ethereal, like she's from a different planet. I reach for my phone from the nightstand and snap a quick photo to remember this moment. Then a message pops on my screen.

> Jasper: We need to talk when you're back. I think someone saw the video before I deleted it. Might have a lead on who's been sending the messages.

Then the message vanishes like it was never there.

"Fuck," I curse under my breath.

"Zay?" She reaches for me.

"I'm here, baby." I climb in beside her, and she presses her head into my chest.

I'm not ready for this weekend to end. Not ready to go back to campus and pretend I don't feel her in my chest, in my blood, under my skin. Everywhere.

Not ready to act like she's not slowly becoming my everything.

CHAPTER 36

Luna

I WAKE UP FEELING NEW, like he cracked me open and put me back together.

Say hello to the new Luna.

The blanket is cool against my skin, the pillow still smells like him, and my body aches in the best way possible. Guess who's not a virgin anymore? I smile to myself. I wouldn't want to lose my virginity to anyone but Zayden Aldenhurst.

Because this man knew what he was doing.

Can someone ruin you and worship you at the same time? The way he fucked me so hard but then touched me like he was afraid I might break.

I groan and roll onto my stomach, burying my face in his pillow. God, it smells so good. That clean, masculine, slightly musky scent that makes my toes curl. I close my eyes and take a deep inhale, like I can breathe him into my bloodstream. But who am I kidding? He's already there, and that doesn't scare me as much anymore.

I've heard my classmates talk about how awkward and uncomfortable their first time was, and I can't share the sentiment. Mine was Zayden Aldenhurst looking at me like I was made of starlight and sin while he ruined me slow and sweet and so deep I saw God. Twice. Maybe three times.

I laugh into the pillow. I'm getting horny just thinking about it.

I'm so glad I waited.

I throw off the blanket, still smiling. My legs are a little sore from earlier as I move toward the dresser. I pull the drawer open and grab the first shirt I see and pull it over my head.

"Zayden?" I pad barefoot down the hallway.

The kitchen and living room are empty. My smile fades a little. He's probably in the bathroom.

He's not in the bathroom or closets. My breaths come out faster as I check the guest room and find no Zayden. *If he's playing with me, I don't like this game.*

Suddenly, I'm eight again, watching my sister Rylee—the person I love the most in the world—leave. The air around me thins, and I can't breathe.

"Zayden?" *He wouldn't leave me, right?* Not after everything. Not after the way he touched me, held me, looked at me. My vision blurs as tears burn behind my eyelids, hands shaking as I check all the doors. Nothing.

Until I see the basement door cracked open, and I run down the stairs two at the time. The cold hits first, then the sound of blades fills the silence.

And I see him on the ice. A small smile tugging at his mouth as he spins, lands, and glides across the rink like it's his own private escape.

He's in a white T-shirt and gray sweatpants, and he looks so beautiful and free that it hurts to look at him.

I feel so stupid. He didn't leave, *idiot*, he was just skating, and I panicked like a total freak.

What's wrong with me?

I turn to go back upstairs before he sees me like this.

"Luna?"

I freeze, glancing over my shoulder to see him jogging toward me, barefoot, with worry written all over his face.

"Hey, where are you going?"

"I–I'm just…" I point toward the stairs, trying to keep myself together. *I'm going back upstairs so you don't see me break down.* "I woke up and you weren't there, and...I—"*thought you left*. My voice cracks a little. "But I'm fine now." I turn toward the stairs again.

"Luna," he says softer now, stepping into my path. "Stop running." His hands come up slowly, like he's afraid I'll bolt again. "Talk to me."

"I thought you left," I whisper, the words catching in my throat. "And I freaked out... And I didn't want you to see me like this." My lip trembles, and before I know what's happening, I fall into his chest.

His arms wrap around me like instinct. "Hey, hey, hey. Shhh. I'm here," he whispers.

"I'm a needy mess," I choke out. I hate feeling like this.

"You're not." He leans in and presses his forehead to mine. "Even if you were, I'd still want you to be my needy mess." He kisses me softly before pulling away to look at me. "I'm sorry. I didn't mean to disappear. I just needed to clear my head. But I promise to leave a note next time."

His thumbs brush the tears from my cheeks, but I can't meet his eyes.

"Look at me."

When I finally look up at him, what I see in his eyes stops me. Not because he's angry, but because he's looking at me like he sees me.

"I already told you. You don't have to hide anything from me." His voice is soft but still has that deep vibration that always does crazy things to my insides. "I want to see all of you, Luna."

"You don't know what you're asking for."

"Yes, I do," he says, brushing his thumb along my jaw. "I want the Luna who skates like her life depends on it. The one who fights for everything. The one who glared at me in the hallways and called me out in front of my whole team."

"You deserved that one." I chuckle a little.

"I know." He grins. "And it was so fucking hot."

I roll my eyes, but he's not done yet.

"I want the Luna who smiles at me like I'm not broken," he says, voice rougher now. "The one who teases me until I lose my mind. The one who's bold enough to make me watch while she takes care of herself—" He closes his eyes like he is still thinking about it and it still wrecks him. Then he dips his head, smile brushing against mine. "I want the Luna who takes up space. Who goes after what she wants. Who falls apart for me."

My heart cracks wide open.

He pulls back just enough to meet my eyes again.

"I want the Luna who's scared, too. The one who thinks she's a mess," he says quietly. "You're not a mess."

I blink, my chest aching from feeling so much.

"I want all of you."

"Even the one with abandonment issues and childhood trauma she still hasn't figured out yet?"

He nods.

"The one who doesn't think she's good enough for anyone to love her?" I murmur. "Or the one who's so stubborn she would rather drown in silence than admit she needs someone?"

"Especially her," he says quietly.

I've never felt this much before. Not for someone. Not like this. And I don't know what to do with it.

"I hate you, you know that?" I say in a breathless, watery laugh.

He smiles. "Yeah?"

"You broke me," I whisper, half laughing and half crying.

He smiles knowingly.

Because he knows what I'm really saying.

I hate you for making me feel things.

I hate you for seeing me when I wasn't ready.

I hate you because I'm starting to like you a lot, and that terrifies me. Because it's too fast and too soon.

"What kind of migraine retreat is this, anyway?"

He laughs.

"You should have put emotional meltdowns as one of the side effects."

He brushes my hair behind my ear, still smiling. "You didn't read the fine print?"

"Fucking fine print. I want a full refund."

He chuckles. "Let's go back upstairs, yeah? I'll make you dinner."

"Okay."

CHAPTER 37

Zayden

THIS WEEKEND HAS BEEN, so far, the longest and shortest weekend of my life. It was supposed to be a break for her, to help with her migraines. But so much has happened that I don't know how to go back to normal after this.

After her meltdown earlier, I made her pasta, and dinner ended with her being the dessert. Now she's lying on my chest with one of my earbuds in her ear, fingers brushing lazily across my chest as we listen to Taylor Swift.

I don't move, or even blink too hard, like if I do, I'll wake her or ruin the fragile quiet holding us both together.

I love seeing her like this, the girl beneath the glares and the mask. Because I know how it feels to wear one.

It's exhausting—pretending all the time. Keeping everything locked inside. But this weekend feels like a detox.

She shifts slightly, lifting her head to look at me, eyes barely open. I hold my breath and just watch her as she looks around, frowns at the pillow next to me, then moves toward it anyway.

She stays there for like two seconds then sighs before dragging herself back to my chest. I bite down a smile, keeping still as she adjusts.

"Better," she exhales, and just like that, she's asleep again.

I adjust the blanket around us, and I don't remember the last time I felt this content. I want to stay like this forever, but in a few hours, we have to go back and pretend.

❄

I DON'T REMEMBER FALLING asleep. One second, I was listening to her breathing, and the next, I'm waking up to her trying to move. My arms are around her waist, my face pressed into her stomach. She's trying to escape slowly like she doesn't want to wake me up.

Too late, little storm.

I groan and tighten my arms around her. "Where do you think you're going?" My voice comes out rough, still thick with sleep.

"Zayden, I have to pee."

"Don't care. I haven't had my special breakfast yet." I brush my nose to the soft skin above her center.

She huffs. "You want me to wet the bed?"

"Yeah. You will. After I'm done with you." I grin, not opening my eyes, but I can hear her little gasp.

Her whole body tenses as I slide lower beneath the covers, trailing my hands down her hips. "And I'll drink every drop," I murmur against her skin.

"Freak," she moans as I settle between her thighs.

I groan at the first taste of her, dragging my tongue along her opening.

I glance up at her from between her legs. "It's your fucking fault I'm a freak." I press deeper, hungrier, burying myself in her like she's the only thing that's ever tasted right. "You made me insatiable."

Her body is mine to worship.

I shift her thighs wider as I suck harder, tongue curling just the way her body likes it. Then I slide two fingers in, finding the spot that will make her gush like a waterfall.

"Zayden—wait—I'm—"

"I know, baby. Make a mess of me and this bed."

And she does.

Legs shaking, hands grabbing for anything as she comes hard, squirting all over my face and mouth. I hold her still, letting her ride it out as I drink in every drop like I said I would.

She's still gasping when I crawl up her body and slide into her with one push. I try to go slow and savor the moment, because I don't know when the next time I'll get to feel her again. But the moment I think about going back, my hips move on their own, thrusting harder and deeper than I wanted to.

"Zayden..." she gasps.

The version of me I have to be again—the cold, broody hockey player who doesn't feel anything.

Thrust.

The way I won't get to hold her like this in daylight, won't get to kiss her skin or breathe her in.

Thrust.

"Fuck," she moans, nails digging into my back.

My dad and his fucking threats.

Thrust. Deeper and harder.

"God, you're so deep," she whimpers.

The fucking video, the messages, the secrets.

Thrust.

Thrust.

Thrust.

I fuck into her everything I can't feel when we get back. Each thrust makes her cry out louder—curses tumbling from her lips as her body tightens around me.

"Oh fuck...right there. Yes! Please don't stop."

And I can't stop even if I wanted to.

Then she touches my face, her fingers trembling as they brush the corner of my eyes, and that's when I realize they're wet. Not from sweat, but from tears, and I didn't even feel them coming or know why they're here.

I blink, but more fall. Onto her skin, her lips, and her throat. She doesn't flinch or ask why.

Then I slow down.

"I'm sorry," I whisper. "I'm so fucking sorry—"

"Baby, it's okay." She brings my face to hers, and something in me calms.

I kiss her like I need her to feel all of it. The fear. The ache. The quiet desperation in my chest. Her arms wrap around my back, legs curling tighter around me, and I flatten my chest against hers because I need more of her skin. More of her breath. More of anything she'll give me.

I roll my hips into her, deep and slow. I want to stay buried inside her until the aches in my chest settle. She whimpers into my mouth as I continue kissing her. Then she comes around me, and I follow right behind her. Our bodies shake as we kiss each other through it, swallowing each other's moans and groans. She's pulsing around me as I release every drop inside her.

Mine.

She's been mine since she saved me that night at the frozen lake.

We don't move for a while. Her breathing evens out while I'm still catching mine. Still buried deep inside her. She feels like home.

"Come on, let's clean up." She shifts under me, nudging me gently to move.

I pull back and slide out of her. My gaze dips down to the mess between her thighs. She rolls out of bed, pulling me behind her, and I let her.

"Shower caps?" she asks as we walk inside the bathroom.

I nod toward the top draw beneath the sink. She opens and pauses when she sees two of them, a black and a blue.

She bites her lips like she's trying not to smile, then she grabs the black one and holds it with a teasing smirk. "Bend down, big guy."

She's tall, about five feet seven inches, but I'm six feet five inches, so she still needs to stretch on her tiptoes to reach my head.

I oblige, leaning forward as she adjusts the cap over my head.

She grabs the blue one next, and before she can do anything, I take it from her. I turn her around and place it over her head, making sure all her braids are tucked in.

"We look cute." She smiles, looking at our reflection in the mirror. Then she walks to the shower, turning the faucet and frowning as she tests the temperature.

When it's perfect for her, she reaches for my hand and pulls me in with her. The water is hotter than what I'm used to, but I don't complain.

I brace one hand against the tile as I let the water fall against my shoulders. My chest still feels tight, like I'm mourning the past couple days. Then her arms wrap around my waist, her bare skin pressed against mine, and I breathe a little easier.

She reaches for a wash cloth, adds some soap, and slowly rubs it over my back and shoulders. We take turns washing and rinsing each other quietly. When we step out, the cool air hits my skin.

She grabs a towel and starts drying me off before I can reach for it, and I let her. I can tell she needs to do this. Then she drops to her knees to dry my legs, and I'm standing there, unable to process the softness of it all until I feel her pause.

I glance down and catch her staring at my dick.

She tilts her head, eyebrows raised like she's genuinely confused by my physique. "How," she says, almost to herself, "is it that big when you're not even hard?"

I blink.

"You're literally walking around with a third leg."

I laugh and pull her up to kiss her. She kisses me back, her body pressing into me where I'm getting hard again.

Then she pulls away, pressing her hand into my chest. "Zayden." She's breathless and smiling. "If we keep going like this."

She stares down at my already hard length. "You're gonna have to carry me out here."

I raise an eyebrow. "You say that like it's a bad thing."

She shakes her head, limping a little as she walks toward the bedroom. "¿Cómo se supone que voy a patinar mañana, maldito cabrón (How am I going to skate tomorrow, asshole)?" She groans, looking for a hoodie from the drawer.

"Wait, what was that?" I follow her into the room, grinning like the fucking asshole she thinks I am.

She glances at me over her shoulders and says, "Nothing."

"You called me an asshole, and it was fucking hot." I step behind her and wrap my arms around her waist. "You're so lucky you're sore right now," I whisper against her neck, and her body shivers. "Because if you weren't, I'd fuck you so hard, you'd be using every fucking Spanish curse you know." I let my hard dick tease her ass a little, and she fucking moans. Jesus Christ, help me. "And next time I'm fucking you, I need to hear every single one of them." Her body arches slightly into me.

I pull back before I lose my restraint and push into her perfectly tight ass hole and grab a pair of sweatpants and a T-shirt from the drawer.

She grabs one of my hoodies and a pair of my sweatpants. I dress quickly, even though I probably need a cold shower. Once I'm done, I glance over at her. The sweatpants are a little too big on her, so she has to roll the waistband to keep them up, but she still looks ridiculously hot. She could be wearing a plastic bag and still be the most beautiful thing I've ever seen.

I walk over to her where she's leaning against the dresser. My hands rest on her hips, and I lower my forehead to hers, just breathing her in for a few seconds. She slides her hands under my shirt like she needs to feel me.

"Come on. You need food and some yoga to help with your soreness."

She looks up at me, eyes wide like she wants to say something but is too scared to say it.

"I know," I whisper, brushing my lips against her forehead. Then I scoop her up into my arms, and she doesn't even fight me this time, just tucks her face into my neck.

I carry her to the couch and gently set her down, grabbing the blanket off the backrest and laying it over her legs. She watches me move around the kitchen like she doesn't want this weekend to end.

Me neither.

CHAPTER 38

LUNA

I'M sore in places I didn't even know could get sore. A reminder of everything that happened this weekend, which should be the last thing on my mind as I push open the heavy doors of the Aureum.

I walk through the entrance hall, past the rows of golden nameplates honoring Champions, Olympians, and multiple generations of Aldenhursts, toward the dome ceiling lounge between the rinks.

The figure skating rink is on the right, so I should be heading there, but I don't. Instead, I stop at the mezzanine balcony that overlooks the hockey rink on the left.

Zayden is out there with Coach Aldenhurst—his dad—running full-on suicides with the puck. His dad stands near the center, holding a stopwatch.

He starts at the goal line, keeping his puck close as he explodes toward the blue line. Then he whips back and skates toward the red line, moving at a speed that should be impossible.

He stumbles barely at the red line, but he recovers quickly. He slams the puck back under control like it insulted him. Like his failure wasn't allowed to exist.

My chest twists, because I know the feeling.

To anyone else, it might look like regular private coaching. But I know better.

As if he senses me, he glances up toward the balcony, and I

stop breathing as our eyes meet. His face softens for a second. All the tension from earlier disappears, and I see him.

My Zayden.

The ones who took care of me, cooked for me, laughed with me, the one who saw part of me that no one ever has before.

It's only a second, but it's enough for me to forget where I am, and that no one can know about us. Especially his dad, who's looking between us now.

Shit.

I look away and hurry toward the right stairwell. By the time I make it to my rink, my heart is pounding in my chest.

Real subtle, Luna. We're supposed to keep this a secret, not get caught staring at him. I drop onto the bench to change into my skates, but my hands won't stop shaking.

I press them into my thighs and close my eyes to steady myself, but my mind is back at the cabin—back to him.

Sunday morning.

He made breakfast while I sat on the couch, watching him. Every so often, he'd glance over at me and smile. I tucked each of them somewhere precious, because I wouldn't get to see them as often when we went back.

We did yoga after, where he sat behind me and helped me stretch my sore thighs. Later in the afternoon, we skated together. And when we stepped onto the ice, everything else disappeared. Every time we skated together, it felt like my body remembered his. Like we'd done this many times before. I didn't have to think, just move. I already knew where he'd be. How he'd catch me. It felt like a secret conversation between us.

When it was time to leave, we kissed by the door. One of those long kisses that said so many things at the same time.

Thank you for the best weekend of my life.

I don't want to leave yet.

"Luna?"

I blink to find Nico sitting on the bench beside me. Wait, has he been here the whole time?

"Did you hear anything I just said?"

"Sorry. Just zoned out for a second."

Nico raises an eyebrow, that knowing smirk pulling at the corner of his mouth. "Let me guess. Hockey boy?"

I whip my head around so fast, it's a miracle I don't pull a muscle. "I have no idea what you're talking about," I mutter, trying to sound chill but absolutely failing.

"Oh, so it's a coincidence you both disappeared this weekend?" he teases, his voice way too loud for my comfort.

"Keep your voice down," I hiss, glancing around, making sure no one is listening.

Nico laughs and pats my shoulder. "Relax, Luna. I can keep a secret."

I tighten my laces and follow him onto the ice, trying so hard not to limp. I bite back a wince and keep my face neutral, even when my body is screaming.

Fucking Zayden. I blame him for fucking me so good.

But Nico notices and glides toward me. "You good?"

"Yep," I say through clenched teeth as I push off the ice and wince.

Nico smirks. "Damn. Hockey boy destroyed you, huh?"

"Shut up, Nico," I mutter, and thank God there's a big distance between us and the next pairs.

"Hey, no judgment," he says, skating beside me now. "I'm jealous, honestly. You know how many people on this campus would kill to hook up with Zayden freaking Aldenhurst, myself included?"

"Nico." I glare at him. "You can't just say his name. Besides, I didn't know Zayden was your type."

"Zayden is everyone's type."

I roll my eyes at him.

"Next time, maybe tell hockey boy to go easier on your legs. We kinda need them, Ice Princess."

"I hate you."

"Didn't you say you hate hockey boy, too? Is this your way of saying you love me?"

Dios mio.

I limp my way through practice. When Coach calls me aside and asks if I'm okay, I lie and say it's just a strain and should be fine in a couple of days.

After practice, I take the back exit, because I'm kinda avoiding Zayden after what happened. The truth is I don't know how to act around him right now. How do I go back to how we were before, pretending to hate each other?

As I reach the little alcove with the vending machine, strong arms wrap around my waist and pull me into the small space between the hall and the machine. My heart jumps only for a second, because I already know who it is before I even see his face.

I turn in his arms to face him, and he buries his face in the crook of my neck like he needs to breathe me in.

"Zayden…" I whisper, brushing the back of his neck.

"I just couldn't go the whole day without touching you."

My heart does stupid flips in my chest, and I melt into him. I need this as much as he does. I barely slept last night. I felt like a stranger in my own bed. The pillows didn't feel the same anymore, not after sleeping on his warm chest and falling asleep to the sound of his heartbeat. It's terrifying how much I missed him.

He pulls back just enough to look at me. His eyes are tired, like he barely slept. His thumbs brush my cheekbones like he's memorizing them. I lean into his touch without thinking, my body not caring that someone could walk by and see us.

"No one really uses this exit," he says, as if he can read my mind. "And the camera can't see us from here."

I lift an eyebrow. "How do you even know I'd come this way?"

"Because you always take this exit after a bad practice."

How does he know that? I do take the back exit after bad practice. Because I don't want to see or talk to anyone, and I need my favorite chips.

I swallow the lump in my throat. "How long have you been waiting here?"

"Long enough to get these before you could." He pulls out a small bag of plantain chips and presses into my hand.

I blink down at the bag in my hand.

"Long enough to know I wouldn't survive the day without holding you."

"I didn't know broody boys could be this clingy."

His mouth curves just a little, but it's tired—like whatever happened at practice drained him.

"You okay?" I ask, softer now. "I saw you with your dad earlier..."

Zayden shakes his head once but doesn't really answer. "I will be. After this."

Then he kisses me.

It's not rushed, not greedy. Just...necessary. The kind of kiss that says he needed to feel something real. When he pulls back, his eyes stay closed, and he rests his forehead against mine like he can't let go just yet.

"What are you doing to me?" he murmurs, barely audible. Like he doesn't expect an answer.

My heart flutters wildly in my chest. "I don't know," I whisper.

"How's your head?" His thumb gently traces the curve of my temple like his touch could erase the pain if I have one.

"It's fine," I whisper through the weird pressure in my throat.

He's studying my face like he's making sure I'm not lying to him, telling him I'm okay when I'm not. And the tenderness of it all is too much. He leans down and presses a kiss to my temple that nearly breaks me. "You'd tell me if it's hurting right?"

I nod and blink back the pressure behind my eyelids. "I'm fine really, but I wouldn't mind a little orgasm. You know, for medicinal purposes."

He stares at me for a few seconds like he knows what I'm doing and decides not to call me out on it.

"Just say the word, Tempestina Mia," he mutters, sliding one hand down to my hip, fingers teasing the waistband of my leggings. "I'll make sure you don't have to worry about a migraine all day."

I hate how much I want that. I want him.

"Not here, Hockey Boy," I whisper, smiling a little.

He growls low in his chest like I just denied him his favorite meal. His brows draw together, and his lips press into a pout. The broody hockey player is actually pouting. I'm saving this moment right here for when I see him looking all broody. I have to bite down on my lip to keep myself from laughing.

"You're adorable right now." I gently cup his face in my hands and press a kiss to the top of his nose.

He gives me a glare, but it's all for show. "Meet me at the library later. North wing has a secret section. I promise there are no cameras. And barely anyone goes there."

"When?"

"Lunch."

"Okay." I smile at him.

Then his lips find mine again, slower this time, like he doesn't want to let me go. "Go, Luna," he says roughly. "Before I change my mind or someone sees us." His eyes are still on me, lips parted like he wants to say something else. Instead, he leans against the wall, running a hand through his locs. "And don't look back."

I walk away, and I don't look back like he asked, but I still feel him like a bruise. The door closes behind me as I start down the path toward my dorm. Then I receive a notification on my phone, and I think it's a reminder for my therapy session later, but it's another anonymous message.

> Unknown Number: Hope your little getaway was worth it. Just be careful, Aldenhurst doesn't like when people get too close to their secrets.

I stop walking and glance around, making sure nobody is following me. For a second, I can't move. A shiver runs down my spine as I shove the phone back in my pocket and keep walking like nothing's happened.

But inside, my heartbeat won't stop racing.

Someone knows we were at the cabin.

CHAPTER 39

Zayden

She disappears around the corner without looking back, just like I told her to.

Good girl.

But damn, it's pathetic how much I already miss her. She's gone, but her scent is still here. I close my eyes and breathe it in like a starved man. Then I pull out my phone and shoot a quick text to Jasper.

> Me: A3 vend. Code red. Last twenty minutes.

Jasper will know what to do. Wipe the last twenty minutes from the camera feed near the vending machine. I can't risk anyone seeing the footage of when I pulled her toward the wall. Not when we still don't know who accessed the last Shadow Rink footage before Jasper could pull it.

I'm about to slip the phone back into my pocket when I receive a notification. I glance down, expecting a sarcastic *on it* from Jasper or a middle finger emoji, but it's another anonymous message.

> Unknown number: Did you enjoy your little weekend getaway? Everyone has weaknesses, and we both know who yours is. Do you even know what your family is capable of? Can you protect her from them?

Everything in me stills, and just like that, all the warmth she left behind evaporates.

I reread the message again. Whoever this is...they're watching, and they know about the cabin. And they know something about my family that I don't. And I have no idea who they are or what the fuck they want.

Fuck! I slam my fist into the wall behind me and welcome the pain that shoots through my knuckles. I need to find Jasper and find out who the fuck is behind these anonymous messages. Their little game ends here.

I push off the wall, chest burning, and take the same exit Luna did. By the time I reach the dorm, I'm shaking. The walk back did nothing to cool me off. I'm still burning inside.

I scan my key card and shove the door open and head straight to Jasper's room. He's sitting at his desk, headphones half on, typing something fast like he's deep in another code sweep. He barely glances up—until I toss my phone onto his desk. It lands with a sharp thud right in front of him.

He pulls his headphones down, blinking. "Uh—what the hell?"

"Read it."

He picks up the phone and reads the message. His face changes fast.

I pace the room like a caged animal, fists clenched at my sides.

"You said you were close. I need a name. Like now."

He nods, already clicking into some tab. "I'm working on it, Z. Whoever this is? They're good. But I'm better. It's definitely a student on campus."

"I'll do anything to protect her, even if it means burning the fucking school to the ground," I say through gritted teeth. "You know that, right?"

Jasper doesn't look up from his screen, but his fingers pause on the keyboard. "I know. That's why I'm not letting this go either."

I exhale slowly then glance toward him again. "And the other thing?"

He leans back, cracking his knuckles. "Still trying to access the deeper archives. The footage from the night Ellias died? It's buried. Not just password-protected—scrubbed. I've been pulling from old backups and ghost files, but it's going to take time."

He pauses, dragging a file into a new folder. "I did find out something, though."

That gets my full attention. "What is it?"

"Ellias had a sister. That part wasn't in the student files, but I cross-checked an old yearbook article with hospital birth records. Same last name, same region."

"A sister?"

"Yeah. They were born four years apart. She'd be around nineteen now. University age."

"Have you found her?"

"Not yet, but I'm close. I think she might've changed her name, because her records disappeared about two years ago. I've got a few leads, though."

"You think she knows what happened to her brother?"

"Maybe. If she doesn't, she might be looking for answers. And if she does, she'd be playing it smart."

I stare at the wall, tension building in my chest.

"I tried reaching out to some of the students who were at Valcérre that year," I mutter. "Some don't even remember Ellias."

"What?"

"They said he was only here for one semester. First year."

"Bullshit," Jasper says.

"Exactly," I snap. "It's like someone wiped him clean."

"We have a dead student. A missing sister. Sealed footage. And you and Luna are in the middle of it all."

I run a hand over my mouth, trying not to lose it. "Why Luna? Why pull her into this? She has nothing to do with this."

Jasper shrugs. "Maybe because she's new. Maybe because she's stubborn. Maybe because...they knew you'd care."

"We need to find whoever's behind this. Because if something happens to Luna..."

I can't even finish the sentence.

"We'll keep her safe. Just trust me to handle this part." He looks up at me. "You've got class, don't you? Go, I got this."

I glance at the time. "I'm not going anywhere until we figure this out."

"No offense, but you being here isn't helping anyone. Skipping class is going to draw attention, and we can't afford that right now." He shoots me a look over his shoulder.

"Fine," I grit it out. "But if anything changes—"

"You'll be the first to know," Jasper says, already pulling up something on a second screen.

I nod and head to my room to get ready for class. I go through the motions, change, grab my bag, but my chest still feels tight. I'm not even thinking about business class right now, I just need to see her.

I move across the courtyard like I don't notice anyone, but the truth is I see and hear everything. The whispers in the study lounges, the side-eyes from my own teammates.

My heart beats a little faster the moment I step into the hallway. I scan everyone, looking for anyone suspicious and listening for anything that sounds off.

Then I hear her laugh.

Not Luna's, but that girl with the red hair she has class with. They're walking toward me. Luna's eyes lock with mine, and time fucking stops. Everything in me stills—except the ache in my chest. Because even though I just held her a couple hours ago, I want to pull her into me again. Feel her against my skin. Make sure she's okay.

So I soften my eyes a little even when I shouldn't, letting her see the things I can't tell her.

I already miss you.
I fucking hate this.
Please, be careful.

Her friend's eyes move between us like she's putting something together, but she doesn't seem surprised.

I look away quickly, slipping my hands into my pockets to stop myself from doing something reckless like reaching out for her. Then I keep walking, but I make a mental note to look her friend up. I don't trust anyone right now.

I should be heading to class, but I'm not in the mood to sit through a one-hour lecture and pretend to care about business marketing. Instead, I head to the cafeteria, grab a salad and lemon water, and discreetly make my way to the library to the section nobody uses.

The old study wing is hidden behind towers of books. There's a love seat, a square wooden table, and a couple of chairs. I blow some of the dust off the table and set the food down. Then I go back to the corridor and pull an old stack of books from the shelf, some shit that no one reads. I place it on the floor next to the bookshelf. It means *occupied* and *do not disturb*.

This part of the library is colder, so I pull out the small fleece blanket I brought with me and place it on the loveseat.

I grab my phone and send a quick text to Jasper to check on Luna's friend from psych class. Then I wait, but every second without her feels like an eternity. The quiet is where I breathe, and think, but right now, it's so fucking loud.

The books on the second shelf look interesting right about now. So I grab the first one I see, something about *Dream and Your Subconscious*. When I open it, the dust makes my throat hitch. I cough into my sleeve and glance around, making sure no one heard. Even though most students don't know this place exists, that's why I picked it.

I open it to a random page, trying to distract myself, but it doesn't work. Then my phone buzzes from where I left it on the table. It's a message.

> Jasper: I got something. Need you back now.

I check the time on my phone. Luna won't be here for another twenty minutes. But I need to know what Jasper found.

I rip a page from the old book I was pretending to read and grab a pen from my pocket. Moving closer to the table, I scribble her a little note.

> *Hey, little storm,*
> *I promised I wouldn't just disappear without letting you know, but I had to go. Something came up with Jasper, but I I'll make it up to you.*
> *Eat something, stay warm, and don't stay too long.*
> *Miss you already.*
> *Z.*

I tuck the note under the water bottle and hope she sees it. Then I grab my bag but pause before leaving. One last glance at the spot where I was supposed to hold her.

Whatever Jasper found better help me put an end to all this.

CHAPTER 40

Luna

This is the longest hour of my life. The professor's been talking for forty-five minutes straight now, and I have no fucking idea what he's talking about.

My knees bounce under the table, and I feel hot and fidgety. I rest my chin on my palm and let my eyes drift toward the windows, where the campus trees blur in a haze of light snow. The view helps calm my racing heart.

I chew the end of my pen, staring at the bullet points about emotional conditioning, but all I can think about is how conditioned I've become—to *him*.

I've never felt like this before. Not even close.

I had a crush on this boy once when I was fourteen, then my mom's boyfriend ruined everything. I don't like to talk about it. But that doesn't get close to whatever Zayden evokes in me.

It's not just a crush. It's not lust. It's…gravity. Like my whole body is tuned to him, and when we're apart, everything tilts slightly off-balance.

Thank God, Serene left early, said she had an emergency. At least I don't have to worry about her asking me questions when I bolt out of here.

I tap my pen against the edge of the desk, glancing at the clock for what feels like the hundredth time. Only twelve minutes left. I'm gonna cry.

I need to see him.

Who am I right now? This is pathetic. But after everything

that happened this weekend, I can't stuff everything back down or unfeel everything I felt.

"That is all for today," the professor says, and the second the words leave his mouth, I'm out of the door.

The library is across campus, and I basically sprint there. It's mostly empty when I walk in, except for a few students gathered around the square wooden tables.

I walk past the bookshelves toward the corner I didn't even know existed. I spot the stack of books first, apparently it's a *do not disturb* sign, and I smile to myself. This means he's here. A weird breath of relief escapes me, because a little part was worried that he changed his mind about us.

Stupid, I know.

"Zayden?" I whisper, walking by the bookshelves.

No answer.

Maybe I got the wrong spot.

Then I see the wooden table with the brown bag and a bottle of water. There's a folded paper tucked under it, and it's a note from Zayden.

I read the note and drop into the seat, grabbing the blanket he left me. It smells like him, warm and a little woodsy, and I breathe it in. My body curls up on the dusty loveseat, and I wrap the blanket around me. I let my eyes close for a moment.

My phone vibrates on the table beside me. The sound forces my eyes open. I reach for it, and the screen shows the reminder for my 3 p.m. therapy session. Which is in thirty minutes. Shit. I must have fallen asleep.

I push the blanket away and stand up. The sudden movement sends a throb behind my left eye. I take a sip of the lemon water he got me before gathering everything and tucking the blanket into my tote bag.

I hurry through the library and across the courtyard. My anxiety spikes with every step closer to my dorm. Therapy's supposed to help with anxiety, not cause it.

When I reach my dorm, I scan my key card and step in. Thankfully, Annika and Sophie aren't back yet. I pull out my laptop and Zayden's blanket and sink into my bed.

I open the laptop and tap the Zoom link. We all drop in at almost the same time.

"Luna, Rylee, Mrs. Del Sol. I'm glad we're all here," Dr. Andrea greets us.

I pull the blanket tighter around me like a shield.

"So, Luna, how have you been settling in at school?" my mother asks.

"I guess I've been fine," I lie, like always, but I don't stop there. "Classes and training are intense. Everyone here's so rich, and I feel out of place, but I'm fine. Why wouldn't I be?" I fake a laugh.

Dr. Andrea remains quiet, but her eyes say everything, and Rylee's watching me, too. My mom is doing that thing where she avoids looking at the camera.

I look down at my hands. "I'm always fine." My throat tightens. "I was fine when I had to figure out how to make my own dinner when I was eight. I was fine when I lied to Rylee about missing the bus so she wouldn't worry about me because it wasn't her job to worry about me." My hands are trembling now. Nobody says anything, so I keep going. "I was also fine when I went to bed hungry or when the kids at school made fun of my hair because I didn't know how to style it."

"Luna." Rylee says my name in a soft, wrecked tone, but I can't look at her yet.

"But you're not fine, are you, Luna?" the therapist says softly.

I shake my head.

"What are you feeling right now?"

"I feel tired of pretending I am fine when I'm not. Tired of being scared, of always waiting for something to go wrong. Tired of trying to prove myself to everyone else, prove I'm worth staying for."

"That's good, Luna. What else?"

"Guilt and resentment. I resent Rylee a little for leaving, then I feel guilty about it. Because she was a kid herself, and she did everything she could to help me. She's always been there when I needed her the most. I just wished she could have taken me with her."

"I'm sorry," Rylee says, her voice cracking a little.

I shake my head. "You didn't do anything wrong."

I inhale shakily and finally acknowledge the one thing I've been afraid to say, and feel, but it's always been there.

"Hate. I hate my mother for not being there when I needed her." I finally lift my eyes to look at her on the screen. "I hate you." I blink, and a tear slips down my cheek. "I hate that you had me when you didn't want me." The tears are hot now, sliding down my face. "Hate that Rylee had to grow up so fast and be a mom, because you were never one. Rylee was the one who raised me." I look at Rylee, who's also crying now.

"I'm sorry," my mother says, her voice barely audible. "I didn't know how to be a mother. After Rylee's dad left, he took a piece of me with him. I was angry, lost, and I blame myself because it was my fault. I pushed him away." She swallows, her eyes on something past the screen. "So when I got pregnant with you, I thought this was it. That you were what I needed to get my shit together. That you would save me." She finally looks at me through the screen. "I waited for you to fix something in me that was already broken." She blinks quickly. "And instead I broke you, too, both of you."

The tears fall again, harder now. I want to scream.

"I hear your apology." I steady my voice. "But it doesn't fix what happened, and I need time to process everything. I'm not ready to forgive you."

"And that boundary is important," Dr. Andrea steps in. "I want you to allow yourself to feel it all, the anger, the hate, the resentment. Let yourself sit with it, but don't do it alone."

Zayden's voice replays in my mind. *"I don't want you hurting alone anymore."*

"Luna, can you do something for me? I'd like you to try journaling. Just a few minutes a day. Just what you're feeling in that moment. You don't have to share it unless you want to. But you've unlocked something today, and I don't want you pushing it all down again."

I nod.

"And to both of you, thank you for being here. Luna took an enormous step today. The next step is to be respectful of her feelings and be patient without expectations."

They both nod.

Dr. Andrea leans closer to the screen. "And Luna, before I end the session, I got to ask you something. I've been your therapist for almost three years now, you've talked around your feelings but never really talked about them. What changed? What triggered this moment?"

I don't answer right away, but I do know.

It's him.

The way he takes care of me, holds me, and looks at me like I'm not too much. The way it felt to fall asleep in his arms, and how much I need him right now.

But I don't want to talk about him here.

"I think I know what triggered it, but I don't want to talk about it yet."

She nods softly. "That's okay. We'll pause here for today. It was a lot, and I'm so proud of you. I'll see you at our one-on-one next week."

Rylee gives me a small smile and my mother's eyes soften before the call disconnects, leaving me alone in my room.

The weight in my chest settles deeper, and I don't know what to do with all of it. My phone vibrates next to me on the bed, and I check the message.

> Rylee: Can I call you? I want to talk, just us, please.

I stare at the message, it's not like I don't want to talk to her, she's just not who I need right now.

> Me: Not right now, but I'll call you soon. I love you.

> Rylee: Whenever you're ready. I love you too.

I don't remember putting my boots on, or grabbing my coat. The next thing I know, I'm standing in front of his dorm, knocking on his door.

The door pulls open, and Jasper blinks at me. "Luna?"

"Is Zayden here?" I wrap my arms around my chest to keep myself from falling apart. This is stupid and I shouldn't be here.

"Yeah, hold on."

He steps aside, and Zayden appears, shirtless.

"I...I'm sorry for showing up like this." My whole body is shaking now. "I just..." *don't want to hurt alone.* I can't get the rest of the words out.

He crosses the small distance between us in less than a second and pulls me into him, pressing my face into his chest like he knows I'd fall apart if he didn't.

"Jas," he says quietly over my shoulder. "Make sure no one saw her come in."

Zayden leads me down the hallway and into his room, and the door closes softly behind us. Then I remember the last time I was here. How he carried me across campus and took care of me without me asking or expecting anything back.

"Can I take your coat?" he asks gently.

I nod, and he carefully slides it off my shoulders before slowly guiding me to the bed. He kneels to untie my boots one at a time.

Then he climbs in the bed. "Come here." He reaches out for me, and I crawl into the space beside him and curl into his bare chest.

"I've got you," he whispers.

The tears come again, and I let them, quiet sobs that shake through my body as he rubs slow circles on my back.

He makes everything feel better, and the ache in my chest softens. I let the warmth of him melt into my skin. And somewhere between the tears and the quiet, I drift into sleep.

CHAPTER 41

ZAYDEN

SHE'S FINALLY asleep on my chest. And for a minute, I just watch her—no, memorize her. The way her lips twitch like she's having a dream. Her lashes tremble; maybe she's having a nightmare. If I could step into her dream and slice whatever dragon she's fighting, I would, because she kept her promise. She came to me when she was hurting, and that alone wrecks me.

I rub lazy circles on her back until her breathing evens out. I brush a strand of her small braids from her cheek. She doesn't stir. Just melts deeper into my chest like she belongs there.

I've never wanted to destroy something more than I do right now. This school, this system, this legacy that keeps breaking the people who don't deserve to bleed for it.

Carefully, I try to ease her off me. She stirs and murmurs something against my skin. Her arm tightens around my torso like she doesn't want me to leave. And part of me wants to stay, just crawl under the covers with her and pretend the world outside doesn't exist. And still, I have to leave her. Because someone out there thinks they can use her. Someone thinks they can hurt her to get to me. And I can't let that happen.

"I know, baby." I press a soft kiss to the top of her head. "I need to take care of something, but I promise we can cuddle all you want when I get back." I smile to myself, even though my chest aches.

I peel her arms from around me, making sure the blanket stays tucked up to her shoulders. Then I grab my hoodie from the back of the chair and put it on. I stop at my desk, grab a pen, and write her a note.

> *Hey, my little storm,*
> *Thank you so much for keeping your promise and coming to me. I have to take care of something with Jasper, but I'll be back soon. Promise.*
> *Btw, you look cute when you're sleeping!*
> *Z.*

I place the note on the pillow right next to her. One more look at her sweet face before I step out.

The second I do, it's like the temperature drops ten degrees. Jasper's leaning against the wall by the front door, arms crossed, his phone screen lighting up his face with that familiar frown.

"Is she okay?" he asks.

I nod. "Sleeping. For now."

"You gonna tell her?" he says, straight to the point.

He found out earlier that Serene, Luna's friend from psychology class, is the one who's been sending the messages. She used a VPN, but she logged in from the student Wi-Fi, and Jasper was also able to trace it.

Serene's also Ellias's little sister. She changed her name a couple years ago and covered her tracks pretty well.

She probably already knows what happened to her brother, and the role my family played in it. She's using Luna to get to me and expose the truth.

If she wanted the truth or revenge, she should've come for me directly, not her. She knew exactly what she was doing, and she's going to wish she never pulled Luna into this.

"Not until I find out what she knows, or what her plan is."

I grab my phone and send Sophie a quick text.

> **Me:** Hey Soph, Luna is in my room. She's sleeping now, but I have to leave. Can you come stay with her until I get back?

> **Sophie:** Is she okay?

> **Me:** Not really, she came to me crying.

> **Sophie:** I'll be there soon.

> **Me:** Thanks. You still have a copy of our key card right?

> **Sophie:** Yeah.

I lock my screen and glance up at Jasper. "Let's go."

"What are you gonna say to her?" he asks as we head downstairs.

"No fucking idea, but she's gonna regret dragging Luna into this."

We don't even bother knocking when we get to her door. She should be alone, since Cameron is keeping her roommate distracted, and Jasper uses one of his devices to override the lock.

The door clicks open, but it doesn't seem like there's anyone here.

"Where is she?" I ask, glancing around the room. The lights are off.

"She should be here. I checked her class schedule, and she had nothing scheduled for today."

We step into her room. Her laptop is missing, and the desk chair is knocked sideways. A drawer is open halfway.

"Shit," Jasper mutters.

I step farther into her room. "She left in a hurry."

Jasper moves to the desk and starts rifling through drawers. "I'll search. See if she left anything behind."

"She's not dumb," I say. "She's been planning this longer than we realized. She got into the school, waited for any opportunity to get to me. Then Luna showed like a fucking storm, and she saw what she does to me and she used that. Got close to Luna, dragged her into this. And now she's running, because she knows we figured it out."

My hands clench into a fists, and I feel like pushing through a wall.

I head for the door.

"Where are you going?" Jasper calls after me.

"To find Serene in whatever hole she's hiding in. She lit the fire and woke up the ghosts. She doesn't get to hide now."

CHAPTER 42

Luna

The second I wake up, I reach for him, but the spot where he should be is empty.

My eyes go wide, and I'm fully awake now.

Don't panic!

The room is dark, except for the lights coming from the window, and there's no sign of Zayden. How long have I been asleep for? That's when I see the small piece of paper on his pillow.

He didn't leave. He's coming back.

I push the blanket aside and shuffle toward the door. My head hurts, but it's not a migraine this time.

When I open the door, I hear whispers. Maybe he's back and didn't want to wake me.

"Zayden?" I take another step toward the hallway, following the voices coming from the living room. But when I round the corner, I freeze. It's Sophie and Jasper. She's laughing under her breath, and he's trying not to smile, and they lean in way too close to each other.

"Luna!" Her eyes go wide when she spots me.

Jasper straightens, too.

Sophie hurries over to me. "You're awake. Are you okay?"

"Uh...yeah. Where's Zayden? I thought he was with Jasper."

"Yeah, he's grabbing dinner," Jasper says.

Sophie leads me back into Zayden's room. I curl back into

the blanket. Even though I slept for hours, my body still feels tired.

Sophie sits beside me. "Hey… What happened?"

I tell her all about the therapy session with Rylee and my mother.

She moves closer and wraps her arms around my shoulders. "I'm proud of you. I know you've been holding it in for years, and it's gonna hurt right now, but we're here for you."

"Thank you," I whisper, leaning into her.

"And I don't think you really hate her, just hate that she was a terrible mother, and you and Rylee deserved better."

Maybe she's right. I don't know anymore.

We sit quietly for a few seconds.

"So…you and Jasper, huh?" I glance at her with a smirk.

"What about me and Jasper?" she asks, a little too quickly.

"Last time I checked, you were hooking up with Cameron. Then I caught you two about to kiss."

"We were not." She flops on the bed, and I lie down next to her, raising an eyebrow.

"So, there's nothing between you two?" I turn my head to look at her. Because if I'm being honest, this isn't the first time I've noticed.

"He's Zayden's best friend, and we get along."

"Uh huh. And that's it?"

"And he's easy to talk to. He understands me." She puts her palms over her face.

"Sophie!"

"I know. It's just him and I are kinda alike. We both don't want to disappoint our family. He just wants to play hockey. Even though he loves tech, and he doesn't want to run his family business. And I want to create the next gen of sports innovation. Gear that changes how athletes move. I'm talking about smart compression, temperature-regulating fabrics. I don't want to be just the stylish little sister who smiles in the press photos."

"Sophie, that sounds amazing. And I'm sure if you talk to Luc, he'll support you. He loves you."

"You think so?" She looks at me unconvinced.

"I know so."

Her smile grows bigger. "You really think I can do it?"

I wrap my arms around her and pull her into a hug. "You can do anything you want. And I believe in you, and Luc will, too."

She lets out a breath, like she's relieved someone else believes in her.

"So, what about Cameron?"

"Well, Cameron and I were never exclusive or anything like that."

"So, does that confirm there is something between you and Jasper?"

She huffs. "You're impossible, you know that?"

"But you love me." I pull her even closer.

She rolls her eyes, but the smile on her face tells me everything. And just for a second, everything feels okay again.

The door opens. "Am I interrupting something?" We both sit up as Zayden steps in.

"Nope," Sophie says.

"Maybe," I say, just to tease him, or maybe to hide the fact that I stop breathing for a second.

He walks toward the bed slowly, eyes locked with mine, and I'm still not sure if I'm breathing properly or blinking. And then he stops in front of me as he leans down, one hand on the bed, the other lifting my chin before he presses his lips to mine.

He kisses me like he's been thinking about it all day. Like he can finally breathe. I melt into it, only pulling back when I remember we're not alone.

"Zayden," I whisper, glancing at Sophie. "Sophie's right here."

"I know," he murmurs. "But out there, I have to pretend, in here, you're mine."

My breath stutters, and before I can blink, he kisses me again. Harder this time, like he needs to make me believe them.

Sophie clears her throat. "All right, I'm leaving." Then the door closes behind her.

Zayden pushes me gently onto the mattress, his hands framing either side of my head. Then he's kissing me again, deeper, hotter. I gasp against his lips, causing a low, deep sound to escape his throat.

God, that sound.

He grabs my thighs and pulls me closer to him. Every hard inch of him pressing against where I need him. My hips shift without thinking, chasing the friction that makes my blood rush hot through every part of me.

Then he flips us until I'm straddling him with my knees on either side of his hips. He rests his hands lightly on my waist, eyes dragging over my face.

"You know, for someone who's broody all the time, you sure are touchy." I slide my hand down his chest, and he grins. I like this version of him, a little too much.

I run my fingers through his locs, twisting them gently, and his eyes flutter closed for half a second before they meet mine again.

"Are you okay?" he asks gently.

"I'm okay." I keep playing with his hair, because it's easier than meeting his stare.

"Luna, please look at me," he says gently. "I want to see you when you talk to me."

Slowly, I lift my eyes until they meet his. He's doing that thing where he peels me open with nothing but his gaze.

"I told you, baby. Don't hide from me. You don't have to be okay with me."

I'm trying, but I've just been hiding for so long I don't always know when I'm doing it. "I guess I'm not okay, but being here with you makes it a little better." I hold his gaze, even though I want to look away.

He brushes my cheeks with his thumbs. "I promise you don't have to hurt alone anymore."

"I know." I press my forehead to his. "Thank you."

When did Zayden, the hot, broody boy I swore to hate, become this important to me?

My stomach growls, rudely interrupting the moment we're having. To be fair, I haven't eaten all day.

He chuckles. "I don't mind staying here with you all night, but your stomach says otherwise."

I laugh, too, curling deeper into him.

"I brought food. We can eat in here, just us. Or we can eat with the rest of the gang."

Instantly, I want to stay here, but wanting to be around him that much is dangerous. So I reluctantly say, "With the gang."

We make our way toward the living room, and I slide in next to Sophie and Annika. They pass me a container of Chinese food. Zayden sits on the armchair across from us, eating without saying much, his eyes on me the whole time.

Then Zayden steps toward us, hooks his hands under my thighs, and lifts me off the couch.

"Zayden!" I squeal as he carries me back to the arm chair, settling me on his lap. "God, you're such a caveman." I bury my face into his hoodie, dying of embarrassment.

Sophie and Annika laugh from the couch.

He reaches for a throw blanket and pulls it over us. "I couldn't take another second watching you from across the couch. I need you in my arms," he whispers into my ear.

"You're so clingy."

He doesn't deny it, just wraps his arms around my waist. The truth is I wanted to be close to him, too.

"So, did you guys find Serene or not?" Cameron asks from across the room.

Zayden goes stiff beside me, and I straighten.

"Wait, why are you looking for Serene?"

"She doesn't know yet?" Cameron asks Zayden.

"Know what?" Sophie straightens, too.

I look between Cameron and Zayden. "Someone want to start explaining?"

Zayden sets me down next to him. "You have to promise whatever's said in this room, stays in here. All of you."

The room goes quiet.

"Serene is the one who's been sending us the anonymous messages." He turns to face me. "She's also Ellias's younger sister. Changed her last name to Vancourt before she enrolled here two years ago." He looks at me like he wishes all of this wasn't true.

I feel the air punch out of my lungs. "What are you saying?"

"She's been using you to get to me, to find out the truth."

"What truth?" Annika asks.

Jasper leans forward. "The Midnight Challenge, the Shadow Rink."

Annika chuckles. "Wait, you mean that story about some hidden rink, where skaters compete against each other, but invite only?"

"It wasn't just a story, and we believe Ellias died during one of the challenges. The school covered it up," Jasper says from his seat.

Annika blinks. "What the hell?" She turns to face Sophie, who doesn't seem surprised. "You knew about this?"

"Not all of it but some parts," Sophie says.

"And now she's missing?" Annika turns to face Jasper.

"Zayden and I went looking for her earlier after we found out who she is, but she's gone."

"Luna, when was the last time you saw Serene?" Zayden asks gently.

"Earlier today during class, but she left before it was over. Said she had an emergency."

Now that I think about it, she looked scared.

"What if something happened to her?" I whisper. "What if she's not hiding? Maybe someone found out what she was doing."

"Hey." Zayden cups my cheek, his thumb brushing along my jaw. "We'll find her."

I nod, swallowing hard, and try to believe it. But somewhere deep in my gut, fear settles in like frost.

Something isn't right.

CHAPTER 43

LUNA

JASPER and I are back at the school archives, and it's colder than I remember. The last time we were here, he didn't have the right tools, but he says he came prepared this time.

He pulls out a slim toolkit and peels back the casing around the reader. "If I fry the biometric," he murmurs, "the system defaults to key card priority. I just need sixty seconds."

I pace behind him, heart hammering against my ribs. It's been a week since Serene disappeared, and no one has seen or heard from her. Zayden doesn't know I'm here. He would have stopped me if I told him. He made me promise I wouldn't do anything reckless. But I need to know what the fuck is going.

A few minutes later, the scanner flashes green. Jasper opens it slowly and pulls out the metal drawer with rows of thick folders. For a second, we just stare at them like we expect them to blow up like a bomb. My heart's beating rapidly in my chest.

I kneel in front of it and sort through the folders. They're labeled with codes: MC101, MC102, and up to MC110. My guess is MC stands for Midnight Challenge.

I grab the folder labeled MC110, which is the most recent one, and flip it open. It is filled with papers, betting slips, pairings, handwritten notes, and more. I pull one out.

Midnight Challenge Report: MC110
Date: Redacted

> *Final round.*
> *Location: Ice Arena D.*
> *Participants: E. Vaughn vs A. Hawkins.*
> *Odds: 3:1 (E. Vaughn favored)*
> *Wagers:*
> *Bettor initials – wager – player chosen*
> *Z.A. - Bet 60,000V on A. Hawkins – Win*
> *M. R - Bet 10,000V on E. Vaughn – Loss*
> *K. D - Bet 3,500V on E. Vaughn – Loss*
> *R.B. - Bet 5,000V on E. Vaughn – loss*
> *K.B - Bet 10,000V on A. Hawkins – Win*
> *Outcome: E. Vaughn did not finish. A. Hawkins declared winner.*
> *Fatality? Yes, E. Vaughn.*
> *Cause of incident: Skate failure.*
> *Internal review: Inconclusive.*
> *No further investigation.*
> *Payout: Approved by C.Z.A*
> *Verified by D.Z.A. Access restricted!*

Hawkins? Why does that name sound familiar?

I look at the bet log, but none of it makes sense.

"I don't get it," I murmur. "If they placed the larger bet on Hawkins…wouldn't they want him to lose? Wouldn't they lose money if he won?"

"No, not if they're the house?"

I blink. "The what?"

"The house. The ones running the bets. The ones holding the money. If Ellias was the favorite, most people, especially outsiders, would've bet on him to win. But if someone knew Ellias was gonna lose, they'd bet on Hawkins."

"Because they were gonna make him lose," I whisper.

Jasper nods. "Exactly. Think about it. If Ellias wins, they pay out thousands to everyone who bet on him. But if Ellias loses? The house keeps the pot. The few people who bet against him get the biggest cut."

"And three to one?"

"For every dollar you bet, you would win three dollars if you bet in favor of Hawkins."

"C.Z.A.?"

"Coach Zayn Aldenhurst, Zayden's father, and if I'm right, D.Z.A is for Director Zander Aldenhurst, Zayden's grandfather," Jasper says.

"No, no. You think the school director is part of it?"

I feel sick, nauseous. A lump builds in my throat. I blink, willing the tears to stay away, but they're already stinging.

"What happened to the winner?"

"Give me a sec. If he was registered here, I should be able to find him." He pulls out the tiniest laptop I've ever seen and moves toward a small desk in the corner, and I follow him. I glance between him and the betting sheet, his fingers moving rapidly across the tiny keyboard.

"Holy shit."

"What?" I lean over his shoulder.

His voice drops. "A. Hawkins… is Aidan Hawkins."

"Wait, the center forward on the national team?"

"Yeah." He turns the screen toward me. "Look."

>*Name: Aidan Hawkins*
>*Age: 23*
>*Height: 6'2"*
>*Weight: 195 lbs*
>*Status: ACTIVE*
>*Position: Center Forward*

Current Team: Valcérre Polar Bears
Previous program: Valcérre University Hockey Division
Accepted into Valcérre's NHP Program post-academy challenge victory. Exceptional discipline and top-tier skating control.
Debut: Valcérre Polar Bears, following NHP placement.

Suddenly, I'm freezing and burning all at once. My chest's too tight, like something alive is clawing its way out. The archive walls feel like they're closing in, like the whole university is closing in on me.

"That's...two months after Ellias..."

Jasper nods slowly. "They fast-tracked him. Right into NHP."

I grab another folder

Midnight Challenge Report: MC109
Date: Redacted
Final round.
Location: Redacted
Participants: M. Lavigne. vs D. Lavaune
Odds: 3:1 (D. Lavaune favored)
Outcome: M. Lavigne won
Fatality? No.
Payout: Approved by C.Z.A
Verified by D.Z.A.

Both files are similar, the house bet on the player they knew would win, but there was no fatality. What happened with Ellias? Did he refuse to throw the game? Or was it something else?

Jasper looks up M. Lavigne and discovers he is the current captain of the Lyonnaise Icehawks and has a multi-million dollar sponsorship deal.

We keep flipping through, and every challenge report, it's the same. The MC108 winner J. Rousseau plays for the Swiss.

> *Midnight Challenge Report: MC107*
> *Date: Redacted*
> *Final round.*
> *Location: Redacted*
> *Participants: F. Belanger. vs (redacted)*
> *Odds: 2:1*
> *Outcome: Win by Forfeit*
> *Notes: Opponent withdrew due to "injury."*

This one is different. The opponent name is redacted. Did they erase him, pay him off, or threaten him?

"Wait, Belanger? That's the head coach for the Saint-Aulaire team's last name."

"The team you played against last time?"

Jasper nods.

If I thought I was shocked before, I wasn't ready for what I'm looking

> *at right now.*
> *Midnight Challenge Report: MC106*
> *Date: Redacted*
> *Final round.*
> *Location: Redacted*
> *Participants: E. Vancourt vs Z. Aldenhurst*
> *Odds: 2:1*
> *Outcome: fatality? Yes. Incident classified.*
> *Winner: Z. Aldenhurst.*

What the fuck?

Bile rises in my throat with the words I don't want to say out loud. "So, someone else died...before Ellias."

I wait for Jasper to say something, anything, to help with the pressure in my chest, but he looks as shocked as I am.

"This whole time," I whisper, "Zayden thought it started with Ellias. But it didn't. It started with his father."

This thing is older than any of us.

"I'm uploading them to my backup drive," Jasper says as he takes pictures of everything as quickly as possible. "We need to go, like right now. We've been down here for too long."

It has been over an hour. Once he's done taking the pictures, I put everything back the same way we found it. Jasper adjusts the lock mechanism on the cabinet door, making sure it seals with a soft click. The biometric panel resets.

"Luna...we have to tell Zayden." He pulls off his gloves as we step away from the cabinet. He's right, Zayden deserves to know how deep this goes, although he already suspected it.

"I'll tell him. Tomorrow at lunch." I pull off my own gloves, glancing around the room one more time—checking that every folder is back in place, every drawer closed the exact way we found it. No fingerprints. No signs we were ever here.

"Okay. But you guys can't keep sneaking out like this. Someone will notice." He's not scolding, just worried about what would happen if they find out we're together.

"I know," I say, and I hate how small my voice sounds.

Jasper sighs then pulls me into a quick, protective hug. "He really cares about you, you know," he murmurs.

"I care about him, too." My throat burns, and I blink again before it gets worse. "Okay. Let's go before I get sappy or something." I chuckle.

Jasper grins. "Yeah. Let's go before we get caught."

All I wanted was to belong here. To prove I deserved to stand on this ice, in these halls, at this school that was never built for girls like me. But if this is what it means to belong at Valcérre, I don't want it.

I want to expose the truth, and their skeletons buried beneath the ice.

I want to burn the whole thing down.

CHAPTER 44

Luna

It's past midnight by the time I sneak back into the dorm, and I'm mentally exhausted. My chest hurts from everything I discovered in the archives. Thank God, Annika and Sophie are already asleep, so I don't have to explain to them where I've been. But a little part of me wishes they were awake so I could check on them. Especially Annika. She's been training really hard for her upcoming ballet showcase.

Once I'm in my room, I close the door behind me and walk to the bathroom. My clothes come off in a second, like they're contaminated, and I drop everything into the laundry basket.

I stop in front of the sink, and the girl in the mirror doesn't look like the one I knew—or maybe I didn't know her at all.

My kinky curls are down, shaping around my face. I reach for my scrunchie and put them up into a pineapple at the top of my head. I spent the whole weekend removing my mini braids, even Zayden helped. It took forever, plus another hour or two to wash and condition them, but I needed something new to match this new Luna I'm getting to know.

Back in school, the girls used to make fun of my hair because I didn't know how to style it, and that's why I wore braids most of the time.

By the time I was eleven years old, I had learned to straighten my hair. I would burn my scalp and damage my curls. I thought if my hair was straight enough, if it looked a little more like theirs, maybe they'd stop saying my hair is too kinky, and my skin is too black to be Latina. Never mind the fact that I speak fluent Spanish and my mom is Dominican.

But maybe I was never meant to fit in. I don't have to be the version of myself they want me to be.

I can be the moon and the sun.

Be bold but also cautious.

Be strong and soft.

Hurt but still learning to love.

Once I'm done brushing my teeth and washing my face, I pull one of Zayden's T-shirt over my head. I turn off the bathroom light and step into the quiet of my room.

The room is dark, except for the light spilling from the window. I crawl into bed, lying on my side facing the lake. The glass is fogged from the inside, but I can still make out the frozen water.

My body's exhausted, but my mind keeps replaying everything from tonight. The betting log. The names. The pattern. My pulse has been stuck in my throat ever since.

The door opens.

I don't move and listen to the sounds of footsteps. Then the soft thuds of boots hitting the floor.

There's a pause long enough to make my heart forget how to beat. Then the mattress dips beside me. His scent reaches me first, cedar, and something sharp that I only smell when he's been skating.

His arms come around my waist as he pulls me back until my spine fits against his bare chest. He slides his fingers under my shirt as he traces lazy lines against my stomach.

I knew it was Zayden the moment the door opened. He's been sneaking into my dorm late at night since Serene disappeared. He waits until Sophie and Annika are asleep, but they know.

Jasper made him a copy of my key card. Said it was for safety, in case anything happened, but we both know that's not the real reason. He comes because he needs me. And I let him, because I need him, too.

We don't say anything at first, just breathe together.

"Jasper told me," he whispers finally, his voice rougher than usual.

My body stiffens.

"That you two went to the archives and what you found down there. And he thinks…he thinks someone might know you were down there. That you might have accidentally triggered something."

"I was going to tell you," I whisper.

"Damn it, Luna." He pulls back just enough to flip me over, his eyes burning into mine. "You promised me you wouldn't do anything reckless."

"I know, but I couldn't. Not after Serene. I needed to know what the fuck is going on. She already dragged me into this, and I can't stop now."

"You shouldn't be the one risking everything to figure this shit out."

And for a second, I see it all—his fear, his guilt, the way he wants to scream and bury his face in my neck at the same time.

"I can't lose you."

I reach for his face, brushing my thumb along his cheekbone. "You won't."

But he doesn't believe it. Not fully. So I kiss him, and he kisses me back like it's the only thing keeping him together. There's no softness in it. Just desperation. Anger. Need.

"I mean it," he says, his forehead pressed to mine. "If something happened to you…because of my family…" His voice breaks. "I won't survive it. I can't fucking lose you, too."

Then he kisses me again. His hand trails down my waist, over the dip of my hip, and settles between my thighs. His pants and boxers are off before I can blink, like he'll lose his mind if he's not inside me the next second.

He slides inside me with one, slow, deep thrust, and I bite my lip to stop myself from screaming and waking up Annika and Sophie.

He moves slowly at first, like he's afraid this will be the last time. His forehead stays pressed to mine, his breath uneven as our bodies fall into a rhythm that feels too real, too intimate for words.

"Promise you'll stop digging. That you'll focus on your skating."

I blink up at him. "Zayden…" I stop when he rolls his hips just right, but it's still not enough. I need more.

"Promise me," he says again, slowing his thrusts like a punishment. "Please, baby."

I swallow hard. "I'm sorry…but I can't promise you that." I can't walk away now.

"Why do you have to be so stubborn?" He pulls back just enough to look at me, eyes wild and tender all at once.

He holds my face, thumb brushing beneath my eye like he can feel the storm brewing inside me. And then he kisses me again. "You drive me fucking insane," he murmurs against my lips. "But I would be lying if I said I don't love that about you."

Thrust.

My breath catches, fingers digging into his ass, needing more of him.

"The fucking fire."

Thrust.

A moan escapes from my throat. I try to move my hips, but his hands tighten, holding me down. Controlling the pace. Making me feel every inch.

"A fucking storm. My fucking storm."

Another deep thrust, and I can feel this one all the way in my throat. A low groan scrapes from his throat, his fingers digging into my thighs like the pleasure is too much, and he's trying not to come too soon.

"You're Luna Del Sol. The moon and the sun. A fucking eclipse. And I'll never take that away from you."

Oh God.

And then he stops.

"Zayden…don't stop…please," I whimper, trying to chase the friction, but he holds me still.

"You want to burn down this fucking school? Then you need to promise you won't do anything without me and Jasper knowing about it."

"Zayden…" I can barely breathe. I'm aching everywhere. My chest. My legs. My throat. My heart.

"Promise me, Luna, or I won't let you come."

Is it bad that I want to strangle him right now? But I also want to kiss him, because I can see the desperation, fear, and worry in his eyes.

"We do this together, promise me, baby," he says, lower now.

"I promise. Now make me come."

He chuckles then pulls out and turns me around before I can protest. "Good girl. I love it when you're bossy."

I push up to my knees, arching my back toward him.

He grips my hips, lining himself up before slides back inside me in one possessive thrust that makes me moan into the sheets.

He groans at the feel of me, buried so deep it's like he's trying to memorize the shape of my body around him. "You're so fucking tight, baby," he murmurs.

One hand stays pressed against my lower back, keeping me in place, while the other reaches around and finds my clit. Then he trusts again, hard, deep, and just the way I love it.

"I'll do anything to protect you," he breathes against the nape of my neck. "You hear me? Anything."

I bite the sheet, stifling the sob of pleasure that rises up as I come around his dick.

He doesn't stop as he chases his own release, and I'm pretty sure Annika and Sophie can hear the sounds of his skin slapping against mine. I couldn't care less right now.

"Fuck, baby..." he groans, hips jerking as he comes. His whole body shakes against mine, and he buries himself one last time, spilling everything inside me.

Then he pulls out slowly, and my body misses the fullness of him. I flip back into my back, eyes still half lidded.

"Be right back." He lets me know before heading into the bathroom.

Zayden comes back with a washcloth. "Let me." He slides it between my thighs and cleans me gently. When he's done, he sets aside the cloth and climbs in beside me.

My head finds the perfect spots on his chest, and he pulls the cover over us.

"Good night, Lunetta." He kisses my forehead.

"Good night." I lift my head to press a soft kiss to his lips.

CHAPTER 45

Zayden

"That's all for today." Coach blows his whistle and ends practice twenty minutes early. This never happens.

A few of the guys glance around, confused, but they don't push it. Most of them are too exhausted to care. I unclip my helmet as I skate toward the bench.

My dad is standing near the board talking to our assistant coach, but something's not right. He shifts from one foot to another, like he's nervous or uncomfortable. Arms crossed too tightly across his chest, his fingers tapping against his elbows like he can't keep them still.

He must sense me watching. His head turns toward me, and for a second, I see something in his eyes that looks a lot like fear or remorse. It vanishes as quickly as it appears. He nods at our assistant coach and walks off without saying another word.

I should say something, but I'm happy practice is over, because I'm tired of pretending that I don't know he has something to do with Ellias's death. Maybe he saw it happen and looked the other way.

And this wasn't the first time.

I hit the showers fast, wanting to catch part of Luna's practice. I put on a hoodie, hoping no one notices me as I head toward the balcony that overlooks the skating rink.

Luna is on the ice going through her lifts with Nico, her curls tied up in a ponytail. A few strands fall loose around her face.

God, she's beautiful.

Not in a way people say when they see a model in a catalog. She's beautiful like gravity, pulling you in without even trying.

She doesn't skate. She commands the ice. It's like watching a tornado in motion.

"Real subtle, Aldenhurst." Jasper leans on the rail next to me.

I ignore him, eyes still locked on her. Watching her skate calms something inside me.

"But I won't lie, though, she's really good," Jasper says as she glides into a perfect spin.

He hasn't even seen half of the things she can do, because she's holding back. He hasn't seen the way she moves when she thinks no one's watching.

I could watch her forever, but if I had a choice, I'd rather be down there with her. Feeling what it's like to move with her, to match her rhythm like we did at the Shadow Rink.

"You still mad at me about the archives?" Jasper elbows me.

"You put her in danger."

"She was gonna do it with or with me, mate. You know how stubborn your girl is."

My girl.

"I went with her to keep her safe." He glances at me from the corner of his eye, and I don't respond, because he's right. And I hate that he's right.

"The only reason you're still mad at me is because you two had make up sex, we didn't, and you need someone to be mad at." Then with a perfectly timed smirk, he adds, "But we can fix that right now. I'm a great kisser."

"Fuck off."

Jasper chuckles.

I turn back to the ice, watching *my* girl. They're doing their backward crossovers. Luna's getting ready for their back press lift, but she hesitates for a second, not long enough for most people to notice, but I do. Something's *wrong*. I can feel it in my chest.

"Wait—" I say, like she can hear me through the glass.

Nico's hands grip her waist, then she pushes off the ice. For a second, she's flying and it's beautiful. But something twists in my chest.

Then she's getting ready to land, but her blades don't catch the way they should. Nico tries to reach for her, but it's too late.

She falls on the ice, bringing Nico down with her.

"Luna!" I shout, but she's not moving.

I'm running toward the stairs before my brain catches up. My skates aren't even on, but I don't care as I run across the ice toward her, almost falling before I catch myself.

Nico is beside her, holding his arm. He looks pale, too, but I can't focus on him right now. Not when she's still on the ground and not moving.

"Hey, baby. I'm here." I kneel beside her.

The coaches and students are rushing around us, and Jasper's talking to the school med, but I can barely breathe.

"Zayden..." she whispers.

Our eyes lock for a second before hers close again.

"I'm right here. You're okay. Help is coming. Just hold on for me, okay, baby." I try to keep the panic out of my voice, but fail miserably. For a second, everything fades, the light, the noises. Moonlight spills across black ice, my breath ghosting white in front of me.

I blink hard, and it's gone. The rink, the lights, the shouts, rush back into focus. I grip her hands tighter. I can't lose her too.

I can't lose her, too.

I meant it when I said I wouldn't survive if something happened to her. I barely did last time when I lost my mom. I went to that frozen lake ready to end everything like she did, but then I saw *her*.

My little storm.

Skating alone, like something out of a dream. She saved me without knowing, and I can't lose her.

The medics burst through the rink, sliding across the ice with stretchers and bags. I want to fight them for touching her. I want to carry her myself.

But I have to let go.

Her hand slips from mine as they lift her.

"Zayden—" she whispers again.

"I've got you, baby," I call out, standing to follow. "I'm right behind you. I'm not going anywhere."

Nico is being loaded onto another gurney. I follow as they wheel them out of the rink and toward the glass doors that lead to the athletes' recovery wing.

"You can't go past this point." A staff member stops me from going in.

"She needs me," I try to argue.

"I'm sorry, please wait here."

I want to push her out of the way and go after her.

The doors close behind them, and I'm left standing feeling helpless.

"Come on, Z." Jasper grips my shoulder.

I don't move until he tugs me away, basically dragging me toward the hallway that leads toward the exit.

I lean back, trying to breathe, but I'm not getting enough air. And Jasper pacing in front of me is not helping.

"I don't think this is a coincidence," he mutters, barely loud enough for me to hear. "I told you we might have triggered something, then this happens." He runs a hand through his hair. "And now Luna… Fuck, Zayden. What if this wasn't an accident?"

His words feel like gasoline on an already raging fire in my chest, because I'm thinking it, too.

My phone buzzes in my pocket.

> Coach: Come to my office.

I show Jasper the screen.

He glances at it then back at me. "You think he knows something?"

I think about the look I saw on his face earlier.

I don't think, I know he knows something.

CHAPTER 46

Luna

"Zayden?" I wake up with his name on my lips. For a second, I forget where I am. Then I remember the fall. Zayden's voice when he called me baby.

"I've got you," was the last thing I heard before everything went black.

I search the room like he might be in here somewhere, but it's empty. That's when I see the folded paper on the tray beside me.

Maybe he was here and didn't want to wake me. That's one of his notes telling me he'll be back soon. A small smile stretches my lips as I reach for it.

I unfold it.

> *Luna,*
> *I promised I wouldn't disappear without telling you. And I always keep my promises.*
> *I'm leaving for the Valcérre national team. They offered me a contract. It's what I've worked for and always wanted.*
> *What we had was never Everything you imagined. It Was a distraction I let go on for too long.*
> *Hockey is the one thing that's always felt Real to me. It's what makes me feel free. It's time for me to focus on that, on the game I love most.*

> *Focus on your skating, and stop digging.*
> *There's Still time to protect yourself. Let this go.*
> *I should've never let in that chaos of Yours.*
> *Our story was always written on thin ice. And thin ice cracks under pressure.*
>
> *Zayden*

At first, I just stare.
Then I reread it.
Again.
And again.
No *my little storm*.
No *I'll be back*.

I try to breathe, thinking that maybe if I focus on the pain in my ribs, I won't have to face the one in my chest.

The same boy who sprinted across the ice screaming baby like the world was ending...just told me I was a distraction.

He told me figure skating was what made him feel free. Not hockey. Never hockey. That was his father's dream. Not his.

He said he was mine. And I believed him. I believed every single lie he told me. I gave him everything. Every piece I'd never let anyone see. Then he left and didn't even say goodbye to my face. And for the first time since I was a kid, I feel small again, forgotten, abandoned.

The tears sting, hot and humiliating as they slide down my face. I press my lips together to stop the sob building in my throat from escaping, but it's too late.

He said he always keeps his promises, but that's bullshit.

What about when he said we'd burn this school down together?

When he said he wouldn't push me away? That I didn't have to hurt alone anymore?

My chest tightens so hard, I can't breathe. I press my hand over my heart, like that'll stop it from shattering completely.

I hate him for making me believe in us.

I hate how much this hurts.

I hate that I let him in.

I hate that I gave him everything.

And still...

I wish he was here.

Because Zayden always made things better. He always knew what to say. How to hold me. How to make it stop hurting.

This time, he's the one who's hurting me, but I refuse to believe everything was a lie.

I know what I felt.

I know what *he felt*.

I know what *we* felt.

No note will make me forget the truth I saw in his eyes.

The truth I tasted on his lips.

The truth I felt every time he held me like I was home. I swipe at my face angrily, but the tears won't stop.

Until he looks me in the eye and says none of it meant anything, I won't believe this is the end of *us*.

He said our story was written on thin ice, but he's wrong.

Our story is carved in the ice. Zayden Aldenhurst is carved into my heart forever.

I press the crumpled note against my chest, tears soaking into the paper. My body hurts from the fall, but this? This is the kind of pain no morphine can help with.

And if they're the reason he left me, they just made the biggest fucking mistake of their lives. Because I'm done being the girl who gets left behind, and nothing will stop me from burning this school to the ground. With or without him.

To be continued...

A FREE PREQUEL NOVELLA

Grab the prequel novella

Hey, Moonlight,

If you're reading this, I guess I couldn't say it out loud. I was scared if I did, I wouldn't be able to walk away.

I just want to say thank you. For last night. For all

of it. For seeing me. For a few hours...a few days, even, you made me feel alive. Like I wasn't drowning.

I hope you keep skating. Keep finding those small moments that pull you back to the surface when it gets heavy.

The world needs your light, moonlight.

And if you ever wondered if last night meant something, it meant everything.

You meant everything.

Thank you,

-Hoodie Boy.

ABOUT THE AUTHOR

Smardline is an Amazon Best-Selling Black, Afro-Caribbean, and Afro-Latina author who loves writing stories about BIPOC characters.

She's always been obsessed with romance—growing up on telenovelas, listening to chansonnettes françaises, and daydreaming about love stories. She still does, but now she gets to write them herself.

Smardline fell in love with reading in middle school and always wanted to see more characters who looked like her. She's grateful to see more diverse stories in the world today and hopes hers adds to that.

ACKNOWLEDGMENT

To my readers, thank you for believing in my stories, my characters and me. You're the reason I get to do this.

To my friend, beta readers/alpha readers, and everything in between Ahsha, thank you for your time, your feedback, and love for these characters. I also want to thank my street team for showing up, and their support.

Thank you to my author friend Akita Sparks for every pep talk, brain storming, vent, and telling me to you got this when I wanted to give up.

And a special thank you to *@scribblebookshop* for giving my book babies a home on your shelves. Your support for indie authors like me makes all the difference.

www.ingramcontent.com/pod-product-compliance
Lightning Source LLC
LaVergne TN
LVHW091718070526
838199LV00050B/2441